D1045267

By the same author

Passion's Shadow

Claire of the Moon

a love story

Nicole Conn

Simon & Schuster

Simon & Schuster
Rockefeller Center
1230 Avenue of the Americas
New York, NY 10020

This book is a work of fiction. Names, characters, places, and incidents either are products of the author's imagination or are used fictitiously. Any resemblance to actual events or locales or persons, living or dead, is entirely coincidental.

Designed by Jeanette Olender
Manufactured in the United States of America

1 3 5 7 9 10 8 6 4 2

Library of Congress Cataloging-in-Publication Data
Conn, Nicole, date.
Angel wings : a love story / Nicole Conn.
p. cm.
I. Title.
PS3553.O495A82 1997
813'.54—dc21 97-23523 CIP
ISBN 0-684-83205-4

acknowledgments

I would like to thank all the angels who have come into my life . . . each and every one of you and especially . . . my dear, sweet Aunt Joy Carol, who taught me how to believe in angels and how to live my dreams.

Acknowledgments

I would like to thank all the angels who have come into my life [illegible] each and every one of you and especially my dear sweet friend Joy Carol, who taught me how to believe in angels and dare to live my dream.

For Gwendolyn,

who loves me unconditionally,

holds me when I can't think of writing another line

and challenges me to be the best I can be

Guardian Angel

Among the many beliefs accorded guardian angels throughout the beginning of time, one element runs true through them all: that each person on earth is assigned a special angel who watches over them, guides them, and nurtures them through every minute of their lives. What most people don't know is that this arrangement is exclusive and binding.

Angel Wings

A brilliant flash of white fills the silent atmosphere of the heavens. The body of a woman floats through the glaring light. Her neck twists into her shoulder at an unnatural angle. It was a seemingly simple fall. A small patch of ice. Death was instant, her spinal cord severed from her own twisted vertebrae.

Subject: Luanne Hunziker, 1892–1937, Earthtime
Incarnate Destination: Angelica
Purpose: Novitiate Angel

The clothes draped upon her begin to hiss strangely as they dissipate from her form, then disappear altogether. Naked, the skeletal structure beneath the flesh becomes a penetrating metallic blue, then slowly effervesces, decomposes. Blood from her veins soaks into the ethereal atmosphere and evaporates.

What is left of her turns a ghostly translucent. Then a light violet ray seeps through her limbs, fills her with a pearly thick magenta. Followed by red. Purple. Green. All colors of the spectrum vibrate through her being. Pure tones simmer, then boil, imploding their hues against one another as a mighty struggle for dominance of one color over another takes place, a dazzling light show inside the woman's deadened receptacle.

Finally a golden hue emerges, bursting through the tortured rainbow, bathing her form from head to toe.

Crackling ruptures draw parallel tears at her shoulder blades. The skin splits open, and two budding sprouts emerge, the size of dove's wings.

An Angel is born.

Angel Carlita.

The Celestial Counsel

"And this mortal shall die in the earthquake scheduled for January seventeenth, nineteen ninety-four, earthtime." Arch Angel Magdalena points to a holographic screen bearing witness to disaster. She is restrained in her presence, not happy about the death, but reconciled to the need for it.

"But why?!" Carlita pipes in. The other angels turn to her. She has now been advanced to an Angel in Waiting, robed in luminous peach, closely resembling her aura color. By custom she is not to speak out of turn, but on Earth, in her other life, Carlita never adapted to custom, and heaven is certainly no different.

Shimmering in a sterling lavender aura, Angel Gabriella floats to Carlita. "Don't you see the futility of debate? These things are written."

"I just don't see what possible use it is to throw away someone so deserving," Carlita says dramatically.

"It isn't necessary that you understand." Gabriella has little patience for this argument. "Fate is. It is as simple as that."

"Please." Magdalena cautions them both, then returns to the hologram.

Carlita watches Gabriella, confused and put out. Granted, Gabriella is a Dominion, an Angel of Intuition. The annals of Gabriella's celestial feats were legendary. How Gabriella had many times outwitted physical and intellectual forces by silent and potent wisdom with astonishing results. Virtues, the order of Angels to which Carlita had been assigned, were more likely to perform miracles of dynamic proportions.

This is a concept that heartens Carlita, for though she has been an angel for only a short time—at least by angel standards—the longer she wafts about with the other novitiates, the less convinced she is that any of them were really doing any good. If angels couldn't perform miracles and make a difference, why were they here? Since they had the power to do . . . well . . . practically anything, why weren't they doing it?

"Carlita, are you with us?" Gabriella beckons. "It is time."

Carlita became alert. They were assigning the charges for the Special Fate Task Unit and she was being given Clancy, a difficult case, which by all rights should have gone to a Superior Angel, someone as advanced as Angel Gabriella, for instance; Carlita's wings were still only in mid-bloom. She'd won the assignment by helping a young boy veer from shoplifting, a small event in and of itself, but the turning point for the young being by which he was gifted a moral compass to lead the rest of his life. Carlita was beginning to understand how important every action was; that's why she wanted to work miracles to right the course of the utterly chaotic mess her earthworld had become.

"Now Angels." Arch Angel Magdalena was speaking. Wings stilled. "As a result of disturbances on Earth, destination charts have been thrown wildly off course and time ripples and space warps have reached a critical mass. Plotting the courses of Earth's mortals has become increasingly problematic. Our priority is thwarted fate convergences: I am speaking of righting meetings that did not happen, of fate that changed before our very eyes, of time ripples that defy the domino effect. There is a lot of confusion among the earthlings. They are hesitant, unable to make decisions. Things that were at one point absolute certainty have now become shrouded in doubt.

"Each of you is about to see brief histories and highlights of your charges. Those of you who have been paired will be working closely together, and for you I have reserved the most difficult assignments. We have angels from all over the universe so we must respect differing angelosophies, but I will remind you, we must all adhere to the Interplanetary Guardian Angel Code."

Magdalena begins handing out assignments, drawing each pair of angels to a floating metallic orb. She takes a majestic breath, spreads her wings, and the orbs metastasize to shimmering side-by-side holographic screens. She stops before Gabriella and quickly glances at Carlita. "Perhaps Novitiate Carlita can learn and benefit from your experience, Angel Gabriella."

"Thank you, Angel Superior." Gabriella solemnly acknowledges the praise.

Magdalena nods, activates their dual screen. Carlita and Gabriella watch. On one side we see a boy's form emerge at a grave site, on the other, a girl walking a city street; both in their teens.

Magdalena's magenta aura quivers now as she addresses the entire flock. "Teamwork is of the essence. But before we review these case histories I must reiterate, so that there can be no room for misunderstanding: We must execute our work so that the mortal makes his or her own decision. Is that clear?"

Carlita starts to speak. "But—"

"No buts. And no grand gestures. It is absolutely imperative the mortal come to a spiritual awakening through the relationship each has to his or her faith and not through trickery and miracles. Yes, we have power over their destinies, but cannot impose it. They individually must find that power within themselves. Do we understand one another?" Magdalena focuses her royal blue eyes on Carlita's.

"Yes."

"Good. Then let us get to work."

Earthtime • May 1965 • New York • Clancy

The day she was kicked in the stomach for complaining about a "tummy ache" at the tender age of eight was the day Clancy stopped complaining.

Her mother had a bad hangover. "Quit your bellyachin'," she had snapped, then laughed at her own double entendre.

Clancy didn't say a word, but the pain grew tighter, more intent, focused like a razor slashing at her insides. Her mind was frantic with the thought she might explode as she wiped the sweat from her brow. So she sang a melody in her head, repeating the incantation with sheer concentration, hoping the pain would go away, but it simply became unbearable. And even her mother, after a few drinks, was more inclined to sympathy when she saw her daughter's scarlet hue as she bent to tuck her in. Although it was awkward, Celia put a hand to her child's face. Inferno.

"Hey, Dick, my kid's burnin' up." Dick, the only one of Celia's boyfriends that came from the human race. He was a traveling hardware salesman, wasn't there much, but when he did show up in his road-wrinkled clothes, he always brought Clancy little knickknacks, cheap souvenirs, samples from his briefcase. Useless, but she treasured them, put them on her rickety bed table, polished them up as if they were jewels.

"Jesus!" He agreed. "Hey, baby girl"—he leaned toward her—"what's the matter?"

But Clancy was a fast learner. She suffered, tight-lipped, pointing to her inflamed womb. Dick took care of it for her. He rested his hand on her tummy and she howled.

Acute appendicitis. She heard the doctor mumble, in the haze of her pain, that they were lucky they hadn't shown up any later. She also heard her mother's parting words, "Shit, Dick, I'm sorry she ruined our date."

Clancy never wanted to leave the hospital. It was so clean. So bright. The white-clad nurses so tender and gentle. They cared for her in a way Clancy hadn't known existed. But three days later she was back in the apartment, closed shades, the never-ending fog of smoke, the murky form of her mother moving unreliably through their darkened cave from which there was no escape, ruled by the tyranny of the unexpected.

"Hey, the next time you decide to get sick" —her mother's cigarette bobbed in her mouth— "don't do it on a night I got plans."

December 1973 ♦ England ♦ Mathew

He stood at the grave site, tears still clinging to his cheeks as his father's partner took him by the arm to lead him away.

"I don't want to go. Not yet." The man glanced at the boy . . . well, he wasn't actually a boy any longer, just fourteen, and with his parents dead suddenly, it made him a man, whether he was ready or not.

"It's time, son. They're ready—"

"Well, I'm not bloody well ready."

The man had never heard Mathew speak in anything other than his gentle, well-bred voice, but now he heard his mother's voice, a whisper that cut like a whip when necessary.

Charles Fenningsworth supposed it was okay for his partner's only heir to stand at the grave site a bit longer. He took out his umbrella, offered it to the boy, but there was no response. He opened it himself, walked several paces toward a tree. It was coming down now. Nothing more certain than death, tariffs, and rain in Cornwall.

Charles cleaned his pipe, keeping an eye on the slender, immobile form that continued to stare into the ground. Well, he supposed he damned well deserved a moment before he had to let him in on the next shock. That their money, his own and the boy's parents', had all been sunk into the business, and that business was going down even as they stood there. The irony of the scene was not lost on Charles. He would be filing bankruptcy Monday, and had, in fact, only been waiting for his partner Kenneth and his wife to return from Paris. That was when their Fiat was blindsided by a runaway delivery truck. Death was instantaneous.

He packed the pipe's bowl with Canadian Rum, his favorite cheap blend, struck a match, and sucked until his head filled with the twining flavors of tobacco and rum. He watched as Mathew peered up at the sky, as if there might be an answer in the dreary gray landscape, letting his face soak in the drizzle. When it began to downpour, and he still hadn't moved, Charles went to him, took his arm. "How 'bout a spot of tea, old man."

They left the cemetery together.

"Well, you see, it's rather frightful, really. While you've been away at Eton, becoming brilliant, apparently your father and I were getting more daft, and the long and the short of it, ol' boy, we're cleaned out. Stock and barrel . . ." Mathew sat by the fireplace, sipping his tea thoughtfully. He could hear Charles's words but they made little sense. His head ached from the tears he had fought trying to keep a sense of grace about his mourning. It would have made his father smile, his mother proud. His mother, who never failed to smell of lavender soap, bending to him at Grandma's funeral, a gentle but firm hand at his chin, wiping a tear with a flick of her thumb: "Suffering's a private affair. Try and be a good boy and wait until we get home."

Charles's words droned on. "We're just this side of destitute. I'm filing bankruptcy after the New Year. Hasn't been much of a holiday at that. Then, well, then we're selling the house and I'm afraid we're going to have to sell yours in the bargain."

Mathew tried to catch up. "As bad as all that?"

"I'm afraid so." Charles went over to him, put a hand on his shoulder. Mathew knew Charles thought of him as a son, the son he'd never had. They'd spent most of their summers with Charles's wife and three daughters. Grew up together. His "Uncle" Charles, so different from his own father, a quiet and unassuming man with a soft and easy charm.

"Point is, after the sale of the house, we're going to have to find a way to keep it all together." Charles took out his pipe. "You'll be able to finish out the term, but after that, you'll have to live here with us. My brother's got a small flat. No luxury, mind you, but I can take up with my brother at the cannery until I get back on my feet. I've already talked about getting you on there as well, after you're done with school."

Mathew bit his inner lip until he drew blood, head lowered, fighting the ever-threatening tears of sorrow and now frustration. He could barely take in Charles's words, thought only that he had stood in torrential rain and felt nothing. Thought of the day his father first took him hunting, the rabbit that Charles—yes, it was Charles who had shot—gutted before his eyes, the tear of flesh, guts shred, blood spilling . . . it made Mathew wonder if his own skin could contain his grief. All he wanted was a quiet corner to think in, the familiarity of his room, somewhere to retreat so he might suffer with dignity.

"You do have one alternative, lad." Mathew glanced at him. "You have a great-aunt, on your mother's side. She's offered to let you live with her and finish your schooling. But, ol' boy, I wouldn't recommend it."

"I don't know of any aunt."

"Well, I guess not."

"I don't want to leave my home."

"And that's how I knew you'd feel. You're family, lad. You know how we all feel about you." Charles took out his pipe as if that were the end of the discussion.

"Why? Why don't you recommend it?"

"Eh?"

"My aunt."

"First off she lives stateside in that damnable desert of Los Angeles, but more to the point, according to your father, he could never decide whether she was eccentric, or just plain knackers. I want you to know, though, son, she's offered to pay your schooling. If you live there. She's getting on. Would like the company, I suspect."

It took Mathew only a minute to decide his future. He would no more be at peace skinning fish than he would living with Uncle Charles, although he loved him dearly. Mathew knew a very simple matter about himself. He could never give up his study. His work.

"Thanks for telling me like it is, Uncle Charles. I do appreciate your candor about the business and your very kind offer to take me in. But"—Mathew stood now, set his teacup aside—"I'm afraid, I rather think it would be best for all if I were to live with my aunt."

Charles spluttered, choking on the smoke. "But son, you can't be serious. The woman's crazy."

"Well, at least I've been warned."

December 1973 • New York • Clancy

It was December 23rd and she hadn't bought one thing. It would have meant nothing to her had she not walked though the Morristown Green, seen the mechanical elves, with their glassy-eyed stares, prim-plastered smiles. She could hear the grind of cogs, tilting back and forth, as the jolly sprites hammered on a shiny red wagon, over and over and over again, accompanied by the tinny melody of "Hark the Herald Angels Sing." *Hark, Clancy, you have nothing for your mother.* So. What was she going to get? A pack of cigarettes? A bottle? Here, throw these under your bed, along with the others. No, she did not want to see her mother. If she didn't buy her a gift she wouldn't have to. Simple.

She was dying for a cigarette herself, so she stopped at a 7-Eleven, picked up a pack of Marlboros. When she came out of the store a bum approached. "Can you spare a dime?"

"No, can you?" Clancy was tough. No one was getting anything from her. She brushed past him and walked the rest of the way to work. This time it was soldering electrical cable. She'd actually lasted two months on this job.

Bright glittering silver that bubbled like mercury, then hardened into a dull glaze about the circuits that blipped and synapsed to another circuit—all interconnected in some divine manner, she supposed. The cable ran about seven feet and shot off in different directions every six to eighteen inches, like ganglia, waiting for a circuit board to be attached to its unruly arms. They had given her the creeps when she first started out, but now they all looked the same to her. Glops of solder points. A puff of cigarette. A fine pink-singed burn on her forefinger where she pointed her number 6 solder wire. She looked at her hands. They were a mess. She sighed. It wasn't like she was going to do a commercial for beauty cream.

"Your hands are your best feature," her mother had said in a rare moment of kindness.

"What should I do? Go about covering my face with them?" she retorted.

"You're such a smart mouth, aren't you? Get me some ice."

That was a year ago. She was nearly sixteen now. She had lied about her age when she got her studio apartment. Apartment, hell. Let's call it a bay window with a shower. So she paid 175 bucks for a window with a view of a neighboring tenement building. But the truth was she liked her window. She had smoked plenty of cigarettes there and had downed many cups of thick instant Folgers. She had planned her life by that window. And now she was waiting for it to happen.

Carlita pressed her lips together, tried to whistle. The other angels laughed the first time she tried, for there were two things an angel couldn't do: whistle and cry. And though there were certainly times she found herself frustrated or sad, the lack of liquid in an angel made shedding tears of relief impossible. But she believed in miracles. Her being here was a miracle in itself.

She had spent most of her incarnations selling herself in one form or another; a beggar-prostitute in the mid-eighteen hundreds in London, a high-class moll at the turn of the century. In her last essence form she had started out as street hustler and ended up running the best-protected whorehouse in Chicago in the thirties, the police her favorite clients. She took girls in, showed them how to take care of themselves, and helped many out of the business.

Then in late March 1937, on the way to make a deposit, she slipped on a ridiculously small patch of ice, fell to an instant and painless death. That was the last of her incarnations for the time being. It had been interesting to study all her lives, much as they were studying Mathew's and Clancy's. It was one of the best things about becoming an angel, Carlita thought. She finally got to see what happened after death, how one got recycled, how it all made sense, these lives of hers, now that she could see them all tied together in the grand scheme of things.

In Angel Basics they'd studied the concept of time—a whole course was devoted to it. It was somewhere in the middle of Einstein's theory of relativity and new age quantum physics that she realized that time was really all rather beside the point, since for earth people you couldn't change what just happened and you had no control over what was about to. And the time in between, well, it was gone while you were thinking about it.

"There's something I don't quite understand," she had said to Archangel Magdalena after a short time on Angelica. "I've been a whore most of my lives. How did I end up in heaven?"

"First of all this isn't heaven," Magdalena sniffed, "well—heaven as earth beings think of it. This is Angelica, realm of Angels. We are not governed by the rules of heaven. We are simply the best of all incarnations on all planes that have been chosen as guides. And you, Prefect Carlita, have been chosen, despite your earth calling, because you are pure." It was true. Carlita had never moved through life with an ounce of avarice or malicious intent. "You are endowed with the best of the earth people's clichés—a heart of gold." And it shone as her chief aura color. She had the rare ability to give, without asking for anything in return. That's why she had made such an extraordinary woman of ill repute. It was all in the attitude.

Which she had to admit colored her reckless desire to save Clancy from the severe dip in her destination chart—fatal if not corrected. Not only in terms of the life she was presently planed in, but in the lifetimes that would follow, which would be utterly miserable if she and Gabriella were unsuccessful. Not that any of Clancy's lives would be without pain. No. Clancy's recurring motif seemed to be pain. But it was the fifth reentry that intrigued Carlita. She still couldn't get clear holographic images when she tried to call it up.

"That isn't a chrono-life that bears interest on our current problem," Angel Gabriella remarked while passing the hologram. "I suggest you keep on track so that we may attend to our charges."

Of all the angels, she had to be paired with Gabriella? "Talk about your fate." She joked with her once, but Gabriella did not respond to Carlita's attempt at humor. They were as different as two angels could be. It didn't matter. She wasn't going to let Gabriella or anyone get in the way of her taking care of Clancy.

As she viewed Clancy's current life she felt an immediate attachment to her. Clancy reminded her of herself. Hard knocks. Desperate situations. But there was an important difference. Carlita had been graced with the gift of acceptance. She never turned bitter, no matter what circumstances were laid before her feet. Not like Clancy, who was in danger of becoming as bitter as the wind that seared into her face that morning.

The morning she lost her third job in a row. She had been late again. Because of her mother.

January 1974 • Clancy

"She's had a heart attack."

"But she's not dead?" The doctor realized it would have been her preference.

"No."

"Hmmm." Clancy stared at the hole in her sneaker. "Now what?"

"She'll have to stay here for at least another week. Then I'd recommend a convalescent home."

"No insurance."

"Hmmm."

"Yeah . . . see my point?" Her face was impenetrable. Not mean, but edged with hopelessness.

"There are social service facilities available. I can give you some numbers."

"Sure." She sounded less convinced the second time she said it. "Sure."

• • •

She stayed home with her mother. For two weeks she nursed her back to a semblance of health. Sponge baths, juices, medicine like clockwork. She bought groceries by forging her mother's name on her disability checks. The government's donation to her drunkenness. She'd sit at night turning the dial on the thirteen-inch black-and-white TV hedged against several pillows at the foot of her mother's twin bed. The hollow clank of a bottle invariably found her foot below the bed. A whole world lived under that bed. Clancy couldn't believe what she had found beneath the sagging twin Sealy.

Amidst the clutter and her cigarettes, there were butted mountains all over the cramped, darkened room, little molehills everywhere. Her mother owned the smallest ashtrays in the world, and refused ever to empty them. Clancy scrubbed, scoured, vacuumed, sprayed Lysol until the can was empty. She bleached the windows of smudge-baked filth and let there be light.

"Close them shades" were the first words out of her mother's mouth as she entered her domain, wheelchair bound.

"*Those.* Those shades" was all that Clancy would say.

"You plannin' on shackin' here?" Nothing about the room being clean. The brilliant shine of order, unnoticed, and then duller and duller as if her mother's funereal presence simply obliterated it altogether. But Clancy didn't answer. She simply began dinner.

"Didn't answer me," Celia continued later. They ate from a large pot of spaghetti. Ragú. Cheap and reheatable. It would last them four nights. She figured it came to 39 cents a dinner.

"Do you have a better idea?" Clancy asked as she threw a napkin at her mother, indicating for her to wipe after the dribbled red whip snaking up her chin.

"I only got one thing to say. Keep outta my sight. And don't bother me 'bout my drinkin'."

Clancy only briefly glanced at her mother, then returned to her spaghetti. "That's two things."

Angel Gabriella perched herself upon a puffy cloud overlooking the Los Angeles shoreline, watching the planes descend and lift off as they made a perfect pattern into LAX. She was checking on a mishap, a dent in converging vortices in time, which would affect roughly three of her charges. She was a true believer in not meddling. Not to a great extent anyway. She was an angel of highest standing, A-Superior Elect Dominion, and she approached her work with a clear and concise objectivity. It wasn't that she didn't care about her charges, but as she'd never inhabited their form, she could not fully empathize with their struggles.

She sighed as she merged with the marine air layer, floated through one of the humans' homes, and stopped at the bed of a young actress who would commit suicide in less than a year. Gabriella's job was to inject a sense of value before this came to pass, so that her charge's next life would be filled with the great work of a painter who abstracted the landscape of human emotion in a way that spoke to millions and touched humanity on a grand scale. The suicide was fated and therefore necessary, and she needed to make sure things were still on track. Not a savory duty perhaps, but essential. There was one thing she could do, however, to relieve the pain of this young girl. She wafted over the bed, put angel's lips to the forehead of this fourteen-year-old, and infused a sense of hope, so that the next three weeks would bring the gift of happy contentment before the child star returned to an earlier despair and began injecting huge doses of heroin to deal with the pain of her life, until she rapidly snuffed it out altogether.

Humankind was primitive in its inability to tap into the inherent core of joy each individual possessed. Gabriella had never understood the need humans had to fill themselves with pain-blocks and joy-feels.

Each of this species had the ability to enjoy forms of euphoria on a much higher level, if only they could simply unlock the secret buried inside each of them, perhaps hidden within the DNA. Maybe that was it. A mutation in fundamental design that made them unable to grasp their own core. There was a constant reach for it nonetheless, whether it took the form of drugs, prayer, extreme measures. One way or another humans were always trying to change whatever it was they were feeling, or transport themselves from one state of being to another.

But she couldn't worry about that now. She needed to focus all her attention and care to her Pairing Unit charge, Mathew. She let herself be whisked along by the wind as she followed the limo just below her that drove him to his new home.

February 1974 • America • Mathew

Mathew's aunt had had him picked up from the airport, but he hadn't yet seen her in two days. The driver had dropped his suitcases at the door and he was on his own. "Welcome to Topanga Canyon, make yourself at home—busy on a project," read the note he found on the large front door, the first of many.

He opened the door to reveal a majestic entrance; a hall dominated by an ornately carved wooden spiral staircase. It was a beautiful home, although he wondered at finding it still decked out in Christmas finery. The second note was stuck to the banister of the stairwell: "Your room, upstairs, first door to your left, or if you have food needs you'll find them in the kitchen, downstairs and to your right." He glanced about furtively, made his way up the stairs.

He stood before a door with a torn envelope that said "Mathew's Domain," brushed his hair from his forehead, a nervous gesture he'd picked up since his parents' death. He sighed, then opened the door to what had been indicated was his room. Quite grand with masculine overtones, burnished mahogany, forest green accents, brass fixtures, again, decked in a seasonal motif. He felt a bit like he had been invited to a Christmas party but the guests had already left.

The deck off his room momentarily eased a growing sense of abandonment when he saw the view—rolling hills meeting in the V of the canyon. Beyond them, the ocean shimmered with the reflection of the sun, so bright that he could not see without squinting. For a moment he forgot where he was. But then he turned and caught his reflection in a mirror.

Death had changed him. Oh, he appeared quite like Mathew, rich blue-black hair, fair English skin, ruggedly handsome as opposed to his delicately featured cousins. But his eyes no longer belonged to a boy.

He walked to the bed, where he found a cocktail napkin with another message: "Shower's to your right. Sorry I'm indisposed, but I've had a terribly important flash and need to attend to it. According to my headache, it should last two days. Maybe three. See you then."

Mathew shook his head, terribly hurt and confused to be left so alone. He wanted nothing more than to cry, but he wouldn't allow himself childish or inappropriate behavior. As soon as his throat tightened he pulled out the notebook he'd taken to carrying in his jacket pocket and let whatever came to his head flow through onto paper. It eased the pain.

When the threat of tears had passed he lay on the bed and stared at the ceiling, contemplating this unknown aunt, her rudeness, her utter lack of consideration. How unlike his mother was this distant relative to whom she somehow belonged. And as if on cue the wind brought into the room a bouquet of wild lavender and the memory of his mother bled through his senses so that he felt the panic rise in him. His mother. God, how he missed her. Missed the way she buttered toast in the morning, as though she had the whole day, graceful movements, never in a hurry, never remiss, quiet tones, genteel reproaches, an essence of fluid perfection as fine as the Limoges teacup that met her lips. But he missed more than her essence. He missed what he could never have. The opportunity to really touch her. Make her see him for who he was. Feel him. The tears began and he could not hold them back. He was exhausted, jet-lagged, and soon fell into a deep sleep.

The light patter of feet woke him. A vision of loveliness met his eyes when he opened them. He propped himself up on one elbow as he watched a woman, maybe twenty years his senior, swiftly braid her long, thick, chocolate-brown hair, then turn to him.

"Oh . . . you awake?" Her words coated in a heavy Argentinean accent.

"I'm not sure. Am I?" Mathew was confused. This certainly could not be his aunt. "Who are you?"

"Maria. I clean and cook for your aunt. She tell me, make sure you have everting you need. Ask to make whatever you want for brekfest." Maria delivered a brown grocer's bag to him and then produced several wrapped packages. "She say give you this when you wake . . . say you sleep many hours." She smiled at him.

Mathew smiled back, then blushed. He thought she was one of the most beautiful women he had ever seen.

"I making tay," she said.

"Tay?"

"English Grey."

"Oh . . . tea." Maria began to leave the room. "Hey . . . wait a minute. Where is my aunt?"

"She working," she replied, then departed, as if that was explanation enough.

Mathew picked up his watch on the bed table and saw that it

was 3:00. He had slept for hours. He rubbed his neck, ran his hands through his hair, and studied the packages in the bag, slowly pulling them out.

Yes. Uncle Charles had been right, he thought. She is crazy. He let his imagination run to images of a drooling hunchback, locked in the cellar. But then he opened the first package and found inside a Dunhill pipe, the wood worn to a smooth-used finish, a note wrapped about the stem: "This belonged to your great-grandfather, his favorite one. May you be inspired by the muse." The second package contained a fine gray and black scarf. The third held what appeared to be an antique Christmas ornament, a shiny bulb, rich royal blue and indigo, with a miniature three-dimensional inset: a fireplace scene, with warming flames, a Labrador wrestling playfully with a kitten upon an afghan rug, a tree with several presents, in one large chair an opened book, in another, opposite, a violin with bow. The scope and detail in the miniature were incredible. A treasure. He read the inscription below the scene: "The most important thing in life is being in it."

Shaking his head, Mathew got up, gently placed the ornament on an antique mahogany dresser, and walked out to the deck. He wanted to visit the view again, make sure it was real. It was beautifully sunny although it was late winter, and he stared at the rolling hills—half green, half desert foliage—and found himself smiling for the first time in weeks. No. Perhaps his aunt was neither crazy nor rude. Perhaps she was simply eccentric and thoughtful. He was now certain he had made the right choice.

It wasn't until his third day there that Aunt Nora appeared. He heard her before he saw her, clambering down from the attic. He was in the kitchen, below his bedroom, drinking Maria's "tay" when she entered.

"Good Lord! I don't believe my eyes." It felt warming to hear her British accent, even if a bit diluted over the years. "You're the spitting image of your mother. Dare say, a bit prettier!" His Aunt Nora, on the other hand, looked nothing like his mother.

Mathew couldn't take his eyes off her. Solid, round, a barrel of a woman, in a bright turquoise tie-dyed dress-length T-shirt, her hair as red and brightly flaming as the burnished sunset he'd seen the night before. She wore bangled earrings that flailed about as she moved and talked, and he could swear he detected a piece of tinsel on the back of her hair. She poured herself coffee, then came around the table to inspect him more closely.

"Well now, let me give you a hug," she said, and practically lifted him out of his chair. He felt his lean body being pulled against hers, which was warm and smelled of perfume and paint, tobacco and cinnamon.

"Sooo . . . how's my weary traveler?" She sat him back down, plopped into the chair next to him, and waited.

"I'm quite well, thank you." Mathew tried not to stare.

"Not quite what you expected, eh?"

"Well, to be perfectly honest, I didn't know about you until the accident."

"Of course you didn't. But see what good things come of tragedy?" Aunt Nora smiled sweetly. "Now you do." She got up and fished around the cupboards for some sugar, which she liberally dumped into her coffee. "Love my sweets, I do." She winked at him, took a few tiny sips, and then stared expectantly. As did Mathew.

"Well?" she asked.

"Well?"

"What did you have in mind?"

"Beg your pardon?"

"What did you want to be doing?"

"Oh. Do you mean today?"

"I'd like to be a little more expansive than that. I meant with the rest of your life. We should make a game plan. Get focused. It's important we plan from the start. God knows when I'll be off and for how long."

"Do you travel often?"

And then Aunt Nora looked at Mathew's troubled face, cupped his chin. "Only in a manner of speaking. No, what I mean . . . well, you might as well know right from the start what you've gotten yourself into. I 'go off' now and again. There's nothing to worry about. It's perfectly safe, but I just want to make sure before I do we have you settled."

"I'm sorry, and I don't mean to appear daft, but I have no idea what you're talking about."

"Of course you don't." Maria entered at that moment with a pad and pencil. "Off to the market?"

"Sí, señora."

"Wonderful. Make sure Mathew informs you of all his favorite little goodies. And don't forget whatever it was I forgot the other day."

"Sí, señora."

"Well, that's that." Aunt Nora got up and followed Maria to the door, as if to see her off. But then at the last moment she followed her out to the driveway and got into the passenger seat of a beat-up Mustang and off they went. Mathew swallowed, then brushed the hair from his forehead. He didn't know whether to laugh or cry. Whatever he had expected, his wildest imagination wouldn't have created the marvel whose bright noise still echoed about the room.

Life began to take a certain rhythm. Mathew would get up, Maria would have tea prepared for him, toast and a hard-boiled egg, not quite hard, just the way he liked it. Before school he'd work on his poetry or short stories and when he got home Aunt Nora was invariably just waking or preparing for bed. Time seemed immaterial to her.

When she wasn't in the attic, she puttered. Everywhere. In the garden, in the kitchen, futzed and made busy, but he could never actually tell if she was getting anything accomplished, for Maria was never far behind doing the real cleaning up. When Aunt Nora was in the attic, she'd stay several days, or until sunrise when she would go to sleep. Or so she said. Mathew wasn't sure. He'd never been up there.

"No enter," Maria tsked at him one day when he began going up the steps to the attic door. "No enter," she repeated.

She turned and went back down the stairs. Mathew trailed after her.

"Maria . . . please, hold on a moment." They stopped at the bottom of the stairwell. "What does my aunt do in there?"

"Work."

"Yes, but what is her work? I have no idea what she does and I can't get a clear answer out of her."

"She make tings."

"But what sort of things?"

"All kind. I go to market. More English Grey?"

"Earl Grey," Mathew said, smiling. "Or English Breakfast. Either will be fine."

"Sí."

"So. When we do get started?" Carlita asked as she shifted from Mathew's hologram to that of Clancy. Gabriella sighed and adjusted her wings.

"Carlita, before an angel can become a guardian she must have wisdom. Do you know what that means?"

"Patience?" Carlita queried weakly.

"Knowledge. And in your case a little composure might go a long way."

"I'm sorry, it just feels like we're sort of wasting time. I mean can't we just get the Cliff's Notes and get to wherever it is that we need to do the work?"

"We're not watching in their time. By the time we're finished viewing their lives, a mere blink of an eye will have passed. And Cliff's Notes hardly prepare an angel for the nuances of a situation."

"Nuance? What does nuance have to do with righting the course of destiny?"

"Nuance is the road map to one's soul."

May 1974 • Mathew

The Christmas tree had finally been removed, but only after shedding a carpet of brittle needles upon the floor. "It's becoming a bloody fire hazard, Aunt Nora," Mathew had observed at dinner one evening. Aunt Nora had looked at Maria, who nodded in silent agreement. So out it went. But Christmas decorations still littered the living room and hung about every crevice of the house. Mathew assumed there was a method or plan to take care of them, and asked Maria several days later if he could possibly wrap the handmade ornaments, pack them off to the basement. She glanced at him, smiled dismissively, as if this were a foolish suggestion.

"No worry. We need to get ready for de thora." And with that, Maria dashed to the kitchen.

De thora turned out to be the infamous Dora, his aunt's best friend, whom he met later that evening. Dora had been married to

Nora's husband's brother. They'd known each other for twenty-five years, laughed when people confused their names. They were as opposite physically as could be; Dora was rail thin, with a pinched face, glasses so thick you could never tell what the shape or color of her eyes really were; all snappy complaints next to Nora's bountiful laughter.

The four of them sat on the deck for dinner eating Maria's spicy barbecue chicken. Within an hour he became accustomed to Aunt Nora and Dora's enthusiastic bickering as they planned one of their many road trips. His mind wandered, lulled by his sated appetite, the gentle breeze, the smell of orange blossoms from below. He felt a sweet intoxication with life here in this "damnable desert of Los Angeles."

He noticed with the late setting sun his skin had become a healthy color he'd never have suspected possible in England. He was healing, although slowly, healing despite the sadness that visited him nightly. He felt awkward and guilt-ridden that he thought so little of his father, a kind and gentle man who'd given him life, but little else. It was his mother, always, who danced shadows on his heart, causing him to remember moments as if they'd just occurred, like the day she got news of his cousin's car accident. She had clutched him close to her, chaos threatening to streak her carefully made-up face, her maternal warmth, ever so contained. His pudgy fingers had found their way into her hair and she immediately pushed him aside. He hadn't meant to touch her hair. He was just trying to slip inside the rare embrace. As a child he had been slapped back and forth between desire and acceptability. And now with his aunt he found himself walking a line between grief and elation. But it was hard to be sad around her. Or around Maria for that matter.

Maria. He watched her carefully as she cleaned up and then followed his aunt into the kitchen to make one of Nora's seasonal specialties, many of which she merely named after the month they drank them in—"April Mist Tide," or "Easter Bunny's Ride Tide." They never quite tasted different, but never quite tasted the same, either. Nora's creations were from an ancient and private recipe and it was strict protocol that no one enter the kitchen while she was up to one of her concoctions, with the exception of Maria. Another mystery.

Mathew stood to help clear, but his aunt dissuaded him good-naturedly. "Why don't you keep Dora company. Get to know each other. Besides," she whispered, "she's in need of a good conversationalist."

Mathew doubted that. Having a conversation with Dora was like talking to a mean old bug. You just wanted it to stay in the corner, and if it started your way you wanted to run. Reluctantly, he turned to the bone-skinny widow staring back at him.

"Uh . . . so what do you plan to do in Santa Fe?"

"A bit a this an' that." She moved her face closer to his. "Why?"

"I was just curious."

"Hrrrmmmppphh." Dora cleared her throat, then turned away dismissively.

"Have you and my aunt known each other long?"

"Long enough."

"I . . . well," Mathew had a flash, "quite frankly, I've been wondering a bit—about my aunt and all—and asking Maria anything is quite hopeless."

"And you think drilling me is going to get you any further?"

"Please. I'm not prying—"

"Then why the third degree? 'F I were you I'd stop wasting time trying to figure out what can't be figured and leave it at that. She doesn't beat you, does she?"

"Of course not." Mathew was appalled.

"Then what's the problem?"

End of discussion. Mathew wondered what his Aunt Nora could possibly see in someone so unpleasant.

"Oh, it takes a while to get used to a person," Aunt Nora had said later. "She's a bit put out, dear boy. Why, did you know Dora and I spent an entire weekend in Las Vegas and I swear she didn't mutter more than three words. Until she hit Keno and won a hundred dollars. She sort of developed a 'jackpot Tourette's.' Couldn't shut her up after that. But do you know what she did with the money? She gave it all to the women's shelter on the way out of town. Dora's a strange one," and here Mathew had to consider the kettle calling the pot black, "but she's got a heart of gold. Just give her time."

But Mathew thought that might take forever, until she tiptoed up behind him one cool-blue night on the deck where he was working on a poem. She read over his shoulder and when he glanced up he caught the misting at the rim of her eyes before it was covered with the thick glass of her spectacles. Dora put a gnarly hand on his shoulder and later that night she sat with him and Aunt Nora giggling like a teenager, gabbing about the good ol' days. Once she "knew you were safe," Aunt Nora said, she let her guard down. It was as if being around his aunt was like taking a happy pill, soothing Dora's mile-deep wrinkles into canyons of mirth. As if his aunt's presence was a tonic that tapped into her vein of humanity.

And Aunt Nora. Well, she just plain rattled him. If Mathew could just come up with an explanation, or understanding of her lapses, her disappearances, he felt it would all come together and he would be fine. But after several days of unsuccessful sleuthing, he went to the source.

• • •

They were sitting in the den one unnaturally cool night. Aunt Nora had Mathew make a fire. She ran her hand across the upholstery of the well-worn burgundy high-backed chenille chair in which she sat. "Got these from Ginger Rogers. She was remodeling her house and gave them to me."

"You know Ginger Rogers?"

"Yes. What a wonderful person she is."

"Are . . . are these the chairs in the ornament?"

"Why, yes, they are."

Aunt Nora got up, wheeled a liquor cart over, and poured two delicate snifters of brandy, then handed one to Mathew.

"I understand the book in the ornament."

"Understand? Is it a puzzle then?"

"Well, sort of. I think, anyway." Mathew took a quick sip, feeling very grown-up. "But I have to say, the violin completely baffles me."

But Aunt Nora simply smiled. "Perfect night for a pipe."

"Yes. It is." Mathew dashed to his room to retrieve his great-grandfather's pipe, the pipe she had given him. He was enjoying the excitement of being treated like an adult. He returned and allowed Aunt Nora to light both his and her own. He choked on the first few drags, clearly a novice.

"Block some of it with your tongue at first. Don't take the whole thing in. You'll get used to it. You were born to smoke a pipe. That's why I kept it."

"But you didn't even know you'd ever see me!"

But Nora didn't respond to the obvious. She never did.

"I think it's time we spoke about your future."

"Certainly." Mathew took another tentative puff from his pipe. "I suppose I need to finish school."

"Yes, well, I took the liberty of enrolling you at Palisades High next year. I know you're used to private schooling, and that's why I put you into Marymount this year; it was the only sensible transition. But it's time you mixed with common folk. Salt of the earth. Not because you're a snob—thank God, you're not—but because of what they'll bring to your work."

"My . . . work?"

"Well, yes. Your writing . . . poetry, stories. Ahh . . . such beautiful stories."

Mathew stopped mid-inhale. He'd never breathed a word of his dreams of being a writer to anyone. How could this woman know this about him? "Have you been . . . have you been in my room?"

"Of course. I've lived here for twenty-seven years."

"No . . . I mean through my stuff."

"Dear lord, boy, why would I go through your belongings?"

"But how do you know . . . I mean about my writing?"

"Oh. That." Aunt Nora laughed then, gulped the rest of her brandy. "It doesn't take a brain surgeon to see you have the eyes of the observer, the mouth of a storyteller, the disposition of someone who lives inside and not out . . . although we'll get around to fixing that, don't you worry. Any fool can see you're a poet."

"Look, Aunt Nora. I'm just bloody well going to come right out with it. I'm completely confused. I have been from the moment I arrived. Nothing in this house makes any sort of sense—"

"Well, you're grieving, dear boy—"

"It's not just that. I can't get a straight answer out of anyone. Not Maria—"

"Yes, I know," Aunt Nora said sympathetically, "her English is atrocious. But don't tell her . . . she thinks she's doing so well."

"And your friend Dora—"

"Oh, darling, Dora's half crazy. She's never gotten over Ralph leaving her."

"And what about you, Aunt Nora?" Mathew was feeling the brandy now, feeling brave, pacing the floor as he began his interrogation. "What is it that you do up in that attic? I mean, what's the bloody mystery? And where do you go when you're gone for two, three days? And why are the halls still decked in bloody holly when it's damn near June? What am I doing here? And how do you know so much about me when I'd never even heard of you until four months ago?"

"Please . . . calm down, Mathew. There's no need for excitement. And please stop waltzing about the room. It's making me dizzy."

Mathew sat. Aunt Nora got up, stoked the fire, poured herself another brandy. "Let me see if I can make it any easier for you." He watched as she repacked her pipe with a blend taken from a canister on the mantel, which he would later discover was mixed with high-priced weed. "Despite your father's unfortunate dislike of me, your mother and I communicated. Oh, not by phone or letter. Just by feel. She did write me when you were five, told me all about you. That's how I knew you would be a writer."

Mathew shook his head. This woman *is* crazy, he thought.

"You know, I've had a rather interesting life. I mean to chronicle it someday. Perhaps you'll help me with that. When I sailed over here I met my first husband, Jake. He was a band conductor. A poet in his own sense. He wrote the most beautiful music. We lived in New York, then traveled here because of his health. He wrote some music for the movies. That's how I met Ginger. What a talent. Such grace . . . such élan!" She stopped, took a deep puff from her pipe, then paused as if musing over a memory. Mathew was afraid she'd detour, but a few seconds later she continued. "Then I had a bit of a . . . break I guess you'd call it. After his death. I was hospitalized for a year. When I came out everything had changed. Rather like I walked from the hospital into a whole new world. I thought I'd been happy with Jake. I thought my world was Jake. But I soon discovered my life was just beginning. Everything was different. Food tasted like colors, the air smelled like orange blossoms, and life was no longer something one simply sat in the middle of. It was a feast for the senses . . . a sensualist's banquet, I dare say, and, suddenly, I knew what it was to be happy. Happy, hell! Pure bliss. And that's all there really is to it."

Now Mathew understood. Nora had had a nervous breakdown and she lived in some delusional reality to deal with her pain.

"What about the attic?"

"Oh, that."

"Yes, that. What is it?"

"My work."

"So why don't you let anyone in . . . to see it, I mean?"

"Because the point is to see it when it's finished."

"But . . . what do you make up there?"

"Oh . . . this and that."

She wasn't being evasive on purpose. She was just evasive by nature. Mathew shook his head. Aunt Nora banged her pipe against the fireplace. "I'm so glad we got this all cleared up."

Mathew stared after his aunt as she left the room, not at all sure he'd cleared up a thing.

The next day he wandered out into the garden where Maria was pulling weeds. He knelt beside her, then lost his concentration when he saw tiny beads of sweat caressing her full cleavage.

"Sí?" Maria asked after several seconds of silence.

"Well, um, Maria . . . what I mean to say, ask, that is, is my aunt, well, she's a bit different, if you catch my meaning."

"Sí, different," Maria agreed, then smiled. "Special."

"Yes, well, that too. But I suppose what I'm leading to is . . . is she quite well? I mean does she take medication?"

"Sí."

"And does she take it regularly? Does something happen when she doesn't? For instance, if she didn't take her medication, is that when she disappears?"

Maria simply shook her head and laughed.

"What?"

"You little boy, but old man in the head."

He blushed and kept his head down, hoping to hide it. Maria stood. "Your aunt, she . . . she no crazy. Only *excéntrica*."

December 24, 1976 • Clancy

Clancy ran as fast as she could, but the bus took off without her. "Dammit!" Now she would have to wait twenty minutes for the next bus, which would be running late from the storm. It didn't help that it was Christmas Eve. By the time it came she was paralyzed with cold. She boarded, then sat shivering on the cold plastic Metro seat, clutching a small gift she had bought for her mother. Never mind that it was her nineteenth birthday. Her mother wouldn't remember. And even if she had, Clancy wouldn't know about it. Just like last Christmas Eve, the evening yawning in silence as a miniature tree blinked, like a visual clock ticking in the cramped corner. They had said nothing the whole evening. Finally Clancy had said she was going to bed.

"Yeah, well don't let ol' Saint Nick bite," her mother said with a laugh, her tepid attempt at humor.

This was the second year she would be spending with her mother. Living with her. No more picture window. No more plans for her life. It actually amazed Clancy that her mother was still alive. Amazed her that her mother's heart refused to stop, even with the guzzling of the booze, the coffee, the hacking through two packs of cigarettes a day. Clancy didn't know what kept her ticking. Perhaps a simple matter of vengeance.

For as long as she was alive Clancy was stuck there. The paltry government check made out to Celia Reardon had been cut in half due to a clerical error, and getting it corrected was about as appealing as unraveling her mother's tangled, knotted hair. So Clancy stopped trying and made ends meet with her tips from Pal's Diner. She also managed to take night classes, as well as her music lesson at the community center. The music lesson was only once a week, but without that two-hour session, she was certain she would die.

"What the hell you think you gonna do with a college education, anyway, Miss Fancy Pants?" her mother would taunt.

"What's it to you?" Clancy would reply.

The first few months after Clancy moved in they kept to themselves, conversation avoided at all costs. In the beginning, a nurse came to take Celia's blood pressure, check her pulse, monitor her lungs twice a week. And twice a week Clancy would endure a lecture about her mother's status barely improving.

"Miss Reardon, your mother should have absolutely no alcohol or cigarettes. And it doesn't take a police dog to tell she's had both."

"I'm sorry, but what my mother does is none of my business."

"But you're the one buying this stuff for her."

"I'm not my mother's jailer. I'm only taking care of her because I . . . I can't afford to have someone else do it—"

"But that's why you are responsible for her care—"

"I am not responsible for her decisions."

The nurse tightened her lips, put both hands on her hips; she wasn't giving up without a fight. "Just because she didn't take care of you as a child doesn't mean you can let her die!"

"Why not?" The question was not asked with anger, just icy calm. The nurse left.

But later she walked to her mother's bed. "Why don't you try . . . just a little bit, to cut down. Slow so it won't hurt."

And that's all it took. Her mother grabbed Clancy's wrist with surprising strength, pulled her close so that Clancy gagged from the sour decay. "Listen you . . . you're nothin' but a little shit, and little shits like you shouldn'a been born in the first place. Now get outta my sight."

Clancy ripped from her hold, ran out of the apartment, ran until her knees gave out. She sat on a bench in the dark. She would leave. She couldn't take it. She'd find herself another small studio. Someplace nearby. In case. But if she did that she wouldn't be able to continue school. Or her music lessons. So it wasn't an option.

The truth was that if Clancy didn't get her mother her skanky rye and Chesterfields, her mother would find them another way. She'd call it in, have it delivered, or crawl to the nearest convenience store if she had to. She knew it eased her mother's pain to have those things. No matter what her mother had done to her—or hadn't done for her—she couldn't stand to see her in pain. And no matter how much she hated her mother, she couldn't leave. So she was trapped. She had to stay. She owed her—at least for that night.

"Clan—Clan's that you?" When she returned, hours later, her mother's semicoherent voice called out to her.

"Clan?" Her mother was drunk. "Clan, don'tya know why it's been so hard for us?" There was something different in her mother's eyes. "Clan, it's . . . it's like you and me, we ain't on the same team. We never been on the same team. Tha's the problem. You came and took him away . . . and me, you took the insides outta me. How could we ever get on after that? After you comin'—takin'all my blood, all my female stuff . . . makin' me bloated an' fat." She lit a half butt from one of the souvenir ashtrays Dick had brought years ago. "No one ever looked at me after you was born. I gave you life and you took mine away. I've tried to love ya. Tried to look at you the same way those mothers on TV do—gurglin', laughin', playin' with their babies like they was gifts of gold. But you . . . you just ain't like that." Her mother's tone wasn't mean. It just was. "No, Clan . . . you just ain't no gift."

Merry Christmas. Happy Birthday.

And then her mother puffed a moment more, stopped talking, closed her eyes. Clancy took the burnt-out butt and put it into the ashtray. Then she stood a long time at the bed, finally understanding why her mother had hated her all these years. It made a kind of sense now, and for that she was grateful.

After that they tolerated one another. An unspoken pact. Celia needed her daughter so that she could drink out the rest of her days. Clancy needed her mother to need her. Stasis. And for the time it suited her fine.

Clancy met Rick at the bus stop two weeks later and lost her virginity. He was long-haired, tattooed all up and down one arm, dangerous, drugged out, temperamental. He was also a fog-brained philosopher who made obscure food metaphors—"Babe, life is a hamburger," "chicks are like potato chips, you can't stop at just one." Clancy didn't mind. He had a strong dick, and used it to batter her into numbness.

They fucked and he smoked Marlboros. There was never a time his tongue did not taste of cigarettes. She stopped kissing him. They met at his "pad" two nights a week, after her English Lit class, and she somehow thought it defeated anything she might have learned. She wouldn't see him the nights she had music. He lasted the year, and then moved on to another Frito-Lay.

◆ ◆ ◆

"Isn't there anything we can do for her?"

"I'm afraid not."

"But I thought we were supposed to ease pain. Guide. Help out."

"We do and we will."

"But then why can't we go help her now while she needs it?"

"Because this is the part of Clancy't life that builds her character."

"Caring for that old witch?"

"It's precisely that she can care for her that will help Clancy in the future."

December 25, 1976

It was their second Christmas together, and the best Mathew had ever had. They had finally arrived at the Lodge, one of Aunt Nora's seasonal homes. They had packed Dora's station wagon until there wasn't half an inch of airspace left and then he and Maria sat in the back, while his aunt drove and argued good-naturedly with Dora in the front seat, a victorless debate: whose psychic was better.

He smiled. It had been a good year for him and he had come to love his aunt's eccentricities. With Aunt Nora he could not only be himself, but was daily discovering his potential, and beginning to understand that the dreams of his childhood could be realized.

"It's okay to heal, dear boy," she had said one day out of the blue. "To let your heart massage the past into bittersweet memories and let the future fill with expectation." There was a long silence as he thought about her words.

"Did you know my mother well?"

"No. I don't think I did."

"It doesn't sound as if you cared for her."

"Your mother was precious when she was young, but somewhere along the line, she closed herself off. I think that tormented her, in her own quiet and civilized way, but make no mistake, it is your mother's graceful charm and drive you have inherited."

"And from my father?"

"His gentle nature."

And in fact, Mathew was all the things Aunt Nora had observed: gentle, charming, gracious. People adored his accent. His lanky awkwardness was developing into lean athleticism, his rugged features into an attractive and tender handsomeness.

He adjusted well to the new school, and spent the year studying, going out with his friends, to the movies, running track, playing football and basketball games at school. He even learned to surf, although it was certainly not his strong suit. He dated occasionally, without serious side effects. In truth, he could not lose his heart because his longing was for one person and one person only. And in the evening he would gaze at her, surreptitiously, mesmerized by her dark Argentinean skin, black as midnight eyes, lashes as thick and lush as paint bristles dipped in oil. It was a fresh hunger, and one that compelled him in a frightening way, and her proximity during the drive to the Lodge had been both tantalizing and maddening.

Upon arriving they immediately built a fire in the double-wide hearth and Mathew felt the sense of home the child in him still ached for. Of all the property his aunt owned, Mathew's favorite was the beach cabin, but the Lodge—named in honor of all the fairy tale remodeled barns of old musicals—ran a close second.

Aunt Nora may have been *excéntrica,* as Maria often said, shrugging her shoulders, rolling her eyes, but her sense about money and investments was right on the beam. Years ago, while traveling with her second husband, Stan, she had bought this ski cabin and several other rental properties littered throughout northwest and southern California. Everything had more than doubled in value over the years and it was the income off the properties that afforded Aunt Nora and Mathew their lifestyle.

His Aunt Nora had an uncanny sense about living life to its finest. The Lodge, indeed, had all the grace and charm of a Technicolor movie, as if the swing gang had dressed the set especially for this scene, so that they could have an "I'll be home for Christmas" memory.

"Here." Aunt Nora handed him an ax. "Chop us our Tannenbaum and make it a beaut."

Mathew wondered, briefly, as he swung the ax, what would happen if Aunt Nora "went out" up here, if she were to have one of her flashes? He stopped suddenly and looked about him at all the white, clean snow. Would she disappear in the woods? Would they find her frozen after weeks of searching? The thought made him shiver, even though sweat trickled between his shoulder blades as he continued whacking at the tree.

He could hear his aunt crooning—"Chestnuts roasting on an open fire"— indelibly off key, as Mathew maneuvered the oversized tree through the door. When they got it upright they immediately set about decorating it. When he thought they were finished Aunt Nora solemnly presented a wooden box with six partitions, holding the sacred ornaments—one for each of them, two sections empty. Exquisitely crafted, each ornament uniquely suited its designated owner: Dora's depicted a woman with a cane climbing a mountain to reach a glorious sunset. Maria's showed a festival of Argentinean culture meeting its American counterpart. Aunt Nora's was a burst of color displaying a canyon sunset. Mathew took out his miniature hearth scene and with great reverence put it on the strongest limb he could find.

Aunt Nora did finally manage to disappear one day, was gone for hours, and just when Dora thought they should call the sheriff, in she tromped, shaking a blanket of snow from her "Santa suit," a crimson varsity sweater from "an old college beau" and an old pair of red repairman's slacks.

"Close the door behind you, Nora," Dora snapped.

"We 've been worried sick."

"Whatever for?" And that was the last they spoke of it.

But no matter how mysterious her treks were and despite her memory snags, there in Mathew's stocking was a tie he'd pointed out to her last April, and a tie pin she'd made with his monogrammed initials, a miniature book of poetry affixed to its side. There was also an original copy of *Wuthering Heights* they'd seen at an estate sale months earlier. He couldn't have been happier.

Aunt Nora came from the kitchen with a tray announcing "Jolly St. Nick Tide" eggnog and brandies. Mathew drank a bit too much, and his cheeks were blazing as he watched Maria open the package that held a lovely summer dress his aunt had purchased for her. He was delighted with the joy Nora's gift brought the woman he loved. Yes, he could say it now, at least in the privacy of his mind. He was feeling so exquisite. So damn alive! It was okay to let the thoughts take form, slide into words, even to savor a fantasy of uttering them to Maria. As if reading his mind, Nora cleared her throat. "You know, Christmas really isn't about the birth of Jesus . . . oh, it is in the clerical sense. No, what it is, is the holiday for romantics. It's the one time of the year romantics get to come out of hiding, show their true colors, get as goofy or extravagant as their natures demand without everyone getting so bloody upset over it all. It's when you get to be as passionate about the people you love as you should be all year-round. So drink up, celebrate, and enjoy."

"But Aunt Nora, you do have Christmas year-round," Mathew countered.

"Well. There you have it." She tipped back her nog, glanced at her nephew, winked, and then laughed heartily, very much like a man, her roly-poly body wiggling.

As the warmth of the drink fused to his head, Mathew momentarily let the thought cross his mind that if there ever was a candidate for a real-life Ol' Saint Nick, his Aunt Nora was it.

August 1977

Her mother died.

Clancy walked in one Thursday evening with Chinese takeout. It had become a weekly ritual: moo shoo pork, chicken fried rice, sweet and sour pork chow mein. They had dinner together and watched *The Waltons*. John Boy and stale fortune cookies.

It was the only night they spent any time together and it had become almost companionable, even caring toward the end, when it was clear her mother's gestures had become tentative. It took more energy to lift her small jelly jar of wine, she hacked more vociferously during each cigarette.

One night, three weeks before she had the final heart attack, Clancy was giving her mother a sponge bath, when she grasped Clancy's wrist: "I'm dyin', Clan . . . I can feel it . . . leavin' me . . . whatever life is. It's leavin' me."

"No. You're just tired." Clancy absently stroked her hand, felt the soft veins sink into the skin. "You're just tired."

But she could see the difference.

"It's good though," her mother whispered, "you can get on." And Clancy knew she meant with her life.

"I'm not going anywhere."

"Yet."

They didn't speak about it again, but that Thursday night when she walked in, Clancy heard a stillness, even through the cackling laughter of Jimmy in *Good Times.* She set the take-out bag down, slowly walked to the bed. Her mother's skin was pale blue and her eyes were open as if she were still watching the tube. Maybe she would, Clancy thought. For eternity.

She called an ambulance, then sat by her mother's bed until they came and took her away.

She had her cremated, but didn't know what to do with the ashes. Didn't know what to do with herself, now that she was free. Now that she could get on with her own life.

She took a day off work, cleaned the apartment, got rid of her mother's old clothes, threw out all the empty bottles and all but one of the ashtrays. Then she took another day off and drank half a bottle of scotch. Though she had anticipated this day, yearned for it, even, once her mother's death was real to her, Clancy felt guilty. And empty. The relief and release, this newfound freedom struggled against a shaming sense that if she had only handled things differently, she and her mother would have arrived at a better peace. The next day she was hungover, but decided she would quit her job, took her savings out of the bank, and traded her car in for a battered '67 VW van, the ugliest yellow she'd ever seen. She called Cynthia, probably her best friend, although they never had intimate conversations or shared warm laughter. They merely sat next to each other in Psych 103.

"You still going to Florida?"

Cynthia had mentioned, during spring break, that she was heading to Florida to train thoroughbred horses. Cynthia lived for horses and was only going to the community college because her parents were paying and letting her live at home. But she vowed she would head south one day to become a female jockey. What little Clancy did know about the horse world would preclude Cynthia from ever becoming a jockey; all five foot, three inches and 160 pounds of her.

"Hey, yeah . . . ya wanna go?"

"Yes, I thought a change of scenery might be good," Clancy answered. By her calculations she had close to four hundred dollars if she didn't pay the rent.

"What about your mom?"

"Oh, I have an aunt who's watching her." She wouldn't tell Cynthia for two weeks that her mother had died.

"Neat. I was just getting ready to buy my ticket."

"Don't have to. We can go down in my van."

"Hey, cool, man. A cross-country trip. And we can save money by sleeping in it."

And that was as much planning either required.

Ocala, Florida. Rolling green hills, beautifully manicured lawns. Clancy and Cynthia were led by one of the other girls to the bunkhouse they would share with the other stall muckers; an old run-down ranch house that housed eight girls in either side with a common room in the middle. Two twin bunk beds sat in an eight-by-ten room, ravaged mattresses, a bathroom with painted-over rust stains, and cracked ceilings. They'd been there only twenty minutes and Clancy had had enough.

"This isn't so bad, is it?" Cynthia's question begged denial.

"Oh, yeah. It's bad," Clancy responded. "But let's make the most of it."

Four other girls were already living there, including the androgynous Shay. At first Clancy could have sworn Shay was a boy with a ponytail, brown scabbed teeth from chew, which Shay was kind enough to spit in the toilet. But Shay had full breasts, bent hips that blossomed into bowlegs from spending the better part of her life upon the backs of horses. Shay was their crew leader. And when she wasn't stuffing her lip with tobacco, or bossing everyone around, she was busy rolling and smoking her stogies, which she littered generously about the bunkhouse.

"Must be new," she said upon meeting them.

"Yes. And we're so excited to be here. I've loved horses my whole life, and I want to be a jockey in the worst way," Cynthia jabbered nervously.

"What about you?" Shay cut through Cynthia and directed a warden's eye to Clancy.

"I'm along for the ride, so to speak," Clancy responded.

"Hmmmph." Shay returned a crisp smile, revealing burnt teeth. "See you ladies in the A.M."

Their days quickly settled into a grinding routine. Up at four, mist swirling, still cool enough to move without sweating, down a bad cup of coffee at the dining room/pool hall, grab a muffin, trudge to the stalls, grab a pitchfork, shovel, and wheelbarrow. Backbreaking work. Clancy didn't mind that. She loved to feel her muscles work, straining to push the limits and fight all the anger that lived in her body. She'd simply take her mind to another place, planning her life. Once again, painting pictures in her head of a world where she did whatever it was she was going to do when she grew up. Play her music. Marry the man of her dreams. Be anywhere but here.

They may look pretty in the storybooks, but these high-bred, spirited stallions were the meanest, nastiest creatures she'd ever seen up close. Next to her mother. Grooming them was taking your life in your hands. But she loved their sleek bodies, the smell of ammonia that no matter how much cleaning, would never go away completely. She felt their sweat creep under her skin as she got closer, and once leaned her head into the thick muscles of the neck, feeling a kinship to the runner, wishing she had its fleet strength . . . running, running, leaving behind.

"Hey, best be careful there." Shay spat, then leaned against the bars on the other side of the stall. Clancy said nothing. "They can be tricky. Seem like they're fine one minute, monsters the next. It's in the blood. Fucked blood." Clancy had never met anyone less charming than this strange girl.

Then in her third week, when she was bending over, picking up a bucket of grain, two hooves grazed her head, kicking at her, frenzied and deliberate. The same horse who nudged her lovingly as she fed him carrots now wanted her out of his stall. Wanted her dead.

Shay slammed through the stall, grabbed the halter. "Hey boy, hey sweety boy, hey, it's okay." She calmed the horse, then helped the shaken Clancy from the barn.

"You okay?"

Clancy was speechless.

"Damn stud should be gelded. It happens. They go off now an' again." Shay's voice was soft. Almost girl-like. "Gotta watch 'em. Just when ya think ya got 'em figured—BAM!"

"Uhh, thank you, Shay."

Shay acknowledged her with a wink. "You'll get used to it."

But that wasn't even up for debate. She walked to the barn next to hers to find Cynthia.

"I'm leaving. Do you want to come with me?"

"But, why?"

"Getting the hell out. I almost just got killed."

But Cynthia was determined to stick it out. So Clancy went to the bunkhouse, packed her belongings, and though fear filled her veins until she could feel it at her fingertips, she knew she was now on her own. She threw her meager belongings into her van and headed out.

It was time for hew new life. She'd get on the road and go find it.

October 1977

"Happy birthday, dear boy." Mathew was dreaming. But then he opened his eyes and Aunt Nora was standing over his bed with a small cake, lit with candles. He tried to focus on the clock: 2:40 A.M.

"Aunt Nora?" He was very groggy.

"It's your birthday. You were born at precisely this moment eighteen years ago." And before he could respond, she commanded, "Up you get, then."

She led him through the darkened halls, their path lit only by the small candles. Once in the living room she sat him in one of the large overstuffed chairs.

"I thought we'd have our very own little celebration. There's something I'm dying to share with you."

Tea service was set out and she poured him a cup, babbling through the entire ritual as though it were in the middle of the afternoon. Then suddenly she jumped to the TV set and turned it on.

"Aunt Nora?"

Top Hat with Fred Astaire and Ginger Rogers was playing. He stared at the black-and-white images, resentful at first, but then as he began to watch Fred and Ginger glide across the floor he became entranced. During the second commercial break he turned and smiled at her.

"Happy birthday, my boy," she said. "May your art be filled with the elements of magic that touch the soul." Aunt Nora toasted.

What could he say to this gift, except a numb thank-you. His gratitude would increase as getting up in the early morning hours to catch old back-and-white flicks became a tradition for them. Their little secret. Their time. Nora warned him now when she intended to haul him out of bed, but there were still those unexpected moments when she'd knock on the door, tiptoe in, and lead him downstairs.

The storylines of those films, overwrought and flimsy beyond description, were worth putting up with for the dance numbers, when Fred with his lithe and limber body, more gazelle than man, would whirl Ginger backward, forward, around and around, their gliding effortless. Mathew came to appreciate beauty.

Later, when videos became all the rage, he collected or taped every Fred Astaire movie ever made. What he didn't understand at the time was how these films worked their subliminal magic on him, unearthing his own sexuality. *You'll Never Get Rich* was a ridiculous farce, but the opening boogie-woogie number that Fred dances with Rita Hayworth pricked in him a stirring different from the flushing eagerness to please with Maria. Primal. His breathing quickened as his eyes were riveted upon Rita's legs, the way her shirt tucked into her shorts, revealing the soft lines of her body, her full, rich hair, bouncing rhythm of the times. It was earthy. Exciting.

But it was the number later in the movie, a minimalist setting that Mathew would remember; Fred warbling "near yet so far" beneath one fake palm tree in the center of a painted-cardboard stage. Rita, decked in a black full-length cocktail dress, low-cut to expose her delicious chest and neckline. Her eyes invite and Mathew felt the kick from sexuality to sensuality. Her teasing tango, subtle, and all the more alluring . . . Just barely. So near. So far. It would categorize his attraction to women for the rest of his life.

◆ ◆ ◆

"She's quite a 'dish,'" Carlita murmured as her wings flailed about her.

"I do wish you'd drop your earthly vernacular." But Carlita continued to prance around epileptically. "Whatever is the matter, Carlita?"

"I was just trying to rewind a bit of the hologram view." Again Carlita signed her wings, trying to mimic Gabriella's flourish.

"It might help if you had the signals in order." Gabriella moved forward and very gracefully signed to the hologram. The images rewound to Mathew watching the dance sequence. "Just remember, you're only approved for rewind. Not fast forward. As you don't know the signals in any case, I suppose you needn't be concerned with that."

"Oh, absolutely not." But Carlita took in every gesture and movement and was quite certain she knew the maneuvers to operate the hologram once she was left to her own devices.

November 1977

A roaring diesel truck woke Clancy from a dreamless sleep. Late morning from the feel of the sun. She had been driving nights, something that had become a habit in the last few days. When the sun came up, the reflection glaring off every man-made artifact on the road made her drooping lids feel like shards of glass, and she would finally pull over.

Life on the road had become familiar; traveling toward an empty tank of gas, stopping at the first reasonable-looking burg, scavenging food as cheaply as possible as she counted her few remaining dollars. Cynthia had sent her meager paycheck care of general delivery in Grand Rapids, so she felt relatively rich this morning as she stretched briefly, then braced herself for the cold outside her van, then made a mad dash to the rest room. The stalls all looked and smelled the same. Urine and Lysol. When she returned to the van, she jumped behind the wheel and went through a series of machinations that worked the motor into an uneven sputter. It didn't do well in cold weather. She pulled out, passing the long line of long-bed trucks, and returned to the freeway.

It didn't matter where she was. Rest stops were all the same; a jumble of "gas-food-and-lodging" in—"remember to pick up your garbage" out. She briefly wondered what the day might bring. After being jailed with her mother for most of her lifetime and working since her early teens, life on the road was bliss. Freedom. Spontaneity. And absolutely no responsibility. No responsibility—it was a concept she warmed to.

She would stop in a small town—where she felt safe—walk the streets and imagine what life would be like in this oak-lined town, with a crumbling movie marquee that showcased films only on weekends. She'd sit in a small but well-attended café, sometimes for hours, reading books she picked up at a garage sale or used book store. When she'd finished, she'd just leave them on the table. She had to travel light. The van could barely carry her without snorting and choking all along the way. Every so often she'd strike up conversation with an older couple or some perfect-looking family, and would get invited for a good home-cooked meal, a hot bath, even television. She'd heartily accept, not because she was sick for company, but because she was trying to stretch her meager budget. It had its drawbacks, however, for once she was back on the highway she would find herself missing the warmth of Tom and Jane Barrow's home and their two-year-old son. Or still smell the kitchen of Mr. and Mrs. Wilson, old-time farmers—all bacony, fried eggs, and dark coffee—where they sat most hours they weren't out riding tractor, feeding cows, hens, pigs, and whatnot, their lives fueled by hard work, simple honesty, and, of course, the livestock report. These people were anchored deep into the earth. But it was their very rootedness she fled.

She now stopped for coffee and cigarettes, glazed doughnut and orange juice. She'd concluded after only three days that criteria for all road food were that it be weak, runny, and/or stale. As the stimulants kicked into her central nervous system, she cranked her radio. "Do You Think I'm Sexy" was followed by a tear jerker she didn't recognize, too maudlin for her patience, so she twirled the radio knob, got caught up in talk radio when she realized she had no idea where she was. She'd been driving for hours and it was dark but she felt like she'd just woken up.

It hadn't been intentional, this heading west. More like a gravitational pull, maybe something as far away as she could take herself without having to swim an ocean to escape her past. "The great escape," she said just under her breath. "Yeah!" and she laughed. Her great escape in a '67 van; fourth gear had popped out somewhere a thousand miles ago, only one side of the heater working; singing along with schmaltzy love songs until she was hoarse; cruising at 48 mph, the fastest this dog would take her. But she was free, and that's all that counted.

She shut her eyes, opened and refocused on the landscape, that over hours became surreal, framed by a long strip of road that faded into black, taillights blipping in and out of the shadows before and after her. Who were in these other cars? Was half of humanity running from itself? Or only a few lost souls. The rest going shopping, visiting the in-laws, on the way to the hospital for a new birth. Her mind wandered into the black that skimmed by and never ended, then tripped its way back to that night. What had made her think of that? Since she'd been on the road she spent most of her time daydreaming, tuning out bad memories with godawful bad radio. No. She couldn't go into that.

She fiddled for the Rand McNally to redirect her thinking, opened the side that said West Coast, let her fingers caress this map—pages that had the crinkled smoothness of a Bible, but had been opened and closed with far more regularity. In that moment she knew she wanted to find a place to settle. Just as she'd got on the road, she was now ready to stop. She thought how simple it was to make the decision as she let her index finger slide left and point its way to her new home. She glanced down to find out where that might be. Portland, Oregon? Sure. Why not?

December 16, 1977

"Mathew, it's time to fly." Aunt Nora waltzed into the kitchen wearing a brand-new Chinese kimono.

"Where? Up there?" Mathew indicated the attic.

"My dear boy, I don't fly up to the attic. I take the stairs, like any civilized person." She walked to him, tousled his hair. "No, darling. We're taking a trip, just you and I."

"What about Maria?"

"I don't believe she's coming with us. Aren't you the least bit interested in where we're going?"

"Well, sure . . . I just thought—"

"Of course you did." Aunt Nora finished for him, although he had no idea what he was going to say. "And I'd love to have her along, but Maria's going to a big family wedding, and well, darling, we weren't invited, so I thought we should take the time and go to New York."

"New York." He was disappointed about Maria, but the thought of New York almost compensated. Great writers, poets, journalists. The round tablers of the . . .

"Yes, and we'll visit the Algonquin," she said reading his thoughts, "although do you really think it's still the same?"

He stared at her, a little startled. Sometimes he wondered if she thought she was talking to her late husband.

"Anyway, pack enough for four days and three nights. We're staying with Esmelda Smythe, a bit of a stick, but good for a visit now and again."

"When are we going?"

"The cab should be here in an hour."

No one could say Aunt Nora wasn't spontaneous.

December 16, 1977

Clancy lived in a basement apartment of a building the city was going to tear down to reroute the freeway. It didn't strike her as ironic that she lived in the underbelly of a building, as she had with her mother, until she had been there two weeks. She was staring at the walls, noticing the damp seepage, leaks that would never be repaired because they would be gutting the building in several months anyway.

It really didn't matter, though. What mattered was that after living in Portland for only a few short weeks, she was flying back to New York in less than three hours.

She had been munching on Cracker Jacks and sipping cheap Gallo wine as she penciled a budget that would get her back to school with her earnings from the split shifts she had been working at "Madame Steak," a restaurant that had an upscale attitude but in reality was just a dressed-up, twenty-four-hour coffee shop for the downscale blue-collar crowd. That afternoon, before her shift was over, she had gotten a call from her aunt Marion, the only person to whom she had given her number. And now she had called to say her uncle Joseph, her mother's baby brother, had died of liver failure, proudly following his sister's drunken footsteps into the grave. Surprisingly, he had left Clancy an inheritance.

Aunt Marion had wired her money for a plane ticket, so here she was, going back already. But only for a couple of days. She would leave the second she could get out of there. New York was nothing but cold and dirty, and it was too close to yesterday.

The funeral was not unlike her mother's. There were only three other people at the service, other than herself and a sedated Aunt Marion, and one of them was the minister, Clancy noted, predictably. What a family, she thought. So well loved and admired.

Clancy stopped herself. Actually, Uncle Joseph had been the nicest of her mother's five brothers, all dead now except the middle one, Sal, whom she had never met. He lived in Los Angeles, but had done something so terrible that he had been disowned by the lot. She never had figured out what could be so awful, especially in light of Joseph's inept philandering, Uncle Tommy's parole status, and Uncle Luke's having to be institutionalized.

After the service they returned to Aunt Marion's, where she made coffee. They sat in silence in what Clancy's mother used to refer to as "that fancy schmancy la-di-da, parlay view" apartment. Uncle Joe and Aunt Marion had baby-sat her there twice weekly. While there Clancy loved to pretend she was a princess, that the other Clancy was a beggar-thief, a Cinderella forced to live in squalor. Uncle Joe had been a maître d' at an exclusive French restaurant and had made good money. At least before his drinking took over. Before he was asked to retire. Before time and Joseph's pride slipped away and the apartment had deteriorated along with their lives.

Aunt Marion's eyes were swollen strawberries. She hadn't stopped crying since Clancy had arrived. Whimpers that made her heart ache. Clancy wasn't sure if she could stay the next two days. If she could stand someone needing her. Again.

"Aunt Marion, maybe I'll just go for a walk."

Her aunt simply nodded.

She walked for hours. When the cold became unbearable she went into a retro beatnik coffee shop, picked up a discarded *Times,* meandered aimlessly through the worn news. Anton Tjiskovsky was playing at Carnegie Hall. The famed violinist. Once she had heard a recording of his at the community college. She had had to leave the classroom, unstoppable tears breaking the determined exterior of her cool facade.

And, now, here he was, to perform, in person. Could she go? The idea terrified her. She felt the tremors beneath her heavy woolen coat. She got up and walked to the café door, then ran back to the table and grabbed the paper with the listing.

December 18, 1977

Mathew wriggled uncomfortably in his rented tux. He'd outgrown his two dress suits since he'd moved stateside, but other than the occasional dinner, there really hadn't been much reason to dress. Mathew loved that about Americans. They were dedicated to comfort. "Dedicated to laziness," Aunt Nora scoffed.

His collar itched, which made it difficult for him to fully enjoy Tjiskovsky's performance. But he would endure anything to get out from under Esmelda, so pushy and annoying with her loud Flatbush accent. They had been in her dust-baked apartment for three hours when he'd developed a teeming headache that would not go away. The next morning Aunt Nora had produced the tickets, magically, the perfect medicine. "Now why don't you take a walk and then we'll catch dinner at the Algonquin and make an evening of it." She didn't have to ask twice.

His Aunt Nora. He glanced at her now. Mouth slightly open, collapsed in her seat, she'd fallen asleep. What a dear, sweet woman she was. That morning he'd discovered quite by accident that Aunt Nora had been a Rockette. Before she met her first husband. There she kicked, next to a younger Esmelda in a small photo framed in wicker. There seemed no end of surprises to this woman who had been kept a secret from the family. Trying to figure Aunt Nora was like trying to understand abstract physics. It was all there, it made sense to those who comprehended it, but for the rest, well, one just had to accept it on faith. And he had. Accepted his Aunt Nora on total faith. There wasn't anyone on earth he loved more.

"Look, she's seated four rows in front of him." Carlita pointed excitedly.

"Yes. I'm aware of that."

"So, is this where it happens? Where they meet?"

"Patience."

Intermission. Clancy sighed. Trying to hold tears back had been useless. She needed to repair the damage, though, and set out for the ladies' room. She left her coat and program, grabbed the purse she'd borrowed from Aunt Marion, and trailed her way through the other patrons, who glanced in admiration at the gown Aunt Marion had lent her. In fact, there wasn't anything she had on that she hadn't borrowed.

When she'd returned to the apartment last night, and found Aunt Marion still silently weeping, she made the decision to go to the concert, even if only to escape her grieving aunt. Then watching the poor woman stuck in the inescapable reality of her future, she asked Aunt Marion to join her. It would be good for her, she reasoned, get her out of the apartment filled with nothing but memories. "I couldn't possibly," Aunt Marion said, shaking her head, but for a few hours her sorrow was diverted as she helped Clancy into her favorite claret velvet evening gown, the one she wore with Joseph on special occasions, when she'd still been young and slender and quite beautiful, as Clancy saw in the black-and-white photo perched on the dresser, the sterling silver frame now aged and tarnished.

Clancy could barely believe her own glamorous reflection as Aunt Marion tried first this pair of earrings, then another, laced a garnet choker about her neck, put her hair up in a loose chignon, then allowed it to drop to luxurious fullness. "No, no—you're more the Rita Hayworth type—best we leave it down," she said, investing all her energy in this younger woman's presence, as if this were the last moment she would ever have interest in beauty, herself.

Clancy now stared at her reflection in the mirror of the bathroom at Carnegie Hall. Her mascara hadn't run too badly. She repaired it quickly, ran a brush through her hair, then decided she would get a glass of wine.

Mathew decided to let Aunt Nora sleep. Once she was out, it was difficult to bring her back. He went into the lobby and ordered some champagne from the bar, sipped from the plastic glass as he wandered through the layers of tuxedos and evening gowns in the hall, patrons chattering excitedly about the performance. He soaked up the experience, completely happy. Suddenly he felt something pulling at him. An awareness of something. Someone. And in that moment he felt compelled to investigate the foyer where prints of Tjiskovsky were displayed; he turned in the direction where Clancy stood.

◆ ◆ ◆

"There's the pre-ripple."

"Yes. Can't they see it? Feel it?" Carlita was beside herself.

A stout woman barged in front of him. "Oh Marcy, I simply can't believe it's you," she gushed. "I mean I thought it might be you from across the room, but I had no idea you'd returned to the States. I mean, after Raul and all, I thought you'd stay scarce."

Mathew momentarily listened to the idle gossip, then realized he had dropped his program, and bent to retrieve it.

Ten feet away from him, Clancy felt a chill run up her neck, a vague disturbance . . . what was it? She turned self-consciously toward where Mathew stood. She saw an obese woman chattering animatedly at her friends, so she turned back to the prints of Tjiskovsky on the wall. She decided to get champagne instead of wine. Why not? Who knew when she'd experience a night like this again. It would fortify her. She didn't much like crowds, and felt out of place, being a single woman, probably the youngest in this crowd, with no escort.

"Oh, move already, you old cow," Carlita urged.

"That was their first ordained meeting," Gabriella informed Carlita.

"Couldn't they see what was happening?" Carlita tried to work her new powers, but it took a few seconds to get the hologram to reverse the images back to the precise moment they were to meet. She reviewed the large ripple, like a clear tidal wave that shook the room. "My God, as clear as day."

"To us." Gabriella froze the scene. "For them it is unrecordable. You see, all they knew was that something jarred them from the mo-

ment they were in. For Mathew it was the woman who bustled into him on his left, see here?" Carlita nodded.

"But there's no one even by Clancy."

"See the confusion on her face?"

"Yes . . ."

"Clancy is aware there has been a shift. She doesn't assimilate that she's experienced a time warp. She simply feels a vague unease. Something's not right, but she has no idea what it is. And in a moment she lets it pass."

They played the scene again. Carlita watched Mathew, who was suddenly bumped by the stout woman beside him. He dropped his program. In the moment he bent to pick it up, Clancy had turned his way, appearing slightly confused, and shrugging her shoulders, turned back to the prints on the wall and then made her way to the bar.

"Could we . . . I mean just a teensy bit," Carlita began self-consciously, "you know—view a little of the destifate screen?" Then rushed on as Gabriella's wings ruffled uncomfortably. "I mean—"

"You know very well it's against Interplanetary Code."

"I know we're not supposed to, but what can it hurt?"

And Gabriella had to admit it. She wanted to see it as well. Of the two she was the only one who had the authority to initiate a destifate screen. "Okay. But Carlita, not a word of this."

"Absolutely," Carlita said, then glanced at Gabriella. She was an angel, after all.

DESTIFATE IMAGERY INITIATED

Rewind. Time Ripple Deactivated.

Mathew whistled the phrase of the Brandenburg concerto that had been playing in his head since the beginning of the intermission. The brooding darkness of Beethoven, the tortured angst of

Chopin were more his cup of tea, but Bach made him feel light, weightless, as if the world were full of endless possibilities. He grinned as the large woman in front of him continued her running commentary on half the debs in New York society. He studied the upper crust here, attending the concert, reminding him suddenly of England, of home. The gentle aristocracy in a culture that had none. He smiled. He felt warmly toward Americans and their attempts at refinement.

He soaked in the experience, completely happy. But then, suddenly, something pulled at him. An awareness of something. Someone. And in that moment he felt compelled to investigate the foyer where prints of Tjiskovsky were displayed.

It was then that he saw her.

A stunning creature in a wine-colored gown. Quite beautiful. Breathtaking, in fact. He simply could not take his eyes off her.

Clancy felt a chill run up her neck, a vague disturbance . . . what was it? She turned self-consciously toward where Mathew stood. She saw an obese woman chattering animatedly at her friends, but before she turned back, she saw him.

Their eyes met briefly. Then she shrugged a bit self-consciously and turned toward the bar. Mathew maneuvered himself around the hefty matron and followed Clancy a few paces behind, caught in the jumble of people, but never losing sight of her.

Clancy continued to replay the divinely mastered instrumentation of Tjiskovsky, the music and champagne burning through her so that she felt the flush in her cheeks. She felt inspired, infused with a hope for her own music that she hadn't felt in years. Damn, it was hot in this crowded lobby. She brushed the hair from the back of her neck to cool herself.

When she lifted the amber hair from her neck, Mathew felt his heart expand in his chest. Exquisite lines of grace, hair swirling, a few loose strands sticking at the nape from the heat—suddenly he realized he wasn't breathing. She turned his way again, and again their gaze drew one another in and he knew, in that moment—a moment of utter perfection, when he saw her as if in slow motion, capturing every aspect of this lovely vision—if such a thing were possible, that he had fallen in love. He knew also that if he didn't speak to her immediately he would lose the opportunity. He pushed his way through the throng of people, all of them oblivious to this crucially important event, until he was almost on top of her.

"Hello there," he said as he stumbled forward, nervous.

"Hello," she said uncertainly.

"Trifle hot in here, eh?"

Clancy turned to Mathew. The first thing she responded to were his gentle eyes. "Yes. It is. Quite hot."

Mathew fanned them both with his program and she smiled in gratitude. He thought her smile was the loveliest thing he had ever seen. He felt the silence grow awkward between them. "You know . . . has anyone ever told you, you bear a striking resemblance to Rita Hayworth?"

She laughed. That was the second time she'd heard that name tonight.

Then he laughed at himself. "I can't believe I just said that. I absolutely deplore that when it's said back home."

"What, that people look like Rita Hayworth?"

"No. Of course not. That everyone rather looks like some movie star or other. But there it is," he pointed at her mouth, "a bit around the mouth. When you smile."

Which she did, for his benefit. "Where's home?"

"Los Angeles."

"Oh?"

"Originally from England," he said, and realized he had sounded more English suddenly. He wanted to impress her. It had worked before.

"What are you doing in New York?"

"My aunt and I are visiting a friend of hers and she thought it would be nice to hear the concert. She very much adores Bach."

"She's got excellent taste."

They stood again in silence. But this time it was filled with an excitement. An energy that swam between the two of them, a current that connected them in some undefinable but very definite manner. As if she knew him, Clancy thought, but of course, how could she? She glanced at him again. What beautiful eyes. Gentle smile, nice even teeth, dimple in his chin, closely shaved cheeks. She had the urge to feel her palm against his skin. Then she shook herself back to reality. Clearly, he was beyond her. An untouchable—way beyond her reach. But he was attentive and sweet. And the only other one here under fifty.

"I take it you're from New York, then?"

"Actually, yes and no. Originally, but I live in Oregon now."

"Oregon? Dear Lord, whereabout?"

"Portland."

"My aunt owns property there. We go to Mount Hood every year at Christmas."

"Really!" And now they were both smiling because this meant they weren't really so far apart.

The lights flickered, indicating the end of intermission.

"Well, I suppose we should be getting back," Mathew said, but neither he nor Clancy made a move to leave.

And then, as if by magic, Aunt Nora was by his side, begging off the rest of the concert, she had a "devil of a headache," she said, and was taking a taxi back to Esmelda's. Would he mind awfully being left to his own devices? Which left her seat free so that Clancy could join him for the second half of the performance that now sounded like the most brilliant music Mathew had ever heard, and even Clancy found the violins sang sweeter, their agony more poignant, their strength more jubilant.

Afterward they stood outside the concert hall. Neither of them wanted to say good-bye and neither of them hailed a cab.

"How does—" He had interrupted something she was about to say.

"I was just going to ask—" But she became shy.

"Coffee?"

"Precisely."

They found a small diner with bad coffee and sat and talked. For hours. During which she decided she loved his eyes best. Then his thick dark hair, almost black, and his rugged jawline under smooth skin—so very English. And his lips were a nice shape, too. They occasioned a self-deprecatory grin when he'd said perhaps a bit too much. She found that adorable—an odd expression, she knew, to use for a man. She loved the way he smiled when he was shy.

He thought her smile the most magical he had ever seen. It transformed her serious face, deep-set eyes—brown one moment, green the next—relaxing the set of her jaw, the tightness around her lips. She had secrets. He could feel it. But when she smiled, her face was altogether striking. He could never tire of looking at it.

They spoke late into the night about everything that had ever mattered to them and much that did not. They walked Central Park when it turned light, strolling closely until Mathew finally took her hand, and she let him, feeling its protective warmth around her own.

And as the sun rose the imagery faded.

◆ ◆ ◆

"I've heard of thunderstruck, but wasn't that awful fast?"

"The ability to fall in love with a soul mate is not measurable in time, my dear. When young, there is less filter. As we move forward in their time it won't be as easy."

"So . . . what happened?" Carlita demanded.

"It doesn't matter because it never did happen."

"But what was supposed to happen?"

"Well, you saw it. They fell sweetly in love, wrote back and forth from Portland to Los Angeles. They had their moments of struggle. She felt she didn't deserve him, he worked hard to prove that she did, and ultimately they married several years later and lived a very long and prosperous life."

"So, then why can't we just shove them together now?"

"It's not that simple. Who they were then . . . the things that happen to Clancy and Mathew between this meeting and the next will change them, will change their perceptions, their ability to trust, feel, hope. All the things that happen to them in life, from this point forward, will shape them differently from who they would have been if they had met at this precise moment when they were supposed to."

March 1979

Gilda," Mathew began, and then recited,

> "In her best slippery bad b-speak,
> the absolute peak
> of femme fatale,
> 'Johnny, let's hate her,' she poses,
> eyes roses, death-as-daggers, the point . . .
> the point . . .

"I want to tie it into Ballin Munson's damn cane." He had been working on a series of poems dedicated to his favorite movies. "You know it as being his 'best friend' and all, but it's really the point that binds them all. Metaphorically."

As always, Maria listened intently, her brow reflecting mild distress and some confusion.

"Do you see what I'm driving at?"

"Sí." She had no idea.

"Good. So I'm not totally off the mark, then?"

"No."

He was about to launch into another idea when she took his hand. "You theenk too much."

He blushed, even before she touched him. All she had to do was get near him and he became a heat-guided missile.

"Come." Maria pulled him forward, picked up a picnic basket she had already prepared, dragged him out of the house to the car. "Let's go. You can't theenk all the time. It's no good for the head."

She packed him in and off they went.

Aunt Nora watched from the attic window. She knew.

The sand felt good in his toes. He'd rolled up his pants, taken off his shirt. The sun had burnished his pale white, now turning him a golden bronze from hours of running. But he felt naked and awkward, his English skin fair next to her dark softness. He'd filled out the summer before, his muscles not large, but well defined. Runner's muscles, lean and agile. She had taken off her sweater, clad only in a loose white halter top. He was afraid to look at her, afraid his eyes would betray him. He looked at the ocean instead.

Surfers played with the waves. There wasn't much to catch a ride on. There was only a mild breeze, just enough to keep one from getting uncomfortably hot.

They didn't talk. They just were together. They'd known each other almost six years now. She'd watched him grow from a tremulous boy, to an eager adolescent, and now, to the precipice of manhood. Changes, tumultuous, painful, all the many evolutions of growing up, while she'd stayed very much the same, Sunday through Monday, Saturdays off, which she spent with her four children. Her husband had been a useless drunk who had gambled away her wages until Aunt Nora had sent him packing.

She glanced his way again, with a question in her eyes that she already knew the answer to. This time he did not blush, nor did he turn away.

She gently touched his shoulder, the tips of her fingers hotter than the pink-singed burn. "It's time," she said, which could have meant anything.

They stopped for ice cream on their way home, picked up a honey-colored pecan praline for Aunt Nora, her favorite, but when they reached the house there was no trace of her. Their eyes met, held. He offered the cone to her. She licked the melted cream, her tongue just brushing his forefinger. His eyes narrowed.

"I'm going to shower, then make dinner. Would you like chicken or steak?" She asked, as if they were a married couple.

"You decide." There was only one hunger he knew.

They walked slowly up the stairs together, Maria a step ahead of him, languorous, there was nothing more sensual than the way she moved. Never in a hurry.

He stopped at the door to his room and watched as she moved down the hall to her room. The one she used on the nights she stayed over or when Aunt Nora entertained too late in the evening for her to drive all the way home to Los Feliz. She did not close the door. He must have stood there a full five minutes before he moved toward it, heard the shower running. What in bloody hell was he thinking? So they'd spent the day at the beach together. That didn't mean she was inviting him into her bed. She was twenty years older than he. She'd practically become a second mother to him. She probably would be flattered by his interest in her, and say in that silky voice, "You silly boy."

The water stopped. She appeared. Naked. She walked from the bathroom into the bedroom. He was still at the open door, paralyzed by her beauty, her soft belly, her gracefully sagging full breasts, thick dark hair at her legs. It took a moment before he realized she was watching him watching her. It could have been forever or merely a second before she smiled.

He tried to mimic something like a smile in return, but he was sure it appeared as a grimace of nervous and awkward frustration. She walked to him, took his hand, led him inside the room, and quietly closed the door.

Her hand trailed a path of quickening desire as she cupped his strong chin, then let her fingernails trace the tendons down his neck, circling both nipples. A sharp intake of breath, his nipples a new part of his body now, and then her palm gently rubbing in small circular strokes down his chest, kneading the muscles in his stomach, down the line of hair to his shorts, then stopping, and holding her hand a half inch away from his fully erect penis, aching now for her to touch him. It seemed an eternity until she did, finally fully owning his desire and then slowly, oh so slowly, leading him to her bed, where she taught him not only how to be a man, but to be a man with a woman.

April 1979

The violin. It stared back at her with demanding frequency as she nibbled on Cracker Jacks at her card table, where she sat and pondered her finances. Two thousand dollars. She kept her inheritance rolled in a sock and stuffed behind a loosened brick in the wall. And the violin: A Stradivarius her Uncle Joe had brought back from Europe. He'd traded his poker winnings for it at a rundown bar while stationed in Italy during the war. "Damn sergeant thought it was just a fiddle!" Uncle Joe cackled every time he told the story.

She had been seven years old when her Uncle Joseph had played Bach's Siciliano on that violin and had turned her body into music. It was the first moment she felt. The first moment she became aware that there was more to being alive than the monotony of food, sleep, and pain. Like a waterfall inside her with no gravity—winding about and throughout her, then coming to the surface so quickly that when he was finished, she was dizzy. She had approached him in awe and asked very quietly, "May I touch it?" And as her uncle was handing her the precious instrument—THWACK!!

"Don't be messin' with adult things." Her mother's knuckles packed quite a wallop against the side of her head. "'Sides, that's for uppercrusts like your Uncle Joe here and his *parlay view* diner. Now come on, missy moonshine, we gotta get home."

But her uncle let her touch the Stradivarius when her mother wasn't there, when he and Marion had watched her the two afternoons and nights her mother worked, and the many other nights she went out. They never had children of their own. "Dead eggs," Clancy had heard her mother gossiping about Aunt Marion to one of her dates.

Uncle Joseph helped stretch her tiny fingers onto the tightened strings at the fingerboard, put the body in the crook of her left arm, leaned the curve of the tailpiece at her delicate chin, and moved the bow over the bridge as if it were a magical wand that produced sound. But sound wasn't enough for Clancy. She wanted to make music.

"Make a song," she demanded, plaintively.

He gave her lessons. From the moment she arrived, she would beg him to help her play. "She's got talent, Mar," she heard him say to her aunt. She glowed inside with her first sense of pride and accomplishment. "Yeah? Well, just don't let Ceel find out." Both remarks made her determined to be the best violinist ever.

By the time she was ten she was quite accomplished, and Uncle Joseph took her to a teacher he'd found through his bookie. They were eating roasted chestnuts at a corner. "She's an old Russky, Vladimira Jones. Her brother's one of my best clients." She stared up at the bookie as he spat little chunks of nutty residue. "Speaks shit for English, but she's the best in this town. On the steep side, but right in your neighborhood."

The first time she met Madame Jones, Clancy was terrified. A sterner face she'd never seen, not even on her mother. Uncle Joseph took her in the first time, but Madame put an unrelenting hand to his chest. "Now you go. Forty-five minutes, come back."

"Why do you want to play violin?" she barked as soon as they were alone.

"I . . . I don't . . . um." Clancy was terrified.

"What makes you think you can *play* violin?"

"Uncle Joe says I have talent."

At which Madame Jones roared, then walked around Clancy three times, appraising her. She walked to a shelf with several violins, delicately picked up one of them, and returned to Clancy. "Play."

Clancy's fingers trembled; she shoved her chin into the tailpiece to keep it from shaking. She couldn't play in front of this monster. Not with this fear in her. The first notes were achingly inept. She braved a peek at Madame, but the old woman's eyes were closed. It gave her courage to shut her own, which led her to the place she went when she played at Uncle Joseph's. A place that was not of words or of this earth, not of anything she could describe in her child's head, but that was filled with light, light so pure it extinguished the existence of her mother and their decaying apartment. A place that teased the pain from inside her and left her free.

She didn't know how long she played, but when she stopped she opened her eyes and saw Madame's eyes narrowed before her very own. Then a miracle. Inside the deep watery wells a smile slowly cracked, opening the stone mountain of Madame's face. "Your uncle is right." And thus began their work.

For one deliciously clandestine year Uncle Joseph walked her twice a week to see Madame, whom she grew to love as a gentle storm, raging on the outside, but safety certain within. She learned to play Mozart, Vivaldi, and her favorite, Bach, most difficult for beginners, but Clancy took to it as if it were as simple as singing. The complexity of the music, the underlining motif of several layers of melodic communication all happening at the same time sprang easily from the place where the music lived. And that's how Bach felt to her: like singing inside.

After that first year Madame Jones gave her a new violin to use. "This for you. Your new instrument. For life." Clancy felt she would melt to the floor with gratitude. She loved the new violin, its seasoned spruce, the burnished auburn finish, smooth maple back, the feel of the gut-wound perlon strings that would toughen the calluses on the tips of her fingers, gritty and hardened, which she ran over and over again along her smooth cheeks when her mother screamed at her. These were hers. She owned this. She loved every part of it, but mostly she loved that it was a gift. Never before had she been given anything so precious.

But then that night happened and with it came the end of the music. The end of any sort of peace between her mother and herself.

She got up, brushed a Cracker Jack from her lap, then walked to the violin, put it in its case, and got ready for her shift.

May 1979

Mathew and Maria slept together only three times, all within a few days of each other, each meeting as potent as the one before. They didn't speak of the obvious: that this could never work. That their desire was mutually driven by hunger on his part, need on her own. It was a passage. Nothing more to be considered. Mathew would forever be grateful for the almost choreographed nature of their encounters, the first a simple matter of spontaneous heat; the second time Maria did things to Mathew he could never have believed possible. He never knew his body could feel the way she made it feel, telling him about himself with touch, as again, neither spoke a word. And at the last, she taught him about a woman, about being inside her, about the outside of her, how to caress the softness of her skin, the hardness of her nipples, the art of moving slowly, touching gently, the tastes and smells that would fill his dreams for months.

But after that last time, it was as if they both knew there was no going back and no returning. Full stop. They never spoke of it, they treated each other much the same, but Mathew was less obviously attentive, more gentle, and Maria rarely met his eye.

A mystery. Which seemed to be the way Aunt Nora and Maria preferred to keep things. But one night he pried information out of tight-lipped Dora refilling her "Maypole Tide," hinting about until she screwed her face up and said, "Yer Aunt Nora saved Maria, poor child. Four kids. Thin as nails. Her workin' in the bean fields and him takin' all that hard-earned money. Gamblin' every last dime away. Nothing wrong with betting a few stakes here and there. But you have to know when the dice are leadin' you down the devil's path. That man would gamble on darn near anything. First time Nora sees Maria she's driving along and there's this woman bendin' over at the edge of the road. Vomiting. Damn near dead. Takes her to the hospital straight away. Course they can barely communicate. Pregnant. Number five it woulda been. But she lost the poor thing. For the best, I say. Aunt Nora hires her on the spot. Well, a couple of years go by and Nora gets the goods on Eduardo . . . finds him gamblin' on the cock fights, walks right in, the only white woman in a crowd of a hundred men, mind you, and grabs him by the cuff. I was there. Waiting in the car. She pulls him out, speaks to him real low, not menacing, just matter of course, and says, 'Eduardo. You've spent your last day on Maria's payroll. I've got INS inches from this place. I suggest you take this ticket to Miami and start a new life.'" Dora gulped from her glass and frowned at it. "I'm feeling a bit woozy, Mathew. Would you help me inside?" After that he loved Maria all the more. But in a different way. Like one loves a legend. Untouchable.

"She's led such a tragic life," he said to his aunt one morning as Maria drove off to the market.

"Tragic? Not tragic, dear boy. I'd call it colorful."

He had dated several friends from high school but was never sexually enticed by their lanky athletic youth, found nothing erotic about their brown slender bodies. They were girls. His mates. But now he wanted . . . something. It gnawed at him, haunted him, created a new tension called yearning. On the surface it reminded him of wanting his mother to know him, know him as he truly was, but this new need did not stem from the ego needs of a child;

this was the desire of a man to be uncovered. Discovered. It felt all mixed up to him. He had no idea how to or where to answer the aching and began to feel half animal, half man. So when his application had been accepted to attend Lewis and Clark, Mathew jumped at the idea, even if it meant leaving his aunt. And leaving Maria, which now seemed a wise alternative.

"My dear boy, you know I have no problem paying for your schooling, but I must reiterate, the best education for a writer is life. Travel. I'll send you abroad."

"But I want to study the classics and learn *how* to write. Properly."

"And?"

"Well, don't you see? I need guidance."

"Pooh. Guidance. All the guidance you will ever need comes from within. That, and to write. Write. Write. Badly. Theatrically. Melodramatically. And then you learn to hone that into fine, pure, lyrical prose, along with huge servings of life. Love. Pain. Torment. Great celebration. Drugs."

"Aunt Nora. I'm going to miss you." He couldn't argue with her, but he felt compelled to go away. "I really think it's for the best."

Aunt Nora sighed. "Well then, I'll call Terrance in Portland. He'll find you a suitable flat, show you around. It's not like here, you know. Lots of rain."

"Rain." Mathew became nostalgic. "I could go for a good dose of rain."

September 1979

Rain. More rain. Clancy couldn't bear it much longer. She'd been holed up for a week. Called in sick every day. Gray. Bleak. Empty.

Empty as her insides. She cried. She had cried for hours. Every day. She felt like she inhabited a form, held together by some glue that kept her insides from falling out, but beyond that she had no relationship to the body that lay in the bed, sore from lack of movement.

It was one of her spells. She had developed them since her mother died. Every few months she'd start to feel not like herself. Unreal. Unconnected to the world or her own body. She'd touch her skin but feel very little. Sounds were muted. Sights alternated between being blurred and then suddenly became sharp and focused. She'd wonder if she were in a dream, not able to attach anything real to her surroundings. And when she felt this way, she'd go to bed.

The spells, in and of themselves, did not frighten her. In a way there was a kind of relief to them. She'd crawl into bed, and sleep hours and hours, of dreamless sleep, and when she woke she felt drugged and groggy so that after going to the bathroom, drinking some water, she would return to the womb of safety.

But this morning she'd been awakened; the dream had come back. It had been some time since it had visited her. The dream that was as real as if she were there. No matter what she did that morning she couldn't shake the realness of her mother's voice, snipping, "Your daddy's comin' to visit," as if she were complaining that the paper was late.

Clancy had never seen her father. Her mother never spoke of him, but one night, after a night's healthy drinking, her mother did something she rarely did. She cried. Clancy had stood quietly in the hallway watching her, this broken version of the steel wall that was her mother, and then the soggy, disheveled face found its way to her own.

"Come here, Clan," her mother whimpered. Her mother

wanted her near her. Little Clancy's heart trembled in her chest. She moved forward cautiously. Her mother yanked her to the side of the bed. "Your daddy's the only man I ever loved." Her mother grabbed her discarded panties from the floor, blew her nose long and hard into them. It made Clancy's stomach turn. "Your daddy an' me, we met at Coney Island. He was a looker. A real looker your daddy was. Not that I was no slouch, mind you. He was rich too. If ya can imagine. Come from some la-di-da folks up at Sutton Place. He asked me to dinner. I knew right off he was loaded. Swank joint, and fancy-schmancy names on that menu I never even heard of. But I more 'an made up for dinner. He liked that fine, so we started datin' regular. It steamed his folks, but good. Oh, they was madder'n a hornet's nest, him takin' up with a lounge singer. But he said I was good. And I was, Clan. I had talent." Her mother gulped the remains of her vodka.

"It was good, for 'bout a year. Then he started doin' what all men do. Started lookin' like there was somethin' better. Even dated a friend a mine once, come back ballin' his head off he loved me. I was the only one for him. But it didn't stop him from wanderin'. Had to think a somethin'—had to figure a way to keep him. So I told him I was pregnant." She laughed bitterly. "'Bout shit his pants over that. No scandal for this boy, and he knew me well enough I'd cause a ruckus. So he married me. City Hall. Your Uncle Joseph and Aunt Marion was our witnesses. First thing he says to me on our honeymoon night, 'You get fat an' I'll leave you inna New York second.' But here's the kicker, I wasn't pregnant. Not then. And I wasn't goin' to get pregnant. I didn't want some brat draggin' at my heels." Clancy felt a sharp blow to her insides, but Celia seemed unaware she was talking to her own child. She was just talking. "So he's askin' me when's the baby comin'. My first period I act like it's a miscarriage. He's pissed, I tell ya. But I got him now. He's mine. And then, I did get pregnant. Goddamn worse day of my life. I find out way too late to do anything about it." And that's when Celia realized Clancy was sitting beside her.

"Jesus, Clancy, what the hell—" But there were no signs of sudden affection. Her grimace was bitter with long-lived betrayal. "Come ploppin' out Christmas Eve like somethin' important, like you was the beginnin' of somethin' special. He left me 'cuzza you! And then I got fat with all the drugs and stuff they put me on and the harder I tried not to, the fatter I got. I lost my looks 'cuzza you. And I lost him 'cuzza you." She gripped Clancy's skinny arms. "And now he has the goddamn gall to wanna see you. You! I'm the one that fuckin' gave up my life! Get outta here. I can't stand the sight of you." She shoved Clancy so hard she fell to the floor. "Get OUTTA HERE, I SAID!!!" Clancy jumped up and ran to her room.

And the dream was as real as the memory. Every movement, word, gesture. There are some moments that can't be forgotten. Even in sleep.

Carlita sighed. This was harder than she thought. Poor Clancy. She knew that if Gabriella were to find out, she'd be in the worst kind of trouble, but she began to visit Clancy in her dreams, early morning hours when things were better remembered. She'd go in, and if there was trouble ahead, she'd just steer things in another direction.

She was having many vivid incarnages herself, one in particular, that she could not shake. She would see herself with a young boy, maybe five, hair the color of pale straw, helping her with what appeared to be bread making, laughing and playing. The little boy's thin arms were covered to his elbows in billowy flour that marked his forehead as he earnestly shoved back loose strands of silky hair, digging into the mixing bowl. Carlita had stood back, amazed by the child's simple beauty, then walked to him and wrapped him in her arms.

That's when she returned to present consciousness. And she realized she'd visited another plane in time.

But when she returned to angel time she continued to feel a strong connection to the little boy, as well as to Clancy, and she was confused.

"You're getting too close to your work," Gabriella had warned when she first told her of her incarnages.

Perhaps. But how could she not?

Just as now, she had made the decision to make a bit of an adjustment in Clancy's recurring nightmare. A minor alteration, a slight tweak. She would simply swirl into Clancy's consciousness and distort her mother's image into that of her own. So that when Clancy's mother asked her into the room, she held out loving arms, soothing and gentle. And as she held her in the dream state, Carlita felt a connection to the dream image of Clancy that was as real and familiar in holding this child as if she were her own.

September 20, 1979

Straight and hazy, sun melting tar. Mathew had been on the road for ten hours, past Sacramento, just past Redding, the I-5 one long, lazy snake. He was tired, but excited too. Aunt Nora, Dora, and Maria had thrown him a farewell party. Dinner at Gladstone's, then back to the house, where they drank Aunt Nora's "Gettin' Educated Tide," upon which they got good and tipsy.

Aunt Nora gave him a leather-bound journal for his poetry, with handmade paper right from the raw elements of the canyon, Dora got him more tobacco for his pipe, and Maria gave him a silk shirt for special occasions, whispering in his ear, "Be good."

Now he drove with no regrets, but still missing them all, even Dora, along with the house, his room, the land, the smells. He pulled off the highway at Yreka to gas up before the long haul through the mountains.

September 20, 1979

Clancy pulled off the exit at Yreka, wondering at the strangeness of the name, what it meant, and how in the hell it might be pronounced. She'd hit a bird. She was sure of it. What if she'd clipped its wing? What if it was suffering? She couldn't stand it. What were the chances, she asked herself five times in the last minute, of its being alive, even if she did find it? She glanced at the fuel gauge. Empty. She'd pull into the gas station first and refuel. No. She couldn't. She had to go back.

Mathew pumped the gas, paid the cashier, and got back into the car. It was getting nippier the further north he drove. He'd given up on the radio; feeling contemplative he slipped in a cassette of Chopin nocturnes. He pulled out, passed a VW van, a hideous shade of yellow, and headed north.

"Talk about your fate . . ." Carlita groaned. On replay of the hologram they saw the ripple, how it crushed the innocent molecules of time and threw the baby bunting into a different course of destiny, attempting to right itself as it flew in front of the VW bus, clipping its wing against the rearview mirror.

"That's just it. Earth people think fate is something that just plops into their laps. They have no idea how complex it is."

"So . . . ?"

Gabriella's wings tightened, ruffled, and then she released them. "Oh, all right."

Carlita watched carefully as Gabriella summoned the screen to rewind to right before the time ripple occurred. "I'm off to speak with Magdalena. She has apprentice spirit guides she'd like me to interview. When you're finished viewing, simply do this." Gabriella signed several hand/wing symbols that faded the screen to its resting place, a myriad rainbow glitter. "Do you have it?"

"Sure."

"And I have your word that after you've watched the destifate recap you will deactivate the screen."

"Of course."

Gabriella smiled, reassured, and floated off in a graceful exit.

Carlita stared at the holographic portal. This was the first time she'd been left alone with it. She'd do exactly as she had been told. Well . . . almost.

DESTIFATE IMAGERY INITIATED
Rewind. Time Ripple Deactivated

While Mathew pumped gas, a beat-up VW van, painted a hideous yellow, pulled up to the pump across from him. He expected an aging hippie to clamber out, but instead a young and attractive woman jumped from the van, auburn hair pulled back in a loose ponytail. He watched her as she walked around her van several times, obviously agitated, speaking to herself. Then, as if giving up, she turned to the mountains and threw up her arms in a gesture of defeat.

Mathew paid the cashier, got in his car. He was tired of the radio, so he put in his favorite Chopin nocturnes and was about to pull out when he saw the woman walk up to the van and remove the driver's side windshield wiper, bent like a cheap clothes hanger, rendering it useless. She put her hands in her hair, ran them through, forgetting she had it tied up. Angrily she freed it, and now it blew in a mad swirl about her face. Mathew stopped mid-motion, struck by this beautiful frustrated woman, compelled to help her.

He rolled down his window. "Anything wrong?"

His voice startled her. She tried to smile politely, but she was too cold. "Is anything right?"

"Beg your pardon?"

"Nothing. Everything's fine. Thanks."

But Mathew could tell she was in a jam. He got out of the car, walked over to her, and took the pathetic wiper. "What happened?"

"You wouldn't believe it."

"Try me."

"Well, to begin with, about two hundred miles ago my fourth gear popped out of place—I've had it fixed three times—which means I have to hold it while I'm driving; my heater's broken; there's a very strange noise coming from either the engine or the transaxle or whatever the hell it's called, and while coming over the beautiful snow-filled mountains without any chains, my defroster stopped altogether so I had to get out several times to wipe frost off my window, and the last time I slammed the door I realized I had the wiper caught in it." She seemed numb by this point. "How's that?"

"Quite a story, actually. First off, let's get you out of this cold." And before she could say a word he led her to his Mustang and opened the door.

"You're not going to murder and rape me on top of all this, are you?"

He smiled. "Hadn't entered my mind." She got in.

They sat there for a moment, a Chopin nocturne filling the car. Finally she turned to him. "Thank you." She smiled, bleakly. "I thought I might just go stark raving nuts and be institutionalized here in some godforsaken dot on the map called Yerka."

"Y-reeka."

"I wondered. You're not from here."

"England originally, but I've lived here for, oh, six years now."

"Haven't lost a bit of your accent."

"Guess some things just stay with you."

"Isn't that the truth." And they both knew she wasn't referring to accents.

"Look. I was about to find a place to stay for the night, so perhaps I could find a way to help you with your situation."

"Oh, no. That's—"

"Please. Let me. You're in trouble. I'd like to help."

"But I don't even know you."

"Mathew Prendergast." They shook hands, their eyes holding one another's longer than was necessary.

"Very British." She smiled now and it lit up her face. She reminded him of someone, but he couldn't place it, only the feeling of it, which stirred from his loins, to his heart, back to his chest, which felt suddenly fuller. She hadn't really noticed him before, but now she saw that his eyes were kind and helpful, and felt the first sense of calm since she had headed over the summit. "I suppose that makes you safe."

They drove around, found a small room for him to spend the night, laughed at the hokey drapes, bad decor. "Now that's settled, let's see to your wiper."

They got back into the car, traveled down the freeway a few miles to another gas station. They found a replacement wiper and returned to the gas station at Yreka, where they had the attendant repair it.

"I don't know how to thank you," Clancy said as she smoked a cigarette in the overheated garage waiting room that smelled like diesel fuel and old candy bars. It was dark now, past eight. "I've got quite a drive ahead of me."

"Then let me buy you some dinner and fill you full of coffee before you go."

"I couldn't."

"Please. Otherwise I'll be unbelievably bored the rest of the evening."

"I . . . thanks, but I really should get going." But when she traveled inside his deep blue eyes, she knew she wanted to stay. "Okay. But I have to make it quick."

"Well, I don't think we're going to find a seven-course meal anywhere up here. Probably nothing more than a truck stop, I'm afraid."

They had greasy burgers and fries, split an apple pie soaked with vanilla ice cream, drank gallons of tinted coffee, and talked as if they'd just invented the concept of communication, until Clancy glanced at her watch and screamed. "It's three A.M."

"No!"

She showed him her watch as evidence and then before she could take her hand back he touched it gently, held it for a moment longer than need be. They looked at one another. She smiled, held his eyes with a gaze so penetrating his stomach fell somewhere near the vicinity of China.

Mathew paid the bill and without saying a word they got back into his car and drove to his room. They entered and turned to one another. He put out a hand. She took it. He drew her close, could smell the China musk she wore, slicing into his senses, becoming a place called home. He drank in the sweet fragrance of her hair, thick and smooth, as he swept it into his hands, heard the moan escape her lips as he drew her closer to his.

• • •

ZZZOOOoooooooommmmmmmm. "What the—?" Carlita watched the hologram as it jumped through time zones, parallel realities, shifting planes. What had she done?

She'd been merely floating, utterly absorbed in the story before her, when all of a sudden the hologram went crazy. She tried to follow the movements Gabriella showed her, got them all mixed up because now the hologram was jumping into images of future lives. "Oh, Jesus! Ooops, excuse me, oh my, what have I done? What have I done!?" She made another set of movements, and another, and finally the images returned to normal speed. But the scene was of a different time and place.

She had watched Gabriella enough to get a bearing, signed to the hologram, and put her hand up in the indication for time.

Subject: Wyila, known on earth plane as the following
Incarnations: Dame Margaret Winston, England 1856–1902
Wild Bird, Ojibway 1903–1907
Carole Lombard, Americas, 1908–1942
Clancy Reardon 1957–2036
Current Plane View: Erik F. Kents, 2059–
Birth child of Mira Kents and Tarek Simon
Screen Time: 2065
Screen Place: United California
Screen View: Activated

The screen materialized to a small room and in it Carlita saw the back of a young child as he played with an old Erector set, his fine hair barely pulled back into a ponytail. Then as he turned to full view, Carlita's wings ruffled uncontrollably, her aura glared a brilliant golden shower, an inner essence shiver.

"Oh my heavenly—" She knew this boy. She knew him as clearly as she knew herself. But she couldn't think of how. Where. When.

And just as another form was to enter the room, Carlita felt before she heard Magdalena behind her.

"Prefect Carlita! What are you doing?"

"I . . . I, well, Gabriella and I were viewing our charges and the screen went absolutely wild."

"The screen does not go absolutely wild, Carlita, unless provoked. What have you done?"

"To tell you the holy truth," Carlita answered on several levels, "I haven't a clue."

September 20, 1979

Clancy inched forward at snail's pace trying to see the bird from the other side of the median, horns blaring as cars passed her. She took the next exit and returned to the scene of the mishap. Sure enough, there was the bird, wing broken, staccato heart hammering in its chest. She picked up the weightless fledgling, saw its tiny terrified beaded eyes, glazed in shock and pain. Was she supposed to kill it, put it out of its misery? Or should she nurse it back to health?

She drove with the wounded bird by her side until she made Redding. By then she'd decided to let a vet determine its fate, this bird she'd laid beside her leg, wrapped in a T-shirt to keep it warm, this bird she now felt obligated to save. No, not obligated. She *needed* this bird to survive.

Ever since she'd left Portland, ever since that dream—the dream in which her mother turned into a beatific and gracious beacon of warmth, summoning her to light—Clancy believed she had been given an option. When she woke that next afternoon, sleeping a straight fourteen hours, she knew that she had a choice: she could spend the rest of her life sleeping, hibernating away from the cold reality of life, or she could do something with it.

She had thought once she was far enough away from her mother and the memories of childhood she would begin to see life in a different way. But going to Portland hadn't been the right decision. She should have known. Charting your destiny by throwing a dart in a map was hardly mature decision making.

The rain in Portland. The gray. The indecision of the sun on the infrequent days it did decide to make an effort and shine forth. They had all worked themselves into a leaching depression. The only escape had been sleep. Lulled by the patter of rain she would find herself hypnotized into the netherworld, although she discovered the more she slept, the less rested she felt. Almost as if the imagery of her dreams, whether she could remember them or not, required more energy than real life.

The only way out of it was to head south. Sun. Warmth. She and "Tweety Bird."

"So how many more time ripples do they go through?"

"Just one. But it's the critical one, because in a way, after this point their lives change irrevocably. So that when they meet, because of the circumstances, they find it difficult to connect. Even when they know what they share is unique and special."

"Ummm, Angel Gabriella?"

"Yes, Carlita."

"I . . . I don't know if Arch Angel Magdalena told you about the hologram going wacko on me—"

"Yes she did." Gabriella sighed, but not ill-humoredly. "It's not an uncommon mistake. If the truth be known, certain vibrations result-

ing from extreme emotion can trigger such activity. And knowing you, Carlita, I'm sure that was the cause."

"Well, I must admit, I did get a bit carried away with the simple beauty of it. So, what happened with them?"

"Much the same as before. Only now, Mathew, having been with Maria, was so wonderfully gentle and loving with Clancy, it gave her the seed of trust. Something she'd long since lost. Maria was a positive by-product of a time ripple. Unfortunately, that is not the case with the next one, as you will see."

"Um, Angel Gabriella?"

"Yes, what is it now?"

"I've asked Arch Angel Magdalena if it was possible to have been assigned to someone I might have known . . . or will know in an incarnation."

"Certainly not," Gabriella responded. "We'd never assign an angel to someone they've known on any plane, Earth or otherwise. Even if the relationship was positive. No. That would be courting disaster."

Still Carlita wondered if perhaps they had made a mistake. For the pull she felt toward the young boy was very strong. And the boy's essence felt so very much like Clancy. And it must be. It was Clancy's future vision screen she had witnessed. No one else's.

"I've told you time and again, you're getting too close to your work," Gabriella said. "I knew this was going to happen. You have to keep a certain amount of detachment, dear, if you expect to make a good angel."

"But, I thought you were supposed to care . . . deeply—"

"Deeply. But remotely."

Carlita puzzled that over a good long time. Every time she found herself alone at the hologram she was tempted to inspire movement at the screen. And just as she was about to rationalize the need to do just that, to find out more about Clancy and how best to help her, Gabriella would inevitably return.

April 1981

The drone of the lecture teased his ears but did not penetrate them. He was reading a letter from Aunt Nora.

> . . . and since her mother has fallen ill, Maria has left, and so I will have to find someone who can take her place. No one can take Maria's place. But then no one knows that better than you.

Mathew scratched the lobe of his ear, feeling his face redden.

> Dora's had another fall, the old fool. Refuses to wear her glasses and then complains she can't see anything, even the steps right before her. I've been doing some tremendous ornaments with all my free time. I hate to sound like the doddering aunt, but I do miss you, terribly, dear boy. Hope the studies go well. The canyon smells like God's florist shop, the ocean his pond. The wind is fresh and the birds are singing love songs.

His heart so ached for Aunt Nora and home at that moment that he gathered his books and walked from the class, got in his car, and drove to the large studio loft where he lived in one of Aunt Nora's properties.

Home. That's what he needed. Home. He wasn't happy here. Hadn't been all along. Higher education was an expectation from a long line of schooled Prendergasts. It was avoided only when one was linked to the chains of poverty. The only time he felt productive were the times he woke in the deep of night, when the quiet filled his head with noise and his stories came tumbling out. He was an excellent student, but his work was flat. The only thing he cared about was writing, and he'd struggled with the guilt of that since the day he arrived. Aunt Nora had been right.

But then, when wasn't she?

June 1981

Clancy met Lisa while waiting tables at Mirabelle's. "Fine French Food Served with a Flair," read the menu and advertisements. Lisa trained Clancy. "Don't worry. No one knows how to pronounce anything on the menu, so be creative."

It was true. The owners, Phil and Stella Bernstein, had jumped on the restaurant bandwagon along with many other young "boomer" professionals, hunting for some glamour in the land of glitz and gimme. Lisa said it best the time she argued with Phil over French onion soup, when he informed her he was serving it with noodles: "You're a raconteur, not a restaurateur!" Lisa slammed the lid down on the soup warmer. "This is not your aunt Millie's homemade chicken soup. Why don't you just throw some friggin' spatzle in it?"

It almost got her fired, but what Phil lacked in taste he made up for in decency, and he respected Lisa's right to speak her mind. Not that it changed his. Mirabelle's French onion noodle soup became something of a specialty.

Their first few training shifts Lisa restricted her communication to waitron-speak. She thought Clancy might be a snobby back-easterner out West seeking fame and fortune. And Lisa didn't trust actresses. She knew better. She was one herself. But when she found out Clancy was attending Cal State to get a bachelor's in business, she let her myriad personalities leak here and there, began to tell jokes, and pretty soon they were laughing about the Mexican cooks who couldn't speak English cooking French for the Jewish owners in L.A.'s American Valley.

They began going out for beers after work and pretty soon movies on their days off. They spent long hours figuring out how to make their work and school schedules jibe so they could spend all their free time together. And since very few free moments went by without their being together, they decided to become roommates.

They found a two-bedroom guest cottage with a window-ledge home for Tweety Bird. The cottage was spacious and beautiful but in dire need of a domestic overhaul, which Lisa negotiated for reduced rent. But Jack, a once famous producer who owned the estate, could have cared less about the rent. He enjoyed the sight of their silky youth, the sound of their hysterical laughter as they talked endlessly at his pool, paying no attention to him whatsoever, treating him like an eccentric old uncle who told great stories but was essentially harmless.

"I used to be an amazing cocksman in my time!" Jack once boasted as they drank margaritas. "But not to worry. Nothing gets the ol' boy up anymore. Not implants. Nothing. But I do believe, I have orgasms in my dreams. Somethin' like them anyway."

They stared at him a moment, then Lisa got up, refilled his glass. "Poor baby." Returned to Clancy. "How long has it been since you've had sex anyway?"

"Before you were born," Jack said, then laughed. "But you know . . . I don't miss it."

"Neither do I," Lisa said in agreement, then dipped into the pool, and when she resurfaced, gasped, "unless, of course, I'm ovulating."

Clancy didn't miss sex either. What she missed was something else. Something she couldn't put words to, but it didn't matter. She had Lisa. She had never had a friendship like this, and intuitively she knew it was the kind that would last forever, would never be stranded in small talk no matter how much time passed, the kind that was devoted to darkest secrets, heartiest laughs, the drive of the young and the desire of the naive.

It was the happiest she could ever remember being.

August 1981

Mathew was having a crisis in faith: his belief in his value as a writer. He had spent eighteen months sitting in classrooms spinning words through his head, perfectly woven tapestries of text and theory, seamless narratives that repeatedly granted him the reward of "job well done." But there was no heart to his work. No core.

Mathew knew his greatest assets were discipline and persistence. Outside of his school papers he wrote reams and reams. Every night the voices in him screamed, bellowed, cried sloppy tears, mourned loudly—but did they make any difference? Did they have an echo that rang truth, talent, insight?

"Well, you did damn well for yourself in that school up there," Aunt Nora said by way of reassurance when he returned. But getting A's wasn't what he had been searching for. He hit a place he'd never been before. Depression. Confusion and lethargy led to hesitancy. These unfamiliar feelings pulled the strings of movement to his days, slow and awkward one moment, bouncing off an idea the next, and then, just as quickly he'd go slack, return to ambivalence.

"Why don't you send some of that work somewhere to be seen?" she asked one morning as they drank tea on the deck.

"It isn't ready. Not by a long shot."

"What isn't ready about it? It's got guts; it's got heart and soul. True, it's a bit rough in places, but nothing that can't be smoothed out."

"I'm not smoothed out."

"Vagabonding's what you need," Aunt Nora said later that night as she handed him a "Summer Breeze Change Tide," as if they'd never left the earlier conversation. "You need to take a journey."

"I don't want to travel, Aunt Nora."

"You don't have to travel to take a journey. Physically, that is."

"Well, I'm not keen on planetary escapades like your canyon hippie friends are into."

"I'm not talking about that, am I? You need to take a journey to yourself."

"Myself?"

"Naturally."

"Now how in the hell does one bloody do that, Aunt Nora? I mean, if one could bloody just call it up, we'd all do just that, now wouldn't we?"

"There's no need to sound bitter, boy. Besides, it doesn't suit you one bit." Aunt Nora sniffed. "Why don't you get our pipes and bring the tobacco on the hearth. The stuff in the purple tin." And it was then that Mathew first got stoned with his Aunt Nora. It wasn't like she even needed it; her frame of reference was always a bit askew. But as usual, Aunt Nora gave him what he needed that night.

His limbs loosened, he could feel the muscles elongate right inside his legs, his shoulders relaxed; he twisted his neck, breathed deeply, and smelled the burnt summer air, cooled now by the ocean mist.

"You know, your biggest problem is you haven't been bit by love," Aunt Nora said hours later, or so it seemed.

"Well . . ." Mathew thought of Maria.

"I'm not talking about sexual discovery," she said, as if she followed his every thought, "I'm talking about bloody balls-out Heathcliff and Cathy, Scarlett and Rhett—the Bogart and Bacall kind of rapture."

"I . . . I just haven't found the right woman yet."

"Ye know, lad, there's 'nother way about gettin' to the heart of the matter." Aunt Nora's accent always got thicker and slanted to her Scottish upbringing when she got buzzed. "And that's to get to yer core. By livin' in humanity. Bein' in it. Feelin' it."

They were simple words, but Mathew heard them somewhere deep inside himself. They began Mathew's initiation into the real world. And the world beckoned him, like Dorothy following the yellow brick road, but this road was the dusty trails up the mysterious upper reaches of Topanga Canyon where he played with Nora's hippie friends, took his first hit of acid, flew above the canyons with the wingspread of an eagle, opened his imagination and added delicious interpretation to his senses. This twisted trail led from the blood-splattered linoleum of an emergency ward where he volunteered, life and death a roll of the dice like the tumbling cubes that left the grimy hands of his coworkers, seasonal cedar-stained carpenters gambling away the few dollars they made daily. Paths he tread softly in the shadows of sweltering sidewalks in South Central, where he feared for his life but sat with gang members, dope fiends, kicking junkies, pregnant fourteen-year-olds. This road led to the bureaucratic paved government issue tile of the unemployment line, the creaky floorboards of a rusty tanker where he got a part-time job with a fishing crew. This road was marching up Santa Monica Boulevard's rainbow of a different color where he met with artists, poets, actors, screenwriters; the wannabes, been-there-done-thats, love-you-mean-its. This road was thick tar that baked as it hit the ground, working on a road crew, thick-chested, muscle-popping, blue-collar bullies, with hearts made of cotton candy. This byway held spindly rows of dirt clods exploding like little bombs as he picked beans and tomatoes with the illegal aliens, dusty sweat stuck like glue.

It was a pilgrimage that wound from downtown Los Angeles to the flat, godforsaken valley, up shaded canyon trails, down to the curl of blue waves at the beach, and in the end he felt like he had walked every mile of every road, taken every detour.

More important, though, he wrote miles and miles of words that lived the journey with him. And that's when he became a writer.

December 1981

Tweety Bird sat on her shoulder, nibbled at her ear. "Tweety Bird, can you stop that?" Clancy nudged her back. Tweety Bird jumped to the top of her head.

"Oh, great, bird on girl." Lisa walked in with the mail. "Wait, I'm gonna take a picture."

"Must you?" Lisa had swiped a Polaroid camera from the last set she had worked on and now insisted on documenting their lives, step by painful step. But by the time she returned from her bedroom Tweety Bird had already returned to Clancy's shoulder.

"Ugghhhh, why doesn't that damn bird ever just stay cute."

"Tweety Bird is always cute. And besides, she's not a poser."

"Yesssss you are . . . huh, TB, come on darlin', jump on mama's head." Lisa spent the next few minutes trying to coax Tweety Bird with everything from sweet talk to Triscuits. "She's too smart to be a bird," Lisa would say when she did something really precocious. But Clancy already knew that Tweety Bird wasn't a bird. She was a little spirit. The gentlest, lightest, lovingest thing in the world.

That afternoon, the day she had clipped Tweety's wing, she had driven like a madwoman until she made it to Redding, terrified the pathetic feathery ball at her side would die before she found a vet that was open. It took away the windshield wiper moment. She didn't really care if she could see, so long as she got the bird to safety.

"Naw, won't die. Jest a busted wing's all." The vet was an old-timer, grizzled and lean in his farmer jeans. "I'll wrap that wing if ya want me to."

"Yes. But then what?"

"Then it heals."

"No. I mean, I'm on the road, I'm not from around here."

"Well . . ." He scratched his chin, figuring. "Well, I'll tell ya, I'll wrap it—"

"It? Can you tell me what it is?"

"Hmmmm." He flopped the bird, the size of a small finch, over gently into the palm of hands that could have doubled as baseball mitts. "Looks to be a painted bunting. Not ordinary breed 'round these parts. Usually winters to Panama. Wonder how it got up here? Though I heard of them found all the way up in Oregon once." He lifted and inspected the bird with squinted eyes. "Little missus."

"A girl bird. How can you tell?"

"Male bunting's damn sight purtier. Not like in our world. With birds, they get all the looks." He cackled over that one. "Yep. Now I'll wrap her up real tight like. Chances are she won't fly again. You could take her to an aviary when you get where yer goin'." Then he fixed her up, gave Clancy a bottle dropper to feed her, instructed her to sog up any breads she was giving her, and if she could catch a worm or some bugs it "would be a nice bit of supper for the little patient."

Clancy thanked him, he refused pay, saying he was only too happy to help someone good enough to pick up a wounded animal. She was only too mortified to tell him she had been the perpetrator. It was okay. When she saw the beady eyes rivet on hers as the bird's body rested in the vet's mighty hands, this bird became her responsibility.

The next day Clancy rented a rundown motel room for a week

to settle until she could either find a cheap apartment or hunt down her Uncle Sal. But she ended up spending most of her time fretting over the bird. Finally the bird calmed down when she took it in her hands, whispering soothing "there now"s until she could feel the tiny bones stop their struggle. "You're safe with me, sweety, Tweety Bird." And that's how she got her name.

After four weeks the bandages had unraveled and Clancy didn't have to go to a vet to know by the very unnatural slant to the wing and the awkward position to Tweety's body that this bird was never going to fly. There was no way she would give it to an aviary. Tweety would never make it. She had seen enough nature shows to know animals were unkind, that weakness invited attack.

So it was that Tweety Bird became what other people referred to as her "pet," but for her, it was more like salvation. At the end of that deep long depression that sent her southward, finding this bird was often the reason she got up in the morning. She had taken care of it and it had survived. So it was a bit of a gimp. What she lacked in the ability to fly, Tweety Bird more than made up for in her morning chipper, her sweet love sounds as she chewed at Clancy's ear, the fluffy feathery dusting against Clancy's neck when they lay on the bed, Clancy reading. Maybe Tweety was reading along with her for all she knew. That great things come in small packages never rang truer for Clancy as Tweety Bird now jumped back up on her head.

"Ah, there she goes." Lisa got the Polaroid, grabbed her shot.

Clancy stuck out her tongue and then stopped. "Is that the mail?"

"Yes." Lisa picked it up and handed it to her. Clancy rifled through it, knew exactly what she was waiting for and didn't want to see.

"God, this is worse than I thought."

"What's the matter?"

"I've managed to screw up all my classes. Again." Clancy sighed, holding her report card, then letting it drift to the floor with the rest of the mail.

"Could it be that you hate your classes?" Lisa hinted sarcastically. "Could it be that business school pumps out nothing but nerds and schmucks? Or that you've been working three part-time jobs? That you run around like a chicken with its head cut off? Give yourself a break. You didn't really want to get into marketing anyway."

"True. But, Lis . . . when am I going to get it?"

"What's the rush?"

"I'd like to start my life sometime this century."

"You're living it." Lisa assessed her. "Looks pretty good to me."

Lisa held Clancy's eyes, then Clancy turned to Tweety, leaned into the soft chest. "Make it better, Tweety."

"Come on, Clancy." Lisa set the timer and ran to get into the shot. When it had flashed and the three of them blinked, Lisa jumped up, snapped her fingers. "I've got it! Let's go to Mexico, get fucked up on margaritas, and live happily ever after."

"Great."

"I'm serious."

"Okay. Let's go."

Lisa realized that Clancy was really game. "What about all your jobs?"

"I'll call and give notice." Clancy tsked at Tweety Bird to move, snaked underneath the couch, brought out an old cigar box, nudged the tip of the violin case so that it was showing.

"Hey, what the hell's that?" Clancy opened the wooden corona cigar box and pulled out five one-hundred-dollar bills.

"No, that." Lisa pointed at the case.

"Nothing important," Clancy answered and teased the money in front of Lisa's face. She had been saving it, all this time, and she still hadn't refurbished the goddamn violin. Why not go to Mexico? What the hell?

They tangoed the night away, slept during the day on the hot sands of Mexican beaches, sipped exotic fruit drinks loaded with rum and tequila, smoked hash from some hippies they ran into, baked until they burned, laughed themselves silly into the early morning hours, and sobered up in a darkened alley with four Mexican *delincuentes* threatening rape but settling for the rest of their money and Lisa's prized quartz watch she'd gotten for high school graduation.

Desperately ill from something they'd eaten, or from the water they'd guzzled to cure their hangovers, they spent the next morning emptying their insides outside a bus terminal. Finally Lisa was able to get in touch with her mother, who wired enough money to get them home.

When they returned to L.A. they fell into fevered sleep and it wasn't until Jack checked on them that they realized how sick they both were, rushed to the hospital, dehydrated, suffering from a particularly virulent strain of Montezuma's Revenge.

So that when they returned home, they had nothing to show for their jolly trip south but a whopping hospital bill for which neither had insurance, having quit their jobs. They both lay in their sickbeds, staring anywhere but at each other, ready to blame the other for their own immature behavior, lack of judgment, and humiliated embarrassment at being two naive young Americanos who'd fucked up *mucho* royally.

In a few months they would laugh about it. It would become their Frick and Frack performance at parties, embellished with each telling, until the entire fiasco was one hilarious string of comic events that showed their bravado and resourcefulness at having survived the ordeal.

Only Clancy would lie awake later those nights after the story's umpteenth performance, face flushed with sickening shame. It didn't seem to matter how close she got, she never got *there.* She hated herself for being so young. So stupid. Such a royal loser. Her mother had been right. She "wasn't no gift." And to think, with another three weeks' savings from the three jobs she worked at so diligently, the reason she had the damn jobs in the first place, she would have been that close to getting the violin fixed. But then she wondered what was the point, and while she was at it, did this life of hers have a point, and if so, was it going to reveal itself, preferably in the very near future?

March 7, 1983

"... she poses
Death as dagger eyes, tranquil beauty lies
beneath the swagger of the target
of the man who's got the market
on her heart that's at the point
of Ballon Munson's cane."

Applause. Lisa sat at the bar waiting for Clancy at Café Cuervo. She'd heard of the "movie poet" from some of her pals, but this was the first time she'd ever seen or heard him. He was charming. His poems were fun. And he was quite attractive, even handsome, but more than that. He was refreshing. Yes. That's what he was next to all the movie industry people she usually hung out with or dated.

She'd been partying with the crew from *Fatal Lessons,* a low-budget suspense noir thriller, and had told Clancy to meet her here so they could catch *The Big Chill.* But since Clancy was late, she was killing a few minutes watching the poet as he sat at a table sipping his coffee.

Stuck in traffic, Clancy pondered her life while sucking in the fumes from the truck in front of her, self-loathing filling her lungs along with the exhaust. She had just finished dropping out of the business school. She'd hated it. This now made about twenty-three possible careers she'd killed in mid-track.

After the Mexico debacle, Clancy had made a commitment to pick something and finish it. But since then she'd flip-flopped so many times she couldn't even keep track. First she became manager of a radical clothing store, quit because the owner, a pampered ex-actress with a lot of money and no talent, didn't really care that the store was running itself into the ground. This venture had started well enough. They had all started well enough.

The acupuncture/herbalist came next. She traveled with Gus, who'd invented an herbs-on-wheels, modern medicine wagon bearing tonics for the wealthy. He intended to franchise the idea and take it national and she'd be in on the ground floor. But what she ended up doing was driving an ice cream truck for the holistic, a broken-down Datsun with a couple of coolers of ginseng tonic in the back, outfitted with an obnoxious horn that did not encourage buyers to flock from their homes for a healthy pick-me-up. So she quit.

Next she enrolled in classes to be a dental hygienist. "They make great money," she explained to Lisa, who simply said, "Hello????" The idea being that when she made enough money as a hygienist maybe she'd figure out what it was that she was supposed to do. Three days in, she decided no amount of money was worth scrabbling about in a bunch of grimy mouths. So she quit.

Next came, in some order, real-estate, selling insurance, phone solicitation, more waitressing, managing a fast food franchise. She saw herself whirling into a funnel of classified ads, a vacuum of endless jobs, going nowhere, swallowed up.

She'd quit and quit and quit again. "You ain't no gift" pounded itself into her brain as her headache got "THIS BIG," and she lifted her hands from the steering wheel in frustration, slapped them to her forehead in agony. She would never become anything. If only she were like Lisa and had something that called to her, something she was born to do. She realized she was crying. Here she was, trapped in traffic, broiling in 95-degree, smog-baked heat, weeping at the perfect metaphor for her life. How stuck could one be before time simply began to crawl backward? She wiped the tears away and then glanced at herself in the rearview mirror. What a loser.

"Get a grip, Clancy," she whispered under her breath. She was late already and with this traffic she was never going to get to Café Cuervo. She veered off to the parking lane and zipped to the next exit and decided to take the side streets. Which could also be a metaphor, she thought grimly, as she wiped the last of her tears.

"Did you know you have Cary Grant's chin?" Lisa stood at Mathew's table now. He looked up. Lisa, classical bone structure, high cheekbones, beautiful patrician nose and lips, wed to long sandy-blond California hair—an interesting mix, Mathew decided.

"Does everyone in this bloody town always resemble someone?" Mathew teased.

"Pretty much. My roommate's a ringer for Rita Hayworth. But only when she's being nice."

He laughed. "Can I buy you a drink?"

"You can buy me two."

Clancy rummaged in the backseat for her *Thomas Guide*. These were surface streets whose names were not vaguely familiar. She was sure she was heading toward the Valley, and she thought if she just kept winding her way in this general direction, she'd get there. Maybe she should stop and call Lisa, tell her she was going to be late, but then noticed the neighborhood she was in. Perhaps not.

After fifteen minutes of crisscrossing the far side of town she was confident that she would be only a half hour late. And that's when she saw him.

"I'm supposed to be on my way to *The Big Chill*."

"Oh, don't let me keep you," Mathew said.

"You're not. My friend is late." Lisa checked her watch. "Do you want to go? Have you already seen it?"

"No," Mathew replied.

"I'm not trying to pick you up." Lisa smiled seductively.

"No. I mean no, I haven't seen it. And yes, I'd like to."

Lisa glanced at her watch. "Then let's call it a date."

The bum. Splayed on a shrub wall of an apartment building, fat gut puffing in the air. Looking like he was having problems breathing. Clancy was at the stoplight. Staring at him. Had he just passed out there? Was this his regular spot? She didn't think so, given the surroundings. She worried. What if he was in pain. What if he'd just had an aneurysm.

"Jesus, what's it to you, Clance," she said under her breath.

The light turned green. She decided to let it go, but several blocks later thought about Tweety Bird and made a U-turn, headed back to where the man lay. She studied him from the other side of the street. She could tell from his labored breathing that he was alive. Shit. She made another U-turn and parked her car, got out, and slowly walked toward him.

Lisa walked up to the bartender, leaned over, and shouted above the music and the noise to tell Clancy, if she showed up, that she had gone ahead to the theater.

She motioned Mathew over to the table where Seth Sharp and Sylvia Peron, the leads in *Fatal Lessons,* shouted introductions. Then she led Mathew out.

"Seth and Sylvia are having a torrid set affair," she said matter-of-factly once they were out on the street.

"Isn't that sort of par for the course?" Mathew asked.

"Yes. But with Seth it isn't whether he's going to sleep with his lead, but how many other women he's going to rack up during the course of four to six weeks."

"Busy guy."

"Busy asshole."

Mathew glanced at her. One tough cookie, he thought, been around. But then, just as suddenly, she turned to him, smiled the most gentle and genuine smile, and took his hand, then uttered in a perfect English accent, "Thank you ever so much for escorting me to the cinema, young man."

Clancy could smell him from two car lengths away, memory of her mother's decay charging into her senses. She tiptoed toward him, then realized he was out, and walked the rest of the way.

"Sir?" Then laughed at herself. Sir, indeed. There was only one kind of rank for guys like this. "Hey . . . hey, you okay?"

There was no response. She nudged his shoulder. He slobbered out a snore. She nudged it again and he stirred.

"Whassa . . . whassa matter?" Then his glazed eyes focused on Clancy. "Whatja doin? Whatja doin' disturbin' my nap?"

Clancy stepped back. "I just wanted to make sure you're okay."

He bolstered his fat gut upright, hacked up some phlegm, and spit it into the grass. "Okay? Okay . . . yeah, I'm great. How 'bout a drink? Wanna you and me get a drink?"

Clancy turned and ran back to her car. What a fool she was.

"So where was the ripple?"

Gabriella rewound the hologram that showed the apartment complex, the bum walking none too steadily down the road. When the time warp occurred the ripple knocked him over like a wave, into the shrubbery, where he passed out.

"Clancy's car arrived at the stoplight not five seconds later. Otherwise she would have caught Lisa before she left for the movies and met Mathew."

"Oh, dear, Angelica," Carlita sighed, "now what?"

"Well, unfortunately this is the time ripple that causes the most disturbance. It really hurts our situation. Not so much because of Mathew and Lisa. Lisa actually turns out to be a conduit later on."

"Conduit?"

"Yes, there are special earth beings that are placed on this plane as conduits. They end up being a bridge for two people who must meet. They don't know they're conduits, of course, but they facilitate pairing."

"And how does one become a conduit?"

"They have to have an extraordinary openness. Much has to pass and filter through them. Many of them lead alternative lifestyles, are writers, actors, same-sex couplers. They have the ability to let things

happen within them that may cause great pain, but then manage to let go for the best of a situation."

"And what about Clancy?"

"That's where our trouble begins."

She ordered a Coke and downed it. She had run from where she finally found a parking spot to Café Cuervo. All that effort and Lisa had left. She supposed she could meet her at the movies but when the bartender told her she'd left with some guy, she decided it probably wasn't the best idea. She was about to pay her tab and leave for home when she and the rest of the patrons in the bar heard the sound of a swift and resounding *thwack!*

All heads turned toward Seth and Sylvia, now standing, facing each other. "No one fucks around on me!" Sylvia grabbed her purse and turned to leave. "You fucking prick!" she screamed and walked out the door.

A long beat of silence passed as everyone was struck by the moment, as embarrassing as it was bonding. There was no way to ignore it, so Seth simply smiled sheepishly, made several small bows, and said, "I could say it was all part of a scene we were rehearsing . . ." Seth stated wryly, ". . . but she's not that good an actress."

Clancy smiled reflexively.

Seth rubbed his pinkened cheek as he glanced around. Catching the glint in Clancy's eye, he offered her his most charming grin.

Not wanting to encourage him, she turned to the bartender. "How much?" she asked, then without waiting for an answer put a couple of dollars on the bar and walked out.

Seth fell in step with her. She kept walking.

"Hurt?" she asked finally.

"Just my ego." He laughed.

"Did you deserve it?"

"I guess that depends on your perspective."

"Hmmm." She appraised him, now. Handsome. He had a Euro feel to him, which she later discovered was part of his shtick, along with his name: Seth Sharp né John Hinglemeier. Rakish is how Lisa later described him. And he was. Also dangerous.

He continued walking by her side as if they were together. Did she really need this, she wondered? Some guy slapped in a workingman's bar was a good bet?

"Hey. Contrary to what you might think . . . I'm a very decent kinda guy." He pulled out a business card: "Seth Sharp, Actor/Writer," it read in bold Helvetica. They arrived at her car. Clancy hesitated before taking the card.

"It's not a proposal," he said grinning, "but if you'd ever like to grab a beer, give me a call."

"Hey, how d'ya know Seth?" Lisa asked a week later, studying the card.

"I met him the day you stood me up. You know him?"

"Yeah." Then mimicking a gravelly movie trailer voice she intoned, "He was a man in a world of women. So many victims. So little time. With a prick that smoked more than a midnight special."

"Puleeeese," Clancy grimaced. "Speaking of victims, is there an aging blond actress on the show?"

"Yeah . . . Sylvia Peron. His leading lady. They were having an affair, but he started seeing the makeup artist on the side."

"Hmmm." Clancy took the card from Lisa. "He's cute," she said, then threw the card in the garbage.

• • •

But she met him again at the wrap party. Lisa had begged Clancy to go with her, saying that Mathew was working and she didn't want to go alone.

"What does he do? He's always working."

"Ohhh, God, Clancy, he's the most amazing writer, poet."

"Really. All bookwormish and nerdy? Not your style."

"He's not. Either. My style or bookwormish. Actually he's the best lay I've ever had."

"Ooooh." Clancy teased her. "And when am I going to meet this mental Don Juan?"

"Oh no. I ain't lettin' him anywhere near you." Lisa shoved her playfully. Then swallowed. Whenever she touched Clancy, she felt strange. Something about Clancy intimidated her. "Come on . . . just go to this damn party with me. Free booze and lots of great food."

So Clancy had come and now she was bored. People in the industry were like people into flying: they had only one focus, one interest—movieland. So she drank the free booze, too much of it. She was just turning with a mild spin when Seth approached her. She felt the familiar lurch in her stomach. She was either going to vomit or end up sleeping with this man tonight.

She did both.

"Well, we'll always remember our first date," he teased her the next morning as they sipped the bad coffee he'd made.

"*You* might," she said, her tone caustic.

"Kim Novak." He nodded approvingly.

"Pardon me?"

"Aloof coolness."

"Hey, don't throw show-biz vernacular at me this early in the morning."

"Okay, what interests you this early in the morning?"

"Usually some light Bach and a book."

"Ooooh, how intellectual."

"Stimulating anyway." Intimating he was not? His eyebrows shot up. He put a hand out to her. She went to him.

October 1983

Mathew had never met anyone quite like Lisa, who was unusual in several ways. As an actress, she actually worked. She had a recurring bit part on a soap and, as she put it, she did "tons of bad theater. Plus a few T and A's—not mine—I always end up playing the best friend who gets chainsawed into hamburger before the end of the first act. But at least I'm out there." Her toughened shell melted easily and she would shift from a defensive "don't fuck with me" attitude to the lady of the manor in moments. He found her myriad personalities somewhat disconcerting, unlike Aunt Nora, who found them amusing.

"Sometimes I can't keep track." He smiled ruefully, one night while they were having their evening smoke.

"Don't you think that's rather beside the point?" Aunt Nora drew on her pipe.

"Which is?"

"Enjoying each and every one as they come. Seems you've gone and caught yourself a chameleon."

After that first date, the day they saw the *The Big Chill,* they had drinks, then met for lunch two days later.

Lisa was in heaven, deep into her second burger, discussing her roommate, Clancy. "She's really the most brilliant woman I've ever met, but she's hidden. Even from herself." She splopped more ketchup on her plate and dipped another fry.

"Do you always eat so much?" Mathew grinned.

"She just can't seem to understand that if she'd just let down the barriers—only after auditions," she answered, stuffing another fry, "—but she's really the most incredible person. She can be a real shrew to the outside world, but that's not who she really is. I mean I live with her. I know."

"You've given her a lot of thought."

"Oh . . . well, that's because I'm fascinated by her." She offered a fry to Mathew. "She's like a character study. Very complex."

"Do you study everyone?"

"Mostly."

"Do you study . . . me?"

"Especially you."

They became lovers that afternoon. Sweet, slow, gentle love-making. He found Lisa incredibly uninhibited, and wondered at moments if this was also part of the study: how one made love this way or that. After Maria's passionate insistence, he was unprepared for the languid pace, the lack of urgency, the air of detachment. It gave him time to discover new things about his body.

After that, they spent several nights a week together, at movies, dinners, taking walks on the beach, and then would make love in his room. He never saw the "roommate," even though Lisa spoke about her all the time.

"Are you trying to keep her from me?"

"Good God, no," Lisa answered.

They had finished making love and she was reading from the bound galleys of his first book, *Footfall,* a collection of short stories, taken from his "journey to the core," a contemporary *Travels with Charlie* cum southern California twist that his editor was very excited about. It was a start. Not Random House, but a small prestigious press that would theoretically build his career. Lisa had rolled over and remarked, "Clancy would love this. In search of . . ." She stopped, then sighed. "God, it's great, Mathew."

"So what's the deal with her, anyway?"

"She likes to keep to herself a lot. We like to spend our time alone. No guys to cater to. And, she's been away with that guy I introduced to you from the film . . . Seth?"

He nodded, then frowned. "I thought you said he was an asshole."

"Oh, he is. But that's Clancy's type." Lisa leaned on her elbows and affected a German accent," "He's gefucked up." Then she climbed upon his torso, kissed his chest. "Besides, you'd probably fall madly in love with her."

"But I am not an asshole."

"No." She nibbled at his neck. "You're not."

December 24, 1983

Clancy wasn't sure what she felt about Seth. It was difficult for her to really discern if his poetic speeches in the clenches of lust were genuine or simply another performance. He was a great lover: very considerate, almost too considerate at times, aware of his movements, pleased with his skill. And he was a typical actor—"enough about you, let's talk about me"—which suited her, as she didn't like to talk about herself anyway.

After that first ridiculous night she and Seth had spent together, they continued to see one another, several times a week. It made her feel guilty, but she quit a couple of jobs to follow him to various locations. He was charming. It didn't matter where they went; movies, theater, wild parties—people not only knew him, but they seemed to really like him. But there was one particular group around which he was noticeably unpopular. She caught plenty of scathing darts from women she assumed were spurned lovers. But there was more to their looks than simple jealousy. Something else. This group seemed to hate him.

He finished work on his film and was free until late August, so Clancy quit another job. They traveled some, but spent most days at the beach. She read. He surfed. He was quite good and he knew it. Had a great body and knew it. Was incredibly handsome as well. Knew that too. There wasn't much about himself he didn't know, but he treated it all so lightly, it didn't bother her. His greatest asset was his ability to spar, verbally, mentally, and that was what kept her hooked long after her fascination with his looks wore off. At times, when they'd had a bit too much to drink, their exchanges got nasty and she wondered where the rapier-edged wordplay might end up.

And then another film came along and she couldn't afford to go with him and for six weeks they saw very little of each other. She visited him a couple of weekends on the set, but things seemed different. He was different. He was the star. And he took it seriously. She would drop him down a peg or two, which began a new sort of foreplay—and he'd reciprocate by getting steamed and withdrawing. But when they came back together it was explosive, which reassured her they were still heading somewhere.

"It sounds a bit twisted if you ask me," Lisa said one night after listening to Clancy.

"You think?" But Clancy knew it was.

"Yeah . . . I mean Seth is not your generic asshole—he's made a whole inspired career out of it—and he's finally found someone who won't put up with his shit, only now you've had to create a new level of excitement with him because you both know you've got him figured out."

"What is this, Psych One-oh-one?"

"Actually it's from my acting class. You know: 'What's your motivation?'"

But Clancy didn't know. What *was* her motivation. She wasn't in love with Seth. Yes, she was fond of him. He was good in bed. He was somebody to be with.

According to shrink Lisa, who was currently playing a therapist in a TV crime drama, their relationship seemed to have gotten stormier and sicker. Clancy knew Lisa was right. She didn't need his egomaniacal tirades any longer so she broke up with him. He came crawling back, begging for forgiveness. She relented and they proceeded for the next couple of months with his new recurring role in "One More Try."

He promised her a wonderful birthday dinner, said he had a gift for her he'd gotten in Tijuana, where he was shooting his latest action thriller. So she waited calmly for this date that would seal their fate. His last chance, she had told him. It was supposed to be a surprise, but Lisa had blurted out something about the Inn at the Seventh Ray, so she knew that's where he was taking her. Lisa was, as usual, going to Mathew's aunt's house. Clancy still had never met this guy. She felt a stirring jealousy. Lisa was always at his place and she missed her.

When Seth was over an hour late, she called his apartment. No answer. Great. Christmas Eve, her birthday, dressed up and nowhere to go.

Mathew held out the ornament for Lisa. It was the most exquisite thing she'd ever seen, the miniature fireplace scene, the detail, accurate and fine. "It's gorgeous." And then before he put it on the limb of the tree she took another look at it. "Do you play the violin?"

"No." Mathew smiled. "I've never figured that one out."

"Clancy does. Did."

"Played the violin?"

"Yeah, apparently was pretty good at it. But something happened. She won't talk about it. Doesn't play anymore."

"That's too bad." Mathew felt a familiar twist of discomfort, not jealousy exactly, but a sort of nagging. In the months since he had known Lisa, he became increasingly aware that one of the greatest influences in her life was the mysterious roommate. "Tell me, why is it we've never met?"

Lisa shrugged. "Timing, I guess."

"Timing's everything, isn't it?" Aunt Nora whisked in with "Nite Before Christmas Tide."

"Hey, this is great." Lisa smiled after she took a sip. "I love the ornament you made. I don't think I've ever seen such detail work."

"Why, thank you, Lisa." Aunt Nora liked Lisa. But she let Mathew know in no uncertain terms that it didn't matter if she liked her or not. Lisa simply wasn't right for Mathew.

"I was just asking Mathew: who plays the violin?"

Clancy sat on the couch watching shit TV, drinking cheap wine. It was near midnight she supposed. She lit a cigarette and brushed an ash from her slip, having long ago hung up her new dress, giving up on Seth's ever coming. As she took another long drag, she heard her mother's voice, whispered pearly in her ear: *You have become me.* She shivered, then jumped when there was a knock on the door.

It was Seth.

"How nice of you to show up." She pushed the door back into his face, but he caught it with his hand and followed her into the living room, slamming the door behind him.

"Hey, Clance, I'm sorry. I'm really sorry." He was smashed.

"Seth, you're shit-faced. I'd like you to leave. Permanently."

"Hey, baby, don't be tha' way. I'm sorry. I got caught up at the producer's gig, ya know? It's business." Clancy's stance was unrelenting. "Hey . . . I said I'm sorry. And I'm gonna make it up to you." He stumbled forward.

"I want you to leave."

"Well, I'm not ready to leave," Seth responded, petulance brimming beneath his effort at charm.

"Seth. I don't want to fight."

"No fights. Promise. Make love, not war." He grabbed at her. "Come on." He tried to kiss her, but she pushed him away.

"Seth! No!" Clancy was afraid now. "I want you to leave."

"I said I'm gonna make it up to you." His body moved closer, pressing her up against the wall.

"NO!" Clancy struggled, but was no match for Seth's strength.

Anger surfacing, he grabbed both her arms. "You little hotshit princess. Cool as a cucumber." He wrenched her wrists until she could feel bruises forming. "I got your fuckin' number. Think you're better than everybody. Jesus Christ! Who the fuck are you anyway? No one tells Seth Sharp where to get off." She struggled to distance herself from him, but her body was smothered with his, his weight overbearing. She smelled the dense alcohol oozing from his body. "You're nothin', Clancy. Nothin' but a cock tease. An' things aren't over until I tell you they're over. Got it?"

He pulled her against him. She could feel he was hard. This wasn't going to happen. She would die first.

And later she felt as if she had. She lay on the hardwood floor, the blood drying between her bruised thighs. She couldn't move, had difficulty breathing. Short panting breaths. Her split lip throbbed, her jaw ached from his rough chin banging into it as he'd taken her. Shortly after he touched her, her struggle muted, she had gone to another place, not the place where she played music, but to an old place, in the rank dwelling of life with her mother—a place she knew as home, the place where, as Seth had said, she was nothing. "You ain't no gift," her mother shrieked, and thought how funny, as she lay splayed beneath the decorated tree, staring at the cheap Christmas lights. "You ain't no gift." She shut her eyes, willed herself to unconsciousness.

They lay bundled up by the fireplace, on the sofa, early in the morning. Mathew had relit the fire. They'd fallen asleep after they'd made love. He studied Lisa, sleeping peacefully, appearing almost angelic. He smiled. She made him feel good. He wasn't in love with her—he knew that—but he liked her tremendously.

She opened her eyes. "Merry Christmas, Matt."

"Merry Christmas."

She yawned, stretched like a cat, then pulled him to her. The last thing she saw before his lips touched hers was the ornament, the violin, and she thought of Clancy. And missed her. Desperately.

May 1984

At first she would not leave the apartment. Lisa would sit with her for long hours, silently, just being there. She could tell by Clancy's body language if she wanted her in another room, or to stay near, be close to her, even offer physical contact, a hand, a touch, a caress. For weeks she didn't say much. Monosyllabic utterings served her basic needs.

When she could, Clancy began to talk. At first she merely referred to "that night," but offered no other information. Like how she felt about it. What she wanted to do. What she needed.

Lisa didn't pressure. She just listened for as long as Clancy would talk.

"Maybe she needs professional help," Mathew said. They had met at the beach, one of the rare moments they were together since that night.

"Fuck that." Lisa sipped the peanut butter shake they were sharing as they strolled the sand.

"Lisa, this is too bloody serious for you to be treating it like a character study."

She turned on him. "And what do you think some friggin' specialist is going to do? Force stuff out of her that's going to do more harm than good? You have to be careful with Clancy. You have to move slow. She doesn't trust anyone but me."

"I know you're great mates, Lisa, but you are not qualified—"

"You're just . . ." But Lisa let it trail off.

"What?"

"You know." She never said the word, but they both knew what she was referring to. And he supposed he was a bit jealous. Since the day after Christmas he'd all but lost Lisa.

"I still say she needs someone who can really help her."

"And I am the only one who can help her." Lisa stood, angry. "I'm sorry if this wilts your male ego, but you're just going to have to trust me on this. I've gotta go." And with that she was off, leaving Mathew to stare out into the middle of the ocean.

Lisa took care of everything: shopping, dry cleaning, mail—anything that required getting out of the apartment. She paid the bills, supporting them as Clancy drifted into the abyss. It wasn't just the rape that was affecting her, it was something much deeper, and Lisa gave Clancy the freedom to go where she needed. They never spoke about the shift in their dynamic, that Lisa had become the provider and caretaker and that Clancy simply floated through her days in a catatonic state. But she and Mathew constantly argued over whether it was good for her, and he pushed Lisa to persuade Clancy to press charges. But Clancy wasn't interested in legal recourse. And no matter what Lisa told Mathew during their square-offs, she herself knew that it came down to Clancy believing she had somehow deserved what had happened. But all of that was beside the point for Lisa. She just wanted to get Clancy back, the Clancy that had been before that night.

She had to admit her motives weren't entirely altruistic, she thought while chopping vegetables for the stir-fry she was making for dinner. She knew Clancy's depression allowed her to have Clancy all to herself, something she realized she wanted more and more. Mathew had remarked more than once that she was "utterly focused" on Clancy and this afternoon after they'd made love, hurriedly so Lisa could get back to the apartment, said, "You're bloody obsessed with her. You have been from the moment I met you."

She tossed that around as she threw the vegetables into the frying pan, sizzling smoke whirling about her face. Was she? Obsessed? She turned the heat down as she heard Clancy walk in the kitchen behind her. She turned. Clancy was dressed into the forest green robe Lisa had gotten her, her face sadly beautiful and expressionless, as if she didn't dare show any emotion for fear it might crumble her into a million pieces.

"We're having stir-fry with shrimp."

"Hmmm."

"You love shrimp."

But Clancy didn't respond. And then Lisa saw what she hadn't seen since the rape. A tear.

"Clancy?"

And then Clancy's stoic mask disintegrated and she began to

cry. Lisa turned the stove off, walked to her, and carefully, slowly, put her hand to Clancy's shoulder. Clancy collapsed against Lisa's body. Lisa wrapped her arms about her and walked Clancy to her bedroom. They lay on the bed and Lisa held her, smoothing the full dark hair back, not saying anything, letting her cry, cry through the night, until light slivered a pale blue through the slats of the shades and Clancy finally fell asleep, loose and exhausted. Lisa tried to slither out from beneath her, but Clancy held firm. They slept, entwined. A door had opened for both of them. It would change their lives forever.

The next afternoon Clancy came out of her room, fully dressed; she tapped Lisa on the shoulder. "I think it's time for the soldier to be wheeled out to the garden." Lisa turned to her. Clancy seemed different. It was faint, but there was a glimmer of life inside her eyes.

"First tell me your dreams." Lisa was playing Ingrid Bergman in *Spellbound.* They'd seen the film a couple of nights back.

"Didn't have any."

"Voilà! You're cured." Then shifted back into Lisa. "Okay . . . where would the patient like to venture?"

"How about a good old-fashioned movie?"

They went to see *Gone With the Wind* at a revival house. "Talk about your fucked-up fate," Lisa remarked as they left. "I think they should have a Scarlett/Rhett syndrome—you know, for people that are always at cross purposes."

Clancy listened, smiling. She felt human for the first time since that night.

"Sooooo, now what? Dinner? Or do you want to go back to the house?"

"I think I've seen enough of the house, don't you?"

So Lisa drove them through a McDonald's, ordered double bacon cheeseburgers, fries, shakes, and drove them out past Malibu, up Kanan Road to an overlook where they had their picnic in front of the fading ocean view.

"It's beautiful out here."

"Mathew's showed me all around up here."

"Mathew," Clancy said. "You haven't mentioned him much."

"Well, I haven't mentioned much of anything, for that matter."

"Things okay?"

"Yeah . . . well, yes, I mean I couldn't have found a nicer guy," Lisa said, then added as though trying to overcome her own indifference, "I really love him."

"I'd like to meet him."

"We'll go to dinner. Or I'll take you up to his house where his crazy aunt lives. She's the original eccentric."

After sitting in silence for a long time, Clancy turned to Lisa and then, with her eyes more than her words, said softly, "Thank you."

September 1984

He walked through the gated entrance to the back and then to the carriage house. Lisa had told him to just come in and make himself at home. The key was under the mat. When he walked in he was struck by an exotic scent, somehow deeply familiar, a sweet musk that filled his lungs like the misty air did at the beach before a run.

It was half past six and the golden California sun was just beginning to set. He felt a keen sense of déjà vu, tried to recall what associations linked it, then shook his head and decided he would make a drink. He was headed toward the kitchen when he saw her. The sun, a soft gentle glow, cast a halo upon the deep auburn hair, thick and silky. It covered half the sleeping face, but he could see a hint of a smile forming around the lips, as if she were enjoying a wonderful dream.

He couldn't help staring. He felt as if he somehow knew her, but of course he didn't. Sure, he knew her through Lisa. But this feeling was something else. Strange. He felt a shift in his gut. And then she opened her eyes. Shining, half-mast, caught somewhere between here and the glistening promise of a nicer place.

She smiled, and then realized she was staring into the eyes of a stranger. "Who . . . who are you?"

"Thief of hearts?" That's not what he had meant to say.

"Oh. You're Mathew."

"What gave me away?"

"Your accent for one." She sat up. Stretched.

"You're Clancy."

"What gave me away?" She leaned forward to get up and her book fell to the floor. Mathew was there in an instant, handed it back to her. She looked at him, her mind and heart still caught in the other realm. She reached up and brushed back the lock of hair that had fallen forward with his movement. She didn't know what made her do it, then suddenly embarrassed, murmured, "I feel as if I know you."

"I think you do." He smiled.

And then she smiled, again. A smile to melt ice caps. It almost broke his heart because as bright as her smile was, it did not hide the tragedy in the eyes, so that she appeared broken.

He would not be able to identify it as so for several months, but it was in that moment that Mathew fell in love with Clancy.

◆ ◆ ◆

"So it really doesn't matter when they meet." Carlita sighed in awe. "Look at the beautiful light they make together."

"Yes. But notice—whereas Mathew's filters allow Clancy in, as soon as she wakes fully her aura becomes smudged by grays. She feels, but cannot identify it."

Clancy glanced at her watch. "Oh, God, I'm late." She got up, held out her hand. "It's about time we met."

"Yes."

And then she went into the bedroom, and when she came back out she was clad in a summer dress with a sweater thrown over the shoulders. She headed out the door. "Make yourself at home . . . but, Mathew? Don't be stealing any other hearts—Lisa might not like it."

"Ohhhh, but it's so romantic," Carlita gushed.

"Hmmmm." Gabriella found herself unexpectedly touched, but she didn't want to encourage Carlita's impressionable emotionalism.

"I can't wait for them to get together."

"Yes, well, I'm afraid the waiting is about to begin."

October 1984

It was Mathew's birthday and Clancy was going to a party his aunt was throwing for him, having been convinced by Lisa that it would do her good. Even though she had partially resumed her life—she had a job as a book salesclerk, and was taking one night class that fall, she still found it difficult to be around people. It was as if after "that night" her belief in the worst in people was confirmed, that no matter how shiny and polished they might appear on the surface, each one of them had a hoary, evil monster lurking inside that could attack at any moment.

For a long time after that night she could barely remember what happened. Not until the day she started crying. Before then she seemed to lie in a dense fog, a haze of inky guilt and shame in which she could see nothing. Couldn't move. Was paralyzed. All she could do was lie in her bed and stare, thinking thoughts now she couldn't even begin to retrace. Maybe she had no thoughts, only the desire to die. And she probably would have if it hadn't been for Lisa and Tweety Bird, who each day perched on her shoulder, then hopped about the bed, until Lisa put her in the cage at night. Lisa who fed her, made her bathe, kept her conscious, offered soothing tones, loving care, never pushing, just being there, a presence, wrapped in a cocoon of love and acceptance.

And Lisa's care was exactly what she had needed. It was her constant vigil without tampering into Clancy's fragile psyche that finally allowed the tears she thought would never stop. And then she pulled herself together, ventured from the guest house, breathed in the air of Los Angeles—all of it: the exhaust, sidewalks, orange blossoms, desert air—and it filled her lungs with the will to be. That day she walked for hours and knew she had decided to live.

"Night and daytime, Always playtime. Ain't we got fun?" read the salutation on Mathew's cake. He had watched Aunt Nora as she put the final touches on his birthday cake, covering it with purple icing. The guests were just arriving. He saw Dora struggling out of a cab, ran to help her when another cab pulled up behind them. It was Clancy. Wearing a pale blue cotton dress and sweater. His

heart pulsed with a new excitement as she approached him, fading sun again caught her hair, auburn highlights, aglow. He put out his hand.

"Happy birthday," she said, and smiled. That smile.

"Thank you."

"Lisa got a call right before we left. She had an audition for some TV thing and said she'd be here as soon as she got out."

"Oh . . . okay." He felt only a twinge of disappointment.

The party was endlessly delightful. Aunt Nora read a hilarious poem about Mathew, a stanza devoted to every year that he had been with her. Massive amounts of "Matt Tide" were consumed. Dora even danced with him after he begged her, her creaky, arthritic limbs giving him a run for his money. Maria, who was visiting, also danced with him, body pressed close. It was an eclectic group: canyon friends, old school friends of Mathew's, new friends from literary circles. In all, good people, good times.

Near midnight the guests began to leave, until finally there was only Aunt Nora, Mathew, and Clancy in the living room, drinking coffee.

"God, what time is it?" Clancy asked.

"A little past midnight," Mathew answered.

"Well . . . it's time for this ol' broad to get into bed," Aunt Nora remarked. She struggled out of Ginger's easy chair. "Delighted to have met you, Clancy. Happy birthday, my dear boy," at which Mathew got up and accepted a loving embrace.

When they were alone, Mathew sat across from Clancy by the hearth. The fire was just burning itself out.

"I . . . I wonder what's kept Lisa. Maybe I should just call a cab?" Clancy mused.

"I have no problem with waiting. Unless you need to go."

"No." She glanced from the fire to him. "No. I'm fine."

A gentle silence fell. Mathew watched her.

"Lisa tells me you're a wonderful writer."

Mathew blushed. "I think I would call myself a serviceable writer—"

"Don't be modest."

"I'm not. I'm afraid the British reserve keeps me from really getting to where I want to go."

"And where is that?" The question hung between them as their eyes found one another's. He forgot that they were speaking and maybe she did as well for she turned her eyes to the fire, long dark lashes resting peacefully against cheeks blushed from drink and heat.

"You slept with her, didn't you?" Clancy took him off guard.

"Who?"

"Your old maid." Clancy laughed. "That sounded funny; let me rephrase it. The woman, Maria, who used to be your maid."

"But, why . . . what would make you say that?"

"Well?"

He cleared his throat. "As a matter of fact, I did."

"I thought so."

"Is it that obvious?"

"I don't think anyone else would see it. But . . . I don't . . . let's call it intuition."

"Actually, I'm pretty sure my aunt's aware of it."

"I don't think there's anything your aunt isn't aware of."

"Most people consider her quite . . . eccentric."

"She might be. But that doesn't mean she doesn't know exactly what's going on all the time." After a moment she added, "She adores you. In fact I don't know when I've seen a person more adored."

Mathew blushed. "It' not . . ."

"Don't—" Clancy's eyes were direct. "It's wonderful."

He stoked the fire. "You know people, don't you?"

"Know them?" Clancy thought about that a moment. "Yes, I think I do."

"What else do you know?" he asked.

"I know that cranky old Dora isn't as mean and nasty as she likes to pretend. I know that Maria is still a little in love with you. And . . . I think Lisa might be jealous if she were to catch us in this cozy little scene."

"Jealous?"

"Yes."

"But I guess the real question would be, of whom?"

Now Mathew's eyes were direct. She finally glanced away and it was then Lisa showed up, and indeed her eyes burnt a bit more green when she saw the two of them sitting at the fireplace, the glow of the room charged with more than the sparks from the dying fire.

"Now what? The suspense is killing me," Carlita said.

"Well, that's highly inconceivable, my dear, since you're already dead." Gabriella shook her head when Magdalena appeared.

"How are things progressing?" Magdalena addressed Gabriella, barely acknowledging Carlita.

"We're about midway to vortexing," Gabriella answered.

"Good. If you can spare some moments, I would appreciate a consultation regarding an intergalactic intervention."

Gabriella glanced at Carlita, who appeared suitably reverential for Magdalena's benefit. "Will you be okay then, Prefect Carlita?"

"Absolutely." Carlita bowed. For a few moments she simply waited, attempting to act the part of an obedient angel, but her cu-

riosity got the better of her. Carlita attempted a few signings to the hologram. Nothing happened. She tried several more variations she had been memorizing and finally the prism of colors activated. From there she had watched Gabriella closely enough to get the information she wanted to see:

Earth Subject: Lisa M. Burke
Incarnations: Eliah, Court Jester—England 1745–1778
Christina Rossetti, 1830–1894
Clark Gable, 1901–1960
Lisa M. Burke 1961–

Clark Gable? "Now wait a minute," Carlita whispered to herself in confusion, unaware that Gabriella was right behind her viewing the screen.

"Carlita! Just what is it you think you are doing?"

"Oh! I thought you were gone . . ."

"Apparently. What in heaven's name are you doing?"

"Well, um . . . I . . ." Carlita quivered. "I . . . I just wanted to see where Lisa . . . how Lisa fit in."

"Carlita!" Gabriella's frustration was clearly genuine. "If you're going to play sleuth, you're going to have to be a far sight better at deception."

"I'm sorry. But how am I to do a good job, be a decent guardian angel, if I don't fully understand what we're doing and why."

"You do have a bit of a point there," Gabriella conceded. "But it was decided by the High Council Seraphim that novitiate angels would be given only the information that was necessary, so they wouldn't feel the undue pressure of the task before them."

"But Angel Gabriella, all I'm asking is to let me do my job the best I can. Please . . . what's the big mystery?"

Gabriella considered the request for a long moment. "I think you need a bit more of the story first. Then I'll think about it."

March 1985

"So . . . what do you think of our Mathew?" Lisa had asked that first night after his birthday.

"He's wonderful, Lisa. You did good."

"Yes . . . didn't I?"

"Yes. You did." And Clancy left her to go to her room to sleep.

It was Lisa's idea that the three of them spend so much time together. Now that Clancy and Mathew had met, she didn't want to be without either of them. So they would go to movies, out to dinner, up to Aunt Nora's for a spontaneous party. They drank, danced, played pinochle with Aunt Nora and Dora. Every so often Lisa or Mathew would bring along a fourth, a potential boyfriend for Clancy, but she wasn't ready to date anyone. The only person she felt comfortable around was Lisa. And Mathew. She felt safe around him. And she liked him.

What the three of them did best together was talk. They spent hours telling stories, gossiping, critiquing, pontificating. They argued good-naturedly and at times their philosophical debates, although playful, held serious undertones, as it did the night they were out on the deck drinking Aunt Nora's "Dorothy Parker Tide." Lisa had been quoting and performing from *The Portable Dorothy Parker,* and as the evening progressed, she was becoming more like her muse, cynical and depressed.

"'For I loved him, and he didn't love back.'" Lisa finished, bowed, and then flopped into a chair.

"Well, that was short and sweet," Mathew teased.

"I met Dorothy Parker once," Aunt Nora mused. "At the

'Gonk. She was so small you wouldn't expect her bark to be so bitter. She was sitting with a gentleman who was clearly her date but he was flirting heavily with another woman two tables away."

A sudden silence fell over the room. "So. What happened?" Lisa asked defensively.

"I was invited to their table, as well as the woman her companion was flirting with, and we all drank a good deal."

"Is there a point to this story?" Lisa asked.

"I rather doubt it. Except that she never seemed content and lived her discontent through her work."

"And where would we be without all our sordid little stories?" Lisa queried cynically.

"Playing out one's fantasies can be quite therapeutic," Aunt Nora said, pouring from the second batch of tide, attempting to redirect the conversation.

"Nora's right," Clancy said. "Even if things aren't, well, precisely as you'd like them, Lisa, you get to purge all those emotions by playing them out in your body, your fantasies, dreams, embodying the skin of all your characters."

"Yes," Aunt Nora added, "playing all those characters seems to suit you."

Lisa conceded, as she became Tallulah Bankhead. "It's really quite divine, dahling, quite divine."

"And Mathew does it all in his head," Aunt Nora remarked.

"Actors get to do it in their bodies, writers in their heads. What about the little people?" Clancy asked. "People that aren't on a quest or driven by a mission."

"They find different muses," Aunt Nora answered.

"Like?"

"Simple things. Things inside a person that give them the same kind of intense and dramatic release as Lisa's acting, Mathew's writing. It just looks different from the outside, but the final reward is the same. It could be the act of knitting—but in that seemingly innocuous activity a whole world exists in the head of the knitter that is textured, lush, and full of creative energy. They work their dreams right into their projects."

"Like you, Aunt Nora." Mathew smiled at her.

"Precisely. And others simply"—she paused for a moment, searching for the right word—"be."

"Be?" Lisa piped.

"Yes. They just are. And they are fine just being."

"I don't know anyone like that unless they're total stoners," Lisa said.

"What about you, Clancy?" Aunt Nora asked. "What makes an ordinary moment extraordinary for you?"

Clancy sat silently.

"Well it's her—" Lisa started out, but Clancy shot her a threatening look.

"Tweety Bird," she blurted.

They all laughed, but Aunt Nora saw the question in Mathew's eyes as they rested on Clancy's. Their eyes held one another's a long moment. Lisa watched them taking each other in. And Aunt Nora watched them all.

The three of them had taken to hiking Topanga and Malibu canyons. One afternoon, as they were just about to leave the house, Lisa was called for an audition. "Hey you guys, it's a callback for the national." She lit up with excitement and they both gave her the thumbs-up sign. "At least I know I'm leaving you both in good company. I'll call the house when I'm done, Matt, and then maybe we can all go out and celebrate."

"Great," he answered.

When she left, he turned to Clancy. "Still want to hike?"

"Sure."

They took off in his Mustang, climbed high, winding roads that threatened vertigo, and found a turnoff. They got out of the car, stumbled through an overgrown path that opened up into a clearing that offered a view of sheer majesty: a large weeping willow graciously supplied them shade as they sat and gazed out over the canyons to the wide expanse of ocean, a cloud shimmering the length of the horizon.

"This reminds me of when I first moved here," Mathew said. "I couldn't believe how incredibly beautiful it was. I couldn't have imagined Los Angeles could be so entrancing."

"Neither could I," Clancy answered.

"What was New York like?"

"Fast . . . furious. Bleak . . . dirty." The tone of her voice redirected his questions.

"How'd you manage to come here?"

"I'd spent some time in Florida," she began and then told him about her road trip and how she'd arrived in Portland. "But there was something about being on the road, being all by myself, early in the morning, that made me feel, I don't know—this will sound completely contradictory—but that I was supposed to be on this path, to nowhere in particular . . . just where I was at." She paused a moment. "It was one of the only times I ever felt really certain . . . inside that paradox." Then she laughed at herself. "Sounds a bit out there, I know."

"My aunt would think it was very logical."

"I know. It kind of sounded like her." Clancy smiled at him and he stopped breathing momentarily. Then: "She's really something. Quite a character."

"I adore Aunt Nora. I was very lucky after my parents died. I could have ended up gutting fish." Mathew grinned. "Or what if Aunt Nora had turned out to be Dora!"

"Well, yes . . ." She laughed at the thought of Dora raising anyone.

"I missed England, desperately at first. Missed the way it smelled, missed the sound of King's English, cockney in the streets, missed the bloody rain, if you can imagine." He smiled shyly. "And then I adapted. We all do, I suppose. And now I love it. There's something ironically enchanting about a city devoted to dreams, but standing constantly in the face of destruction. Flip sides of a coin—a very unusual place."

"Do you mind my asking . . ." She paused a moment. "I was just wondering about your family."

"I missed them too. At first. But then, it's true what they say about time."

"You think so?" Clancy asked, thinking of her own mother, the intense feelings of disgust, hate, shame, and guilt as strong in her now as they ever were.

"Actually, there are times I think of my mother. Like she's there, somehow. I speak to her in my head." He blushed slightly. "I don't mean like—"

"You don't have to explain." She touched his forearm. "I think I know what you mean. It's sweet."

"I . . . I don't know, I just wish she could have known me—who I am. As a grown man. And that I could have known her better." He picked at a twig. They both sat in silence, letting the breeze play in their hair. He was going to ask about her family, but it was almost as if she anticipated this and redirected the conversation.

"And now you're getting your second book published." Clancy gazed at him with admiration. "I read *Footfall*."

Mathew tensed. He wondered if he would ever feel anything but insecurity about his work.

"It was . . . wonderful, Mathew. Incredible, really. I felt like I was in each of the places, you know? Like I was working with that road crew, or in the hospital. God, some of those passages were"—she shivered—"actually . . . excruciating. But the thing I liked the most was the certainty of 'being' each different lifescape."

"Lifescape. That's a great word. Mind if I use it?"

"Well, maybe," she teased, "if you dedicate your next book to me."

"How 'bout the one after that?"

"Okay." Then she got serious again. "I guess when you wrote about those individual lives, I felt each had purpose, a sense of rightness. And I . . ." She trailed off.

"And you?"

"Nothing. I just think it's amazing. I mean, how do you do it? Just gather all these thoughts, put them down on paper, and poof, there's a book?"

"Well"—Mathew laughed—"it happens something like that."

"You really work at it, don't you?"

"I wish I didn't have to. Work so hard." Mathew's smile was vulnerable. And beautiful.

"What do you mean?"

"I wish it came more naturally."

"Give yourself some credit. I could never do anything like that."

"Sure you could. If it was something you loved."

"The only thing I love besides Tweety Bird is Lisa—" and then she stopped.

"And?"

But she'd already revealed too much.

"What is it?" Mathew pressed. "Lisa almost let it out the other night. Didn't she?"

"I . . . I don't want to talk about it."

They sat quietly for a moment. "You're really quite fond of her, aren't you?"

"Yes." Clancy looked at him and then back out at the ocean. "Yes. I am."

Lisa watched them several nights later in Club 7, a hot smoky dance bar, thick with bodies, sweat, and hormones. Mathew and Clancy were out on the floor, only because Lisa forced them to dance together, said she wanted to sit a couple out. The pulsing beat of a popular dance number segued into a lazy rhythm, not quite a slow dance, but she watched Mathew as he moved closer, then took Clancy in his arms. They moved well together, both lost in the music. The sensual strength, the lines, curves, the hair—all of it made Lisa's breath catch. She took a sip of her beer, lit a cigarette, then studied the two of them. Her jaw tightened as she let the feeling sear through her. Excitement. Arousal. New. Very different. Arousal, in a way she hadn't felt before. It wasn't at the surface, at her skin. This burned from inside.

Later, Mathew could barely keep pace. Aggressive, her mouth trailing his body, taking him in her, making him hard, guiding him to her, meeting him urgently, creating the fire, until he came and she came after, on his leg, grinding into him, above him, caught somewhere in her own fantasy.

She lit a cigarette, kept to her side of the bed. When he tried to touch her, she got up and walked to the window. He lay they watching her.

"Anything wrong?" he asked.

"No." But her tone was unconvincing. She couldn't tell him. Hell, she could barely voice it to herself. This drive, this raw angry desire was awake and hungry. There was only one problem. It wasn't Mathew she wanted to go to bed with that night. It was Clancy.

• • •

They smoked Aunt Nora's pot one night after a festive dinner she gave for the three of them, herself, and Dora. Dora had long since fallen asleep in one of Ginger's chairs, snoring lightly as the fire played gentle shadows on her face. Mathew and Lisa sat to one side of the hearth, propped up by pillows and each other, Clancy sat on the other side. Aunt Nora leaned against the other Ginger chair. She packed another pipe, lit it, and then passed it around.

"Nora," Lisa asked, "I've always wondered why it is you have all your Christmas stuff out. Is it late being packed up or out early?"

"Neither," Mathew supplied. "Aunt Nora believes Christmas should be year-round and this is her way of lobbying for that."

"Christmas." Lisa took a puff and passed it to Clancy. "Commercial. Harried. For the Rich. Irritating . . . what letter comes next?" Lisa was very stoned.

"S."

"Sobering," Clancy quipped.

Silence fell.

"Christmas is simply a wonderful excuse to be extravagantly romantic and I, for one, believe we should be that every moment of our lives," Aunt Nora offered.

"What is romantic?" Lisa asked. "I mean romance is all in the perception of mutual illusion. In fact, romance is a synonym for illusion—"

"Oh, come on, Lis!" Clancy said laughing.

"Seriously. We go on and on about this mythical lightning bolt, when in fact it boils down to an empty vacuum . . . waiting to suck love in. When a person is ready to fall in love, any one of several people could be walking through the door and boom! 'That's the one!' It's manufactured along with the expectations for that other person to be everything you've ever wanted from Cupid's arrow."

"Darling boy, did you know your girlfriend was such a cynic?" Aunt Nora asked.

"Well, this personality anyway." He laughed. "Several of Lisa's personalities are quite devoted to romance."

"Half the time we're doing a relationship in our head. We give it the particular ingredients it requires by devoting hours manipulating all the props: moonlit strolls, candles, a little vino, and some violin. Presto. Then we perpetuate whatever scenario we've created, never having a clue what scenario the other person has created."

"So you're saying that if two scenarios that meet up are compatible, that's when a relationship happens?" Clancy asked.

"Precisely. When the hell do you get to know each other? After you drop the illusions and pretense. Then it becomes too damn much work. End of relationship. Why do you think most of them end so quickly? You think it's because Jane and John Doe share their humanness? No way. It's because they share everything but their humanness. They share a well-developed facade, their front, their best foot forward."

"My, you *are* cynical." Mathew's tone was somewhere between hurt and surprise. "Is that what we are?"

"No, Mathew, you fall into a special category," Lisa said, her voice turning soft. "You don't play games."

"And you?" Clancy asked.

Lisa looked directly at her. This was between them now.

"I've led myself down some paths."

"And?"

"And what?"

"Where are they taking you? If you want honesty and humanity, why don't you just have the balls to go for it?"

"I'm as human as they come, Clan, and that means I also don't want to be squashed in the process."

The glimmering contact was interrupted by a fitful snore by Dora.

"Got yourself a regular ménage there, dear boy," Aunt Nora remarked the next morning.

"I don't know what you mean."

"Why, that you're both in love with her."

"Oh, don't be ridiculous." But as Mathew headed for the shower he knew she was right.

He'd fallen. Hard. All he thought about was Clancy. She moved him in a way nothing ever had.

July 1985

. . . a whisper in the wings of magic,
her flaming indigo hair
the smell of her would take you there
another world of mystery and lore
you'd never been before
and haven't since.

a goddess in revelatory stance
a dreaming angel waiting to dance
to the melody of light and
exposure to the order
that is simply . . . her.

When he was done and the audience finished clapping, Lisa turned to Clancy, pegged her straight in the eye. "Well, we both know who that was about, don't we?"

They had been waiting for Lisa but after a half hour when she hadn't shown, they decided they couldn't tolerate the heat any longer, left her a message, then took a picnic lunch to the beach. The breeze that whipped off the ocean was vigorous and made the heat endurable. After they ate they walked for what seemed hours. Talking. Not talking. And then she glanced at him and they stopped without a word. She took him in, his wonderful jaw line, his fine thick black hair blowing about in the wind, his gentle ruggedness, sweet English lips. She smiled as his eyes spoke and then he opened his mouth, but she put a finger to his lips. "No."

They continued walking.

That night she walked into Lisa's room. Lisa was sleeping. Clancy sat on the bed and watched her for a long moment. Lisa woke. She wasn't surprised to see Clancy. There were many nights Clancy became frightened and crawled into bed with her, so Lisa put out a hand to her, gently cradled her beneath the covers, keeping her safe.

But this night Clancy felt the heat of Lisa's body, aware of the soft stomach at her back, Lisa's legs against her own, and then felt Lisa's hand cautiously move through her hair, stroking it gently, sensuously, until she tenderly pulled Clancy's face toward her own, her fingers grazing her cheek and drawing her closer so that Clancy's lips touched Lisa's. Tender. Loving. Safe. Then she felt Lisa's lips at her eyes, forehead, cheeks, so loving, so caressing, Clancy could feel her body become alive, and she felt a hunger in her she hadn't felt in so long. And the safety to expose it. Lisa's sweetness, Lisa's care for her expressed in every touch of her mouth, her palms now gently clasping Clancy's body to her own, her lips traveling down the length of her neck, hot breath through the material of her T-shirt to aching nipples. Lisa undressing her now, with great urgency but care, until their bodies were exposed to the fullness of heat, desire, and a longing in Clancy to be healed.

"Oh God, yes," Clancy could barely breathe as Lisa loved her, made love to her, lavished all the feelings she had ever had for this woman, as Clancy held onto Lisa, her new lover.

"Does this mean we're lesbians?" Lisa asked the next morning after coffee.

"I guess so," Clancy answered without conviction.

"I suppose this means I have to go stock up on feminist books and get some Birkenstocks." Lisa attempted a wry smile.

"What about Mathew?"

"Shit." Lisa just remembered she had a boyfriend. "Well, this is California. Can't I have you both?"

When Mathew saw them he knew something was different. Lisa was glowing; Clancy's eyes were more alive. There was also a tenderness between them he'd never seen, a protective veil that dropped over the two of them and said "Do not enter." When the evening came to a close, Mathew knew he and Lisa were not going to return to his place, as well as he knew by the glimmer in her eyes, when she had brushed his lips good night, that something in her was gone, and would never return.

When Clancy embraced him she held him a bit longer, gentle touch of palm to his cheek, and then she pierced his eyes with a look that said good-bye, and something else: apology, but also a truth . . . that his feelings for her were reciprocated in some way. He would relive that look for months, trying to understand.

It never failed to produce absolute ecstasy in Carlita when they flew, as they did now, gliding through the galaxy past the shimmering stars—she loved being lit up by their energy—through the strato-

sphere, dipping through Mathew's window, out the open front door as Aunt Nora bent to get the paper, and then onto Point Dume, where they perched and watched Earth's sun rise.

"Do you see now, how this has become so complicated?"

"Yes. Never in all of heaven did I see that coming."

"But you have been courting the future."

"Pardon me?"

"I brought you down to Earth, so that we might have some privacy, Carlita." Gabriella's tone was low and serious. "I won't caution you again. You must stop coercing the hologram into seeing the future lives of your charges. What's important is this particular Earth life."

"But something keeps nagging at me. As if the future holds the key—"

"No, Carlita. You have it backward. The present holds the key to the future, so I must ask you to relinquish whatever tail-brain scheme you have indulged yourself in. Promise."

"Yes, Angel Gabriella," Carlita responded, her wings folded ever so slightly behind her back.

October 1985

. . . and I'm not sure what it was he did. Your uncle Joseph never spoke of him. Your mother wouldn't allow his name to be said in her presence. He may well be dead, but I thought you might want his last known address, which is 4732 Holly Lane, Los Angeles.

I've been having problems with the arthritis, and have been feeling a bit under the weather. I hope your work goes well. Thank you so much for the photos of the old stars. I do so love Claudette Colbert, Myrna Loy, Fred MacMurray, and especially the Joan Crawford shot. I think they should have used her as Scarlett O'. . . .

And that's where the letter ended. It was sent with the last of Aunt Marion's personal belongings. She had been struggling with cancer for the past year, and no one had realized how advanced it was. Apparently, she had never complained. That was Aunt Marion. She just sort of let life take her on its own terms.

And now she had the address of the notorious Uncle Sal. Did she even want to find out any more about her family? She was as good as free now. She walked over to Tweety Bird.

"What do you think?" Tweety jumped to her shoulder and she walked outside with her and sat by the pool. Clancy sighed. She and Lisa had had another fight last night. "I don't see why you won't just come to one meeting with me." Lisa had screamed about the Lambda Lesbians for Life, only one of several new organizations she had joined to claim her new sexuality. That seemed to occupy Lisa's every moment when she wasn't working: attend meetings and fight with Clancy.

"I hate group things. You know that."

"No, you hate lesbians. You hate the idea of a whole bunch of us in one room. You hate to be identified with it."

Did she? No. It wasn't the identification per se that bothered her. It was the loss of Mathew, Aunt Nora, the time they had spent up in Topanga, but most importantly their friendship. Their friendship, which had been the cornerstone of her stability, was now taut and full of suspense as every minute Lisa waited for her to change her mind. And the more uncertain Clancy became, the more adamantly Lisa challenged the entire world to accept this alternative way of loving. But it wasn't about that for Clancy. Loving Lisa was about loving Lisa, and she tried to express that to her when Lisa would return home, repentant, and they would hold one another, clinging, afraid of a love that neither seemed to understand.

"I love you. That's all that matters." It became Lisa's haunting refrain.

"I love you too. That's not even the issue," Clancy would respond. And then they would stop talking and hope tomorrow would be different.

"But it isn't different, is it, Tweety?" She got up from the pool now and walked around listlessly. She returned to the table where Aunt Marion's letter rested and thought of the night her aunt had taken such care to make her look beautiful for the concert, and she remembered the music, and felt an intense pain in the center of her that was longing. A poignant and nostalgic memory pulling at her from a place she couldn't even name. It wasn't the kind of yearning that had propelled her toward Lisa. That had been a need to be touched again, to feel a lover's hand, safety, to participate in some measure with the human race. This wanting was for something she couldn't even identify. She stared at Sal's name for a long time, then turned to Tweety. "Should we look up this old geezer?"

Clancy joined Tweety Bird by her perch at the window. She turned around and looked at the home she had shared with Lisa as a roommate for the past four years. And then shared as her lover the past few months, she reminded herself. As her lover. And then thought of Mathew.

She didn't want to be without either of them.

But it was time to leave.

When he opened the door, she dropped her purse. The resemblance to her mother wasn't uncanny—it was frightening. Uncle Sal was her mother in male form, but more feminine.

"Yes, my dear? Can I help you?" He asked. He was dressed in a sarong, his hair neatly coifed. He was holding a thin cigar stuffed in a gold cigarette holder in one hand, a miniature gray schnauzer snuggled under his other arm.

"Sal O'Halloran?" She didn't have to ask.

"Yes, dear."

"I'm Clancy Reardon, Celia's daughter."

"Oh, my dear Lord in heaven, you don't say." He stood stunned for a moment, then beckoned her in. "Oh do come in. I'm sorry, I lost my manners for a wee second, but it's a bit like a voice from the dead then, isn't it?"

Clancy entered the magical kingdom of Sal O'Halloran, replete with Chinese and Indian art, mixed in with a late sixties decor he'd never outgrown. He led her into a large sunken living room with a burnt tile fireplace, walls of windows that spanned a meticulously attended garden full of exotic flowers and shrubs, and beyond that spread the cityscape of Los Angeles.

"Do have a seat, my dear." Uncle Sal immediately recharged his cigarette holder with a fresh cigarillo. "Now, what can I get you to drink? You look a wee bit like a Chablis spritzer? Or are you one of those smart young ladies into Chivas on the rocks?"

"Actually, a Coke would be great if you have it."

"Hmmm, a teetotaler? Are you sure we're related?"

"I drink, but I'm really thirsty, and a Coke would be great for right now."

He walked behind a bar stocked with bottles of things Clancy had never seen before, as well as trinkets and bar-related gewgaws. He returned with a Coke for Clancy, then made himself a Manhattan with the speed of a professional bartender, which it turned out he had been on and off throughout his life.

They sat with their drinks for a few moments.

"Now, my dear. Tell me. How is your mother?"

He didn't know?

"She's been dead for years."

"Oh, yes. I forgot." Like he'd forgotten to take in the mail. "Marion told me. And how is she?"

"Dead."

"Joseph dead as well?"

"Yes."

"Hmmmm . . . I guess that makes me the last standing O'Halloran."

At that moment a reed-thin gentleman in a burgundy silk robe and ascot walked in.

"Ahhh, Dirk, my dear niece is visiting." Dirk, realizing they had company, pulled his robe tight. "Clancy's her name and she's going to be staying with us . . . aren't you? I mean you haven't gone and gotten a hotel or anything?"

And it was then that Clancy explained that she'd been living in Los Angeles for several years.

"And what took you so long to look me up?"

"Well . . . to be perfectly honest, my mother and I didn't get along so well, and I wasn't sure I wanted to meet anyone else in the family."

"Perfectly reasonable. Our family bred nothing but losers—"

"Except you, dear." Dirk beamed at his lover.

"And now you're in a wee bit of a jam?" Her uncle Sal may have appeared the perfect fop, but he was no fool.

"Yes. I am."

"Worry no more. We've got the most splendid guest room downstairs, your own bathroom. Very large. Lots of privacy. We'd be delighted for you to stay. Wouldn't we, Dirk?"

Dirk put his hand on Sal's shoulder. "Absolutely."

So the outcast of the family, the one they would never talk about, the one excommunicated because of his "forbidden love," turned out to be the kindest, warmest, and most gentle of the O'Halloran bunch, and for the first time in her entire life, Clancy knew what it was to have family.

"Have you spoken to her?" he asked.

"No." Lisa took a sip of Aunt Nora's "Autumn Leaves Tide." "I don't even know where she went." She'd come home one day and Clancy was gone. Her clothes, her meager belongings, stripped from the guest house as if she'd never been there. No trace of Tweety Bird. Anything they'd purchased together remained behind. But the ghost of Clancy was there. The smell of Clancy and her China musk leaked from every corner. Lisa found it would enter her senses when she least expected it.

She'd called Mathew. They had spoken very little in the past months. He was there in half an hour.

"What happened?"

"I have no idea."

"No. I mean, what happened from the beginning?"

"Don't you know?" She looked at him, her expression heartbroken and defensive.

"Yes. Yes, of course I do." They stood with the truth between them. Mathew put his hand out to Lisa. "I do. I knew the morning you told me you wanted to take some time to be alone. I'm not a bloody dope, you know." Lisa had called him the morning after the last night they'd all spent together. They had met for an almost wordless breakfast. She'd said things like "You're wonderful. . . . I'm just not present. . . . I need space. . . . I don't want to hurt you. . . ." But he had told her he was fine. And he had been. He wasn't in love with Lisa. But losing Lisa meant losing Clancy, and that was much harder to bear.

"Guess we screwed up." Lisa's tears were choking to get out.

"No one screwed up. It's just the way it is."

"I don't know, Mathew." The tears fell softly down her cheeks. "I . . . I love her. God, I love her more than anything. I . . . I really have no idea how she feels about me."

"But you were lovers?" Mathew had to hear it spoken aloud.

Lisa's eyes, wet and runny, shone with the painful answer. "Yes."

Mathew sighed. Long and hard. Then took Lisa in his arms, and she felt his strength shielding her. It was then they forged the friendship that would last a lifetime.

November 1985

It was the day before Thanksgiving. Lisa was visiting her parents so she couldn't make it for dinner at the house, and Mathew was disappointed because he and Lisa now spent all their time commiserating over the loss of Clancy, getting to know one another in a way that was natural and real. Without Lisa he felt like a new part of him was missing.

"No good moping about, Mathew," Aunt Nora said. "Why don't you take a run into Santa Monica, go into Herbaceous for me, and get these things I need."

"Sure." Mathew had nothing better lined up for the day. Maybe he'd go for a walk on the beach there as well. He was working on the outline of his new book, and he could think about it while he walked. Do something to occupy his mind so he didn't feel so out of sorts. It was difficult moping about for a woman he now missed as his primary mate and another woman he yearned for but didn't feel he had the right to.

Lisa watched football with her family. She didn't want to be in the snug home with her three perfect brothers, all professionals whose lives made sense, and her showcase parents, both highly esteemed doctors, in their individual practices. Lisa was their adored anomaly, and she gladly pulled out that character so everyone in the family felt good about who they were. But she missed Mathew, wished they could have combined families so they could spend the day together and continue sleuthing the whereabouts of Clancy.

They play-acted Nick and Nora Charles. It brought humor to their misery, and dressed up the reality of their obsession. Mathew made a brilliant Nick, even to the point of growing a thin mustache for the part. They watched every one of the *Thin Man* movies several times over so that Lisa now possessed Myrna Loy's every mannerism, spoke in her lilting movie-tone accent to Mathew's bon vivant William Powell. They played their roles through grocery lines, restaurants, public libraries, even the police station as they hunted clue after clue that led to nothing.

In the meantime, Lisa's part on her soap had been killed off, but now, even if they were renegotiating her comeback from a madman's mansion as an evil version of herself that started killing off bit players as the Salem Stalker, she was uninterested in her career. She'd fired her agent when he tried to put the moves on her, and instead of hunting for a new one, spent her time playing private eye. Yes, Nick and Nora kept Mathew and Lisa from dealing with anything that resembled their real lives.

Clancy walked Val (short for Valium) back to the house. The miniature schnauzer weighed in at eight pounds and was the most inert animal Clancy had ever seen. Hence the name.

The dog would literally pass out on Sal's lap. You could pick her up, throw her in the air—still she wouldn't wake. Clancy wondered if maybe her lethargy was due to her blood pressure, or lack thereof, but the dog proved to be healthy. It simply had no energy.

Tweety Bird would perch on Val's back as she slept, and even sometimes while she puttered around the house. Val was often found draped upon Sal's shoulder like a tatty fur stole as he walked around the house. Sal loved Valium with all his heart, though, much as he loved Dirk, musicals, Gene Kelly, and now, Clancy.

After sharing breakfast with Sal that morning she had found out what had happened back East, when he left home with the "silk shirt on my back."

"You see, your mom and I were great drinking pals for the longest time. She loved to hang at the bars with me, and we both had a wild crush on this maddeningly handsome Italian named Tony who sang Frank Sinatra amore songs, even if he was often more than a wee bit off key. Your uncle Joe came with us one night. We were having a great time and of course by last call we'd all had more than our fair share, and we invited Tony to our table. Tony put his hand on my knee, so I knew he was a wee bit Dorothy like myself.

"We all shared an apartment at the time, and the next day your mom and Joe came home early. They were planning a surprise birthday party for me. But the surprise was on them. There were Tony and myself humping ourselves mad on the living room floor. Well! You can just imagine. Your mother went stark raving hysterical and Joe just stood there with his jaw to his knees. Tony and I grabbed our clothes, your mother kicked me out of the apartment, and I guess that night they had a family powwow and crossed me off the O'Halloran name in the family Bible, and sent me packing.

"Actually, I wasn't all that devastated. There wasn't much in the way of family love, as I'm sure you're well aware. Except for Joe; I missed the dear boy. No backbone, but he loved the ladies. Like I loved the lads. So I hitchhiked to Los Angeles, tended bar at the Queen Mary, and saw my first drag show. Ohhhh, how I loved the costumes and props. I swooned. I simply swooned. And it wasn't long before I started my illustrious career as Lady Lankershim, and the rest, as they say in the biz, is history."

She smiled.

"My dear, you are absolutely ravishing when you smile. You should do it more often." He patted jam on his blueberry muffin. "Now. What are we to do with you?"

"I'm . . . I honestly don't know. I'm having some difficulty making decisions. I don't know what I'm doing. It's been great staying here the past few weeks, Uncle Sal. Letting me be—"

"But it's time to get on with it, eh?" he asked kindly.

"Yes. I just don't know what step to take first." Clancy, who rarely exposed herself in any way to others, felt safe with Uncle Sal.

"And what seems to be the problem?"

"Well, there's this friend. A woman. And this guy, Mathew. And our relationships have become—I don't know, tangled and warped. I've spent all this time trying to figure it out, but haven't come up with anything. My life's a mess, which is par for the course. I don't know *why* I'm doing what I'm doing half the time, and I have no idea what I want to do and every time I think I've got something worked out, I seem to make a mess of it."

"Well, my dear, seems as if you have a wee bit of the human condition."

"What do you mean?"

"Just that there are so few who really do know what the hell they're doing."

Clancy wasn't satisfied.

"Hmmmm." Uncle Sal sipped his tea. "What shall we tackle first?"

"First? I need a job."

"Easy. Next?"

"I'm not sure. Let's get the job out of the way."

So he sent her to Santa Monica that morning. To Herbaceous, which a good buddy of his owned. They were in desperate need of a manager, someone who could whip the herbal/giftshop/new age bookstore into shape. And the only day she could talk with him before he left for Hawaii was today.

When Mathew entered the store, the smells of patchouli, herbs, and incense slammed into his senses. He took the list from his pocket and began his search for the strange ingredients Aunt Nora wanted for the stuffing. He was studying the rack of spices when he smelled the familiar scent, the sweet musky scent of her perfume. He'd heard the tinkling of chimes as the door opened, but it was the smell that told him she was there.

"Clancy?" He said it without thinking.

And as he came around the aisle she stood before him. She blushed, then stammered as if the air had been knocked from her. As it had been. "Mathew."

"Clancy, we've been . . ." What could he say: we've been parading around as Nick and Nora hunting you down? "We've been worried."

She cleared her throat. "Um . . . Mathew, I'm sorry, but I've got to see the owner here about a job. And I'm already late. Could we, uh, talk afterward?"

"Yes."

He waited. Walked around outside. He retraced everything they had just said to each other over and over until he felt sick to his stomach. He was. Lovesick. He tried to call Lisa from a pay phone but her message machine was on the fritz. He tried to remember her parents' number, looked under the white pages, saw 450 Burkes. So he called Aunt Nora.

"I've found Clancy."

"Well, of course you have," she responded

"What . . . what in the hell is that supposed to mean?"

"Nothing, dear boy. Just I don't think she was ever really lost."

"Aunt Nora—"

"Never mind. I won't wait dinner." And then before she rang off: "Be careful."

"Thanks, Aunt Nora."

Then he spent the next twenty minutes rehearsing what he would say to her, but when she came out the door, he lost every bit of it. He thought she momentarily looked relieved, as if maybe he'd left, but then she saw him, rearranged the expression on her face. She walked over to him. A long, awkward pause stretched between them.

"Look, Clancy. We both just want to know you're okay. Lisa's . . . she's worried sick."

"I sent her a note."

"Yes, but it was a bit cryptic, don't you think?"

She shifted her eyes, trying to look anywhere but at him.

"Hey, I know. It's okay," Mathew said. "Clancy, it's okay."

"Is it?" Her jaw tightened and she looked into his eyes. "I've got to get back to my uncle's."

"Your uncle?"

"Yes. I found my last remaining relative buried in the Hollywood Hills."

"There's nothing bloody predictable about you, is there?"

But she didn't take the remark as a compliment. They shifted around an awkward silence.

"I've got to go. My uncle's expecting me."

"Clancy. Please. Can we at least get a number? Lisa's completely broken up over this."

"I . . . I'm sorry. I—please tell her I'm sorry. Tell her I'll call. I'm sorry, Mathew, I really have to go." And she ran to her car.

For a moment he had every intention of following her, but saw the movie car chase in his head. He gritted his teeth and decided he would toss in his silk topper. He'd had enough of playing Nick Charles.

But she didn't call Lisa.

One night, several weeks later, Uncle Sal sipped his Manhattan while they stared at the city lights. Val lay in his lap, Tweety Bird on her shoulder, Dirk was in bed, not feeling well. Clancy told him the story of her mother's death, of her journey from Florida to Portland to Los Angeles, how she met Lisa, then Mathew and his crazy but lovable aunt. She alluded to what happened with Seth, and told of Lisa's care for her afterward and the densely complicated triangle that existed between her and Lisa and Mathew now.

"I adore her. I really do. I don't know . . . I mean it's strange. And Mathew . . ."—she paused; her voice became very soft—". . . is the best man I've ever met. Decent, strong—but gentle, God, he's just pretty much too perfect."

"Don't sell yourself short, my dear."

"It's just that he deserves . . . he deserves the very best. And so does Lisa. And, well, I suppose . . ." Clancy stopped, then shook her head. "And I guess, since I enjoyed it so much, I must be a lesbian . . . or something."

Uncle Sal cupped her chin and turned her face to his. "My dear, I know a wee bit about this stuff, and I really rather doubt that you are."

◆ ◆ ◆

"Now what?" Carlita asked.

"Now . . . we fix a vortex and get to work."

"But how? What do we do, if we're not allowed to use our natural gifts?"

"Oh . . . but we are. With discretion." Gabriella smiled. "For instance, we can take care not to influence thoughts and emotions any sooner than the precise moment. A good way to practice angel magic is to take subtle measures. I think we'll employ an alternate destiny as a starting place."

"I'm confused."

"Of course you are." Gabriella was in rare good mood. It was time for her to use the best of her talents and it brought out a serenely happy side that Carlita welcomed. "March seventh would have been their anniversary had they continued their lives from the meeting at the concert."

"Yes?"

"And so, because that day holds great importance on a parallel reality, it will be easier to dent their defenses. We'll have them meet on that corresponding day in this particular plane of reality."

"But how?"

"I want you to visit Clancy's dreams as I know you've been doing on a regular basis, anyway."

"But—?!"

"Not much escapes me, Carlita." Gabriella cleared her throat. "But this time you have permission to do so. In the early morning, when she wakes and then returns to a hazy beta state, I want you to appear as Mathew."

"And you?"

"I'll be busy preparing Mathew."

March 1986

She was waiting on customers at Herbaceous and he suddenly appeared. But then they weren't there any longer—they were at the guest house, that first moment she had met him, his hair falling forward, his beautiful eyes looking into her own. Then Lisa and she were walking up a steep cliffside, trying to get to the top, struggling to make it. But for every step she took, she slid farther back down the perilous mountain, until the summit seemed like it was miles away. She kept struggling, struggling with all her might. She had to make it; get to the top of the hill. A hand reached out to help her. She thought it was Lisa's, but when she took it, it was Mathew's, and suddenly they were in a strange house, in front of a roaring fire, and Mathew bent to kiss her, and she kissed him back, and her body responded to his as if she needed his lips as desperately as she needed air to breathe. Her arms wrapped about his neck and she drew herself into him, and he held her tightly. A new hunger came from inside her—not the physical hunger she'd felt before, bodies meshing for release, but a deeper core hunger, one aching to be met.

And then she woke.

Gabriella let herself be whisked along by the wind, as Mathew ran below. She watched his strong legs as they pumped, silty sand spraying behind him. Watched as his chest heaved in and out. He ran like a thoroughbred, yet she knew there was a frenzy to his race, a straining to escape the feelings inside. She dissolved her form, mixed with the fine molecules of mist that showered his slender body, and entered his skin, infusing him with renewed hope, grounded vigor. A calm acceptance washed over him. It would be his greatest strength.

He held his notebook, sitting at the same spot he and Clancy had visited together under the weeping willow tree. His mind kept returning to that day at the store, when he'd first seen her. He dashed the lines as they came to him, feeling Clancy . . .

Dream world deep and loamy
I feel your breath in mine
dance on a plane divine
with no regard for gravity

Or pain. For in this waltz
with midnight climes, our lives
may meet again; I feel your touch
more keenly now . . .
It wakens me forever
and sleep will never
be mine.

. . . and then he smelled her before he felt her presence behind him. It took several seconds before he moved, wondering if his imagination had finally overtaken his senses. But when he turned, he saw a vision that would forever be imprinted on his soul: Clancy stood with her hair streaming behind her, backlit in the spring sun, her cheeks blushed from the hike up the hill. There was a hesitancy to her movement and then she smiled, uncertain, but so beautifully real.

"Hi." Her voice was breathy from the climb, breathy from nervousness.

"Hi."

"Am I disturbing you?"

"No." He motioned for her to sit next to him. "No. Not at all."

They sat quietly for some time, neither certain what to say. Mathew wondered how she had found him; Clancy tried to control the trembling beneath her surface. She didn't know quite why she was here. Actually, she did and she didn't. It was as if something beyond her control had made her get in her car, drive to Mathew's house, and then ask Aunt Nora where he was.

"Up on the hill. By what he calls your grand willow tree," Aunt Nora had responded with a knowing smile.

"What are you working on?" Clancy pointed to his notebook. He shut it abruptly. Then realized that must seem ridiculous and became embarrassed.

"I'm sorry," Clancy said, her voice barely a whisper.

The silence between them grew until it filled the canyon. Mathew wanted so badly to touch her. Clancy wanted so badly for him to put his hands upon her. He glanced at her and she at him. She knew she couldn't bear this much longer. And then his hand touched the sweater at her back; gentle fingers touched the nape of her neck, then slid into satin hair.

"Mathew . . ." His name barely escaped her lips as she turned to him, desperate for his touch, her lips finding his, longing for each other, until they lay sweetly entwined beneath the tree, fierce in their connection, she clasping him in her arms, his hands at her waist holding her to him so that she would never leave. Never escape him. Never again.

"What do you think it all means?"

They lay in a queen-size bed in a small hotel near Santa Barbara. Her leg was draped over his as she propped her head upon her pillow.

"Simple things, I suspect."

"But nothing's simple." She frowned.

"What's not simple?"

"This, for one." She indicated their being together.

"As in . . ."

"As in, I have no idea what made me go to the hill."

"How did you find me?

"Your aunt."

"But I didn't tell her where I was."

They both smiled. Of course. It made perfect sense.

"And Lisa," she said quietly, then drew her leg back, so that she wasn't touching him. "I've just destroyed her world."

Mathew knew that was true. He leaned over, brushed a shimmer of Clancy's hair to the side. "She started out with me when it was you she wanted all along. I don't blame her."

"No matter how much I try, I can't get a handle on it. On her. Us." Clancy lay back. "I love her so much. I wouldn't have been able to survive last year without her. She loved me in a way no one ever has. She's unusual, with all her personalities, but I found myself drawn to her as I have been to no other woman . . . and other times, nothing. But can we get back to it?"

"Back to what?"

"What all . . . everything is about? There's not one thing that really makes sense to me."

"You think too hard." And he heard Maria's voice echo in his head.

"And what do you do?"

"I just try to suit up and be there, you know?"

"But 'be there' for what—I mean, how in the hell do you know what that is?"

"Whatever feels right inside."

"Oh come on, don't be so smug. Haven't you ever had to make a hard decision?"

Mathew thought for a long time. "Not really. I've mostly led with my gut, and it's gotten me this far with no major regrets."

"What about this?"

"I don't want to hurt Lisa, but I've never felt more right about anything."

Clancy, though, wasn't sure. She couldn't think of a time when things were simply just "right." She went to great lengths to make it appear she never second-guessed herself, but the truth of the matter was, she rarely went through any decision where she didn't worry about whether it was "right" or not.

He leaned to her, his tongue gently touching the tip of her upper lip, quelling any concerns she might have had about her feelings right now. Her body released the tightly held reins, and she let herself feel the intensity in his delicate touch. His lips searched her own. She answered, hands finding his shoulders, muscular, fine, his smooth skin, soft, trailing to his nipples, arousing him, kissing the dimple in his chin. He felt her wetness, the heat of both of them, growing harder as he entered her, slowly, achingly slow until she grasped him to her. And then she was under him, and he gently took her face in his hands, and made her stay with him, eye to eye, present, contact constantly between them. He left her only in reaching the peak, eyelids fluttering, and then she came and felt his heart envelop her in a place that was as terrifying as it was safe.

"And so you just used me, let me take care of you, brought you back from the fucking dead. . . . You were a basket case, Clancy. And then what? You just throw me out when you get strong enough to go out into the world?"

"No . . . it isn't like that."

"Just tell me . . . did you fake it?"

"No." And it was said with such passion, that Lisa felt somewhat validated.

"Then what? What is it? I mean, we're so good together."

"I can't explain it. . . . It's just not where I am right now."

"Right now?" Lisa grabbed onto a straw. "Does that mean you might come back?"

"Lisa"—Clancy couldn't bear the pain and hope in Lisa's eyes—"I love you. I love you in a way I never knew was possible. But it's not—it's not—"

"What? You're not a lesbian?"

"I . . . I really don't think I am."

"You sure made a good imitation."

"I don't give a shit about being a lesbian or not. I'm trying to tell you, I—"

"You just don't have the balls—"

"No, it's—"

"You're too fucking above it all—"

"No, Lisa—"

"So now I'm less than—"

"If you'll just—"

"What? You come back and tell me you love me like you haven't loved before, but say you can't do this—what the hell do you mean? Do you even know? Have you ever known? Clancy, you run. . . . Run. Run, escape it all. If you don't have the courage to be here, then I don't want you—"

"I'm in love with Mathew." There, it was out.

Lisa stopped mid-diatribe. She was about to say something, several things, but she couldn't. The implications of what Clancy had said played upon her face. She shut her eyes, took in a deep breath. "You're what?"

"I'm in love with him," Clancy said softly but with conviction.

"I've been in love with him all this time. I just wouldn't let myself be, because of you. Because of me . . . what I'd been through . . . I was scared. But mostly I didn't want to betray you."

"Your generosity is so touching." Lisa walked to the refrigerator, grabbed a beer. "And we all know—hell, the entire fucking western hemisphere knew—he was in love with you from the beginning."

"I'm sorry."

"Sorry." Lisa shook her head. "Sorry? Fuck you."

"Lisa—"

"No. Go." Lisa turned to the window that Tweety Bird used to occupy. "Please, just go."

Clancy walked up behind her. She gently put her arms about Lisa's waist, laid her face against Lisa's shoulder blade, smelled the familiar smells. "I'll always love you." Then she turned and walked out the door.

It became the Bermuda Triangle—murky, troubled, and swirling in confusion. Mathew and Clancy continued falling more deeply in love. Mathew and Lisa continued trying to talk around it. Trying to maintain their friendship. But Lisa felt hurt and betrayed. She refused to see Clancy, to even talk about her. And Clancy wouldn't talk to Mathew about her feelings for Lisa.

No. There was no way around it. It couldn't have gotten any messier.

"How sad," Carlita said. "I mean, I've wanted Clancy and Mathew to get together as they must, but I don't know . . . it seems at such a price."

"There is always a price, my dear. Sometimes we just don't know what it is. But with Mathew and Clancy . . . well, they are at their most natural state in union."

"Oh, I can tell. They're simply glowing."

"That's because Mathew and Clancy feel as if they are one. And, indeed, they are," Gabriella explained.

"What does that mean exactly?"

"Simply that Mathew and Clancy complete one another. They have for a thousand years, and they will for a thousand more."

"But why?"

"If I've told you once, I've told you a million times. There is no why to fate. It simply is."

"Have they always been together?"

"There are lifetimes in which they don't connect and there develops a nagging sensation of unfinished business, a sense of loss in them that never quite goes away. They never feel completely right. But it is this lifetime that is crucial."

"Because . . ."

"If they do not complete their union now, it will be the end of their continuing link. Furthermore, it will hold rather grave ramifications for what would have been their future generations."

"Wow . . ." Carlita began to grasp the importance of their mission. "I guess people have more reason for existence than they know."

"Most humans don't realize this. And very rarely do they recognize the absolute importance of their actions. But saddest of all is that they don't understand that each of them has achieved immortality as they are reborn with the ones they love over and over again."

September 1986

Their courtship was elegant and loving. They spent every free minute they could together. Clancy had never been treated like a princess. She would often come home from a day at Herbaceous to an evening of candles, bubble bath, and dinner that Mathew cooked himself.

Mathew wrote during the days while Clancy continued to turn Herbaceous into a thriving success. So successful that Uncle Sal's friend gave her a raise and decided to stay in Hawaii. When Clancy got home in the evenings Mathew was invariably sitting at his desk, working on his second Aunt Maplethorpe Mystery. He was diligent, persistent, and tireless. Clancy was amazed at his ability to create a whole other world by the clacking of keys on his keyboard, that had their own certain rhythm; a gentle hum that coaxed the insecurities from her day. But sometimes she would come upon him unawares, where he would sit and stare off Aunt Nora's deck with a sadness in his eyes that Clancy couldn't read. He wouldn't really discuss it. All he said was, "Poetry was so much more fulfilling."

"Then why don't you work at that?"

"Because poetry serves an audience of three. And, it doesn't pay." He would put his hands in her hair and kiss her and that was the end of that.

They alternated evenings at Aunt Nora's or Uncle Sal's, and found it unusual with both their parents dead that they lived with their aunt and uncle. But even more extraordinary was the fact that everyone got along. "A regular love fest," Aunt Nora quipped. Dora even joined them for bridge and pinochle games while Mathew and Clancy would sit outside in the silent moonlight, listening to the four of them; so thrilled for the fine match, the way they went on you'd think they'd put them together. They genuinely liked each other. The odd sextet paraded around on the beach, the boardwalk, dined together whenever they could coordinate everyone's schedules. They spent Easter at Uncle Sal's and the Fourth at Aunt Nora's, where they had a glorious view of the fireworks. Both Sal and Nora threw quite a party. It was always magically festive, with more food than a battalion could eat, drinks, laughter, conversation.

So life was perfect bliss.

◆ ◆ ◆

Carlita found herself becoming bored. After all, things seemed to be going pretty darn well for Mathew and Clancy, which then prompted her to consider her propensity toward drama, and that it hadn't left her, even as an angel. As much as she yearned for a happy ending, she had been fascinated by all the roadblocks and obstacles. But now that Mathew and Clancy were together, as they were supposed to be, it seemed like a natural conclusion to her.

"It's the subtleties," Gabriella cautioned. "That is where the big things happen. Not in the car crashes and the train wrecks, but in the merest flicker of an eye. That's what you must study."

Gabriella needed to visit with Magdalena and left Carlita with strict instructions to keep on track, to continue to study, very carefully, the progress of their charges. And no more "accidental" meanderings through the cosmos.

As soon as Gabriella left, Carlita found herself struggling, however. What could it hurt? Mathew and Clancy were getting on famously. She watched one happy scene after another, saw them walk hand in hand on the beach, a montage of wonderful, loving moments. She fidgeted. She had had a hunch and her wings would not still until she checked it out. She glanced about her, then signed to the hologram. It jumped sequences in fast motion heading like a lightning bolt into the future until she waved her wing in just the right formation.

The hologram stopped. The year, 2065.

Carlita glanced about her. All she would do was take a peek and then return the hologram back to 1986, rationalizing that it couldn't possibly hurt to see a bit of Clancy's future life:

Erik, with a focus quite advanced for his six years, builds an elaborate structure with an ancient-looking Erector set. His slender bangs fall about his face, his cheeks twist into an expression of determination.

"Erik?" A woman's voice calls to the boy.

"Wait, Mama—almost done."

"Erik, come on, sweetie, it's time for dinner."

Erik sighs with deep frustration. "Mama, I'm not hungry." But puts down the screwdriver and bolt, assesses his creation. He smiles, quite satisfied.

"I'm building you a grand castle."

"Aren't you my little prince," says Erik's mother as she enters the room. She is a tall and slender woman, plain, but possessing eyes that shine with a startling beauty as she gazes at her son. She bends and holds out her arms. Erik runs to her. She scoops him up and his thin little arms wrap themselves about her neck.

Love. It is palpable through the screen. Carlita shivers. She has never been a mother, not in any of her lives, but she suddenly feels an understanding of maternal connection to this boy.

Whew! Carlita could barely handle the emotions she was having. She quickly signed to the hologram, stopped the imagery altogether. She floated restlessly a moment and then sighed, a long siren of a moan. She had to confess to herself—even if it was in direct opposition to the cardinal rule of detachment—that the feelings she had been having for Clancy were very much like the ones the mother in the screen had for Erik. Yes, very much like the love of a mother for its child. As if Clancy were her very own.

December 1986

The smells of Christmas filled Uncle Sal's home. Clancy thought he must be partial to fresh holly wreaths because they hung at every door. "Actually doesn't much care for them," Dirk informed her. "Just that there was a Help the Homeless teenager selling them the other day. Oh, your Uncle Sal got into quite a philosophical debate with the boy, but loved the fact that he was out selling wreaths instead of crack so bought the whole carload." Clancy thought it was a lovely story and wondered why Dirk was so pinched when telling it.

"Can't wait till you open your wee gift, my angel." Uncle Sal paraded around the place like a young boy, full of excitement, with rosy cheeks, generously provided from the Manhattans that disappeared at an alarming rate. Clancy loved her Uncle Sal, in a way she would not have believed possible, but his drinking distressed her.

"Clancy, come on, you make your uncle sound like a drunk," Mathew said when they talked about it.

"Mathew, trust me, he is."

"He just likes his Manhattans, like Nora likes her 'tides.'"

"He's a happy drunk. That's all . . . it doesn't bother me. Not like my mother's drinking bothered me. It's just . . . I worry about him."

"You, my love, worry too much." He tried to lighten the situation. It seemed this was becoming a pattern; Mathew always trying to lighten the situation. Even when it wasn't necessary. It was as if he thought it was his job to make everything okay. As if she needed him to or she might disappear again.

Which was ridiculous. She loved him. God, how she loved him. She didn't know what she would do without him at this point. But, Clancy had to confess to herself, things had changed somewhat. They were still mad for each other, but the love bubble had dissolved and real life had settled in. And there was something going on between them. A drift had started. Maybe he sensed it.

For her it was the gnawing envelope of dependency that had begun to wrap its tentacles about her again, growing tighter, until she began to think she would suffocate from it. It was the same as it had been with Lisa. She had found something so wonderful, so perfect almost, that she wanted to dive in all the way, but when she did she was confronted with the terror of drowning. It made her moody, then resentful. She found herself getting bitter, snapping at him. And that was when he would try and make it better. He had the resources. She didn't. He was successful. So what if she managed a run-down herb store.

"You've tripled its revenues."

"Right. We're taking in a hundred dollars a day instead of nothing."

"Clancy, why can't you just see you've worked wonders with that store."

"Anyone with an IQ over forty could have seen what the problem was." It wasn't false modesty. She just couldn't see that what she'd done was anything special and she became irritated when Mathew tried to make it so.

"That's not true."

"I suppose you can afford to be charitable," Clancy snapped, then shook her head. "I'm sorry, Mathew. That was pretty low." Clancy was referring to Mathew's most recent success, stacked upon so many. His first Aunt Maplethorpe Mystery was being considered for a television series. *Aunt Maplethorpe's Ride* followed the not so loosely based escapades of a young man's coming of age while his dodderingly eccentric aunt, under his care, sleuths her way through the underbelly of Los Angeles to find a crazed killer. It was a tremendous success, something he had been thrilled about initially, and then increasingly more worried about what it meant to his work as a writer of merit, as a poet.

"Have I sold out, Clancy?" he asked her one night while they were taking a walk.

"My God, Mathew—*no!* You're brilliant, the world recognizes it, and you're the kind of success most people only dream about."

"But, am I good?"

"Good?" Clancy had never heard this fear before. "Well, if it counts for anything, I think you're very very good." And Clancy turned his face to her and kissed him on the cheek, then small nibbles at his neck and chin, up to his eyelids, and then her lips found his and they met each other hungrily. Later that night, while she lay awake listening to Mathew's slow and even breathing, she wondered how long they would be able to run away into each other's arms whenever anything was bothering them.

As the weeks rolled by and life became more commonplace, Clancy got her answer. Little roadblocks presented themselves; branches splintered out when least expected, and they became more and more snagged by petty little arguments, nothing serious really, but enough to trip over. And when they did they weren't falling into one another's arms as if nothing else in the world but their desire existed. She found herself becoming a bit more reserved, perhaps even cautious.

But when he was away, how she missed him. She sat in the living room now, by the Christmas tree, rearranging the presents as if she were putting together a window display at the store. Mathew was in New York with the TV people and would be flying home on Christmas Eve. Then they would all gather at Aunt Nora's to celebrate Clancy's birthday and stay the night, to be there for Christmas morning.

"Can't you just wait until after the holidays?" she had asked while he was packing, and then wondered if everything that came out of her mouth sounded like a nag.

"We're under a deadline. That's all."

"I just hate it when you leave."

"Darling, I'll be back in two days."

"I know. I'm being silly." Mathew had come up to her, tried to comfort her in his usual fashion, taking her in his arms. She shrugged him off. But later in bed, she had turned to him, caressed his body with her own, run her hands through his hair, whispered to the back of his head, "Don't leave me." His body automatically moved into hers in the lazy movements of sleep. "Ever," she finished. But he was asleep.

The next morning she made love to him, sweetly and tenderly. "I'm sorry I was so—"

"Baby, stop worrying. It's fine." Mathew kissed her absently.

"Just come back, okay?"

And then he really looked at her, wrapped his hands through her hair, took in the smells of her. "I miss you already." And then he left.

"Phone for you, my dear." Uncle Sal walked in, then tiptoed out to give her privacy.

"I miss you," she said breathlessly in the phone.

"Yeah?" But it wasn't Mathew. "Well, I miss you too."

Lisa.

She was on her second cup of coffee when Lisa entered the coffee shop. A rush of warmth spread through her, and then she shut it off. She had no idea how this was going to go. She would follow Lisa's lead.

"Hi," Lisa said.

"Hi, Lisa," Clancy said tightly.

Lisa slid into the chair opposite her. They examined each other for a long moment, then Lisa averted her eyes. "Hey . . . I know a lot's happened. You know . . . time heals all wounds, et cetera. Bottom line, I didn't want to leave things the way they were."

Clancy waited a moment, then responded, "I don't either."

"Good."

And then the waitress came and took the order for a cappuccino from Lisa, who told her precisely how she wanted it made. "I was in Seattle on my last film and do they know coffee! Now I'm a major junkie."

Clancy smiled.

"God, you're beautiful when you do that," Lisa said spontaneously, then reconsidered. "Hey . . . don't worry—"

"I'm not." Clancy took in Lisa's eyes, did not avert her own.

"Let's just get this part out of the way. I'm a lesbian. Always have been. I just didn't know it until I fell in love with you."

Clancy glanced out the window. Then back at Lisa. "I'm not saying any of this to make you uncomfortable. I'm saying it to own it. Me. I'm a lesbian." And then as the waitress passed, Lisa stopped her. "By the way, you're waiting on a lesbian."

"Cool," the waitress responded, continued on with her coffee pot.

Clancy laughed then. Laughed like she hadn't for a long time. Oh, she laughed with Mathew, and Aunt Nora was always funny, intentionally or otherwise, but with Lisa she had laughed as with no one else. Lisa watched her, then started laughing as well. Full, joyful, a long release. And they continued laughing until they were both near tears.

"Come on. I want to show you what I did with the house." Lisa flagged the waitress down.

"Here's my number," the waitress said as she handed the bill to Lisa.

Clancy and Lisa looked at one another and burst out into renewed laughter. "Leave it to you to pick someone up while you're doing therapy!" Clancy stretched her hand across the table, grasped Lisa's, and held it.

Everything would be fine.

Mathew's plane was grounded in New York.

"When will they let you fly?"

"Not until this storm clears. What's everyone doing?"

"Getting ready to have Christmas without you, apparently."

"I'm sorry, Clancy."

"Mathew . . ." Clancy was terrorized at not being able to have access to him. "I . . . I miss you."

"God, I miss you, darling."

"I can't bear for you not to be here."

"Me too." A voice over the loudspeaker interrupted their conversation. Then, "There's a bloody line here a mile long waiting to use the phone. I'll call you as soon as I know anything."

"Okay."

"Clancy?"

"Yes."

"I love you."

"I love you, too."

When they hung up the phone she walked over to the window, stared out, wondered what was bothering her so. Well, how much more did she need than missing their first Christmas together? But it continued to irritate her, whatever it was.

"Happy birthday, dear Clancy, happy birthday to you," Aunt Nora, Uncle Sal, Dora, Dirk, and Lisa all sang heartily.

Clancy bowed, self-consciously.

They sat in the dining room, which appeared even more festive than usual. Aunt Nora had knocked herself out, putting extra-special touches to her already over-the-top Christmas decor. She also had made a wonderful turkey for the birthday dinner and had concocted "Clancy Tide," which everyone agreed was her best tide yet. They partook liberally until all were quite toasted.

"And now, my dear, presents," Aunt Nora bellowed.

Clancy opened Dora's first, a beautiful silk scarf. Dirk got her two Yanni tapes. "His music is pure divination," he informed her. Lisa had bought her a leather bag, noting that her purse had all but fallen apart, and inside was a small silver-framed picture of them taken years ago, with Tweety Bird on her shoulder, the three of them a happy family. Then Uncle Sal and Aunt Nora came forward with an oversized Nordstrom's box.

"This is from all of us, dear," Aunt Nora said, as she touched Clancy's cheek.

She opened it slowly, hoping she would be able to render an expression that would be worthy of whatever was inside. She glanced at Lisa for support; she was the actress, after all. Finally she plunged in, expecting some godawful fashion Uncle Sal might have picked up. But when she lifted the tissue paper she was stunned. Immobilized.

"Oh . . . my," in a voice that was barely a whisper.

"Hope you don't mind, Clan, but I did a wee bit of breaking and entering."

She lifted the gift, slowly, as though she couldn't bear to touch the pear-shaped instrument, its beautiful wood shined and polished, the strings tight and new, the replaced bridge, new tailpiece. Her violin.

"Uncle Sal . . ."

"You need this, Clancy," Uncle Sal said with conviction.

"What's the fuss?" Dora demanded. "Doesn't she like it?"

"But how?"

"Lisa gave us the idea," Aunt Nora provided. Clancy glanced at Lisa, who met her eyes with an expression of nonchalance.

"All I said was you had this ol' thing laying around forever that was useless and needed to be fixed before you could play it."

"And who said I wanted to play it?" Clancy stood now, and left the room.

"Didn't she like it?" Dora snapped.

The others looked at each other. Uncle Sal sighed. Dirk went to him. Lisa began to follow Clancy, but Aunt Nora stopped her, and went in her place.

She knocked on Mathew's door and before Clancy could respond, she entered. She walked to Clancy, who was standing by the deck window, tears streaming down her face. Aunt Nora gently put an arm around her, let her cry. When she had finished, Aunt Nora kissed her forehead gently, smoothed her hair.

"I . . . I don't want to hurt anyone's feelings, Aunt Nora."

"Of course you don't."

"But . . ."

"But nothing. They'll get over it." And then she turned and looked in Clancy's eyes. "They love you, Clancy. We all do. Don't worry about how they take this. Just know one thing. Without it, you can't heal." Aunt Nora squeezed her hand. Then left her to herself.

Christmas morning was a dour event. Spirits were muted. Mathew tried to call but was cut off before he got three words out. Aunt Nora took out his ornament.

"Here, Clancy. Why don't you hang this for Mathew."

She stared at the ornament for a long time. Mathew had told her in detail about it, that the violin had always stumped him, but now he understood. His aunt could see into the future, what other explanation could there be? Lisa had suggested it was more than likely just a representation of the arts. But now that Clancy saw the violin, and how closely it resembled her own, she wondered.

She moved to the tree, trying to find the best limb to hang it from. She attached it close to the top and then stared at it for a moment. She finally figured out what had been bothering her for two entire days. Mathew had forgotten to wish her a happy birthday.

The first chance she got, Carlita fast-forwarded Clancy's hologram to the future:

Mira's birth is an unhappy occasion, for while her parents are happy that she is healthy and possesses all ten toes, they have been desperate to have a boy. Under the new United California's Population Control Edict, there is only one child per family. Mira will wonder later if it wouldn't have been better for all concerned to adopt the ancient Chinese remedy to girl children.

Being extinguished might well have been preferable to a life born of fractured isolation. Discouraged that Mira has turned out to be a girl, her parents pay little attention to her. They certainly tend to her basic needs, but spend most of their time involved in professions at the Institute for Cloning Hazards. Mira's primary stimulation comes from her computers, all wired from room to room, and they soon become her best and only companions.

Mira is a gifted student, excels at Isolation Learning, advances rapidly through Net School, and is promoted upon early graduation to work as a WIN—web-integrational navigator. At first she is quite pleased with herself and her talents.

Up until this time, it has suited her quite nicely that she has been able to go through each day attending to every need, every detail of life, by pushing a button or speaking into her computer. And in fact Mira takes to naming each computer, assigning specific tasks to each so they may have their own personality. That way she can believe they are her friends.

But when she begins to interact with the faces she sees on her screen daily it becomes painfully clear to her that she is not only quite plain but socially inept. Mira knows it is unreasonable but begins to feel betrayed by her computers and starts to believe perhaps they have not always best served her, perhaps somehow they have let her down. She has always managed alone, but now she realizes she is lonely.

February 1987

"Do you ever get tired of everyone around us?" Mathew asked one night as they lay in bed.

"No. Do you?" Clancy had never had family before. The warmth, kindness, and tight-knit love she felt from Aunt Nora and Uncle Sal and Dirk were things she had only dreamed could be possible, and within that framework she had finally found part of an identity.

"But don't you ever just want privacy?"

"I guess I hadn't much thought of it."

"What would you think of our moving in together? Finding a place of our own?"

Clancy turned to face him, frowned a moment. "I don't know. I hadn't thought of that either."

"What have you thought of?" Mathew was a bit peeved now.

"I do have some thoughts occasionally, Mathew, even if I don't write them down."

"I'm . . . I'm sorry." Mathew snuggled next to her, put his arm around her. "Come on, what do you say to playing house?"

June 1987

They rented a two-bedroom fixer on Point Dume that had a glorious view; a scenic span of ocean from the kitchen northwest to the living room deck facing southeast. They met sunrise with coffee in the mornings, had dinner with the setting sun in the kitchen. Clancy loved it. She never knew playing house could be so fun.

She had decided to cut her hours back at Herbaceous so that she could fix up the house—sanding, painting, wallpapering. It gave her sense of purpose. Their days fell into harmonious routine. Mathew wrote in the mornings while Clancy was at the store, and then in the afternoons, after his second session, he'd give her a hand with the remodeling. They talked for hours while they built their house together, then they would break and take a long walk at the beach. Returning to the house, they made love, then dinner, and fell into each other's arms and deep sleep.

Around the time the house was finished, Herbaceous went under. It seemed the owner had been skimming all of Clancy's hard-earned profits on high-priced weed in Hawaii. She came home one day in the middle of the afternoon. Mathew was at his desk. She walked in and stood watching him. He wasn't even aware she was there, he was so focused on the work in front of him.

"Mathew?"

"Hmmmm?" He continued to write.

"Mathew!"

"Just let me finish this paragraph."

She walked over and put her hand on the keyboard. He looked up at her, stunned. "What are you doing?"

"I'm trying to inform you that I no longer have a job."

It took him several seconds to shift gears into the here and now. "What?"

"I've lost my job."

And then explained to him what had happened. He shook his head.

"Aren't you going to say anything?"

"Oh, Clan." He got up and put his arms around her. That was better. Until he opened his mouth. "We're fine with my income. Don't worry about it."

It was difficult but Carlita managed to find another moment when Gabriella wasn't floating nearby. As soon as she was alone she returned to Mira's story:

When Mira turns seventeen she discovers a hidden net-web featuring a Retro CD-ROM site. At first Mira is apprehensive and it frightens her, clicking on icons that open up into a world that feels disorganized and anarchic. But as she begins to view the movies of the 1930s, old black-and-white slices of a traditionalism that at first appear hokey and mawkishly sentimental, a spasm rips through her gut that feels strangely exotic, and seductively alive.

Mira finds herself drawn to the site, even when she knows she should be working, even when she knows it is considered an anticyber station. As she watches digitized celluloid and prints out volumes of old books dedicated to physical adventure as opposed to the cerebral landscape that is her world, Mira finds herself excitable and agitated. It is then that Mira realizes she is completely alone and terribly unhappy. It is then that Mira comprehends the inevitable: humanity has become completely isolated from itself.

October 1987

"There's no drug like it," he said to her one night while they were lying beside the fireplace, his eyes a brilliant glare. "When I'm inside that screen, nothing else exists. Not time, weather, anything. The characters, places, events; they're what's real. They are flesh and blood, rich and textured, and until I come out of it, I'm not aware of my physical surroundings."

"Does it ever scare you?"

"Scare me how?"

"That you won't come back?"

"Certainly not." He laughed. "No, darling, it's user friendly, this trance of mine."

"Do all writers get it?"

"I suppose they do in one form or another." They were silent for a while.

"Is that what I'm missing?" Clancy asked softly, remembering back to the other plane of consciousness she visited while playing the violin, and she knew how inviting those trances could be.

He took her in his arms. Clancy felt a vague sense of torment, but didn't know where it came from. They were getting ready to tour back East. Mathew's third Aunt Maplethorpe was even more successful than the last and since Clancy no longer had a job, she was free to travel with him to New York, D.C., Atlanta, and Austin.

"I've made it," Mathew had said when he got the call from his publisher, but the tone in his voice was not entirely convincing. Mathew found it difficult to accept this newfound success, for in his mind he was and always would be a poet.

• • •

Getting famous was hard work. They were in New York, three days into the tour. The publicist assigned to Mathew was an old-time song and dance man, who led them around by the nose for two interminable weeks. And Clancy became a shadow, sometimes stuck like high noon to Mathew's side, at other times a long lazy figure of fatigue, following in the footsteps of her commander. It wasn't simply that Mathew was the center of attention. It was that she was nothing. Nobody. A shadow didn't stand a chance in the glare of his spotlight.

And Mathew deserved the adoration. She saw who he was with his fans. Exhaustless. Very warmly British with his charm and the patience of the newly in love with each and every person who would smile shyly and ask for his autograph or prattle indiscriminately as the line bunched up like a Slinky until the publicist, the bulldog, kept the fans moving. Always moving. Radio interviews. Phoners. A TV spot. Bookstores—the tiny cramped literary stores dedicated to the art of writing, and the big sprawling giants, decked in neo–mass market shelving, devoted to commerce. And Mathew worked it. She discovered an unexpected side to him: he was a born performer. She was proud of him. And something else, she whispered to herself in the crush of adulation. She envied him.

She was happy for him. Of course, she was happy for him. But she knew she was also scared. From the moment they had left for the tour she had felt a shift. It wasn't that she was jealous of his fame. Quite the contrary. She reveled in his ability to take it in and still be the perfect gentleman. But it was during the tour that her two greatest fears came to light—that there would be no room for her, and that she needed to make room for herself; to create the space she needed to become somebody. The need to be "someone" compelled and terrified her.

When they returned to their house it seemed bleak after the four-star hotels they had spent the past two weeks in. Clancy became restless. She would tiptoe into Mathew's office, bothering him in the mornings, teasing him into going for walks with her, to the store, seducing him back into the bedroom when she knew he had work to do. He complied, but she could tell he wasn't there. His work had taken on new meaning. It wasn't just the writing anymore. It was the demand of letters, appearances, the administration of a writer who has an agent, manager, publicist. His office filled with files, faxes, and papers until it became harder to find him in the midst of it all.

"I've decided to go back to school," she told Mathew at dinner one night.

"You have?" Mathew glanced at her. "Anything particular?"

"I don't know. But I've got to get focused—get back on track."

"Track? Have you been off one?"

"Look, Mathew, you have a gift, an amazing talent, and you are using it. You're successful. You make money doing what millions only dream about. I . . . I'm nothing. I—"

"Don't ever say that, Clan. You are one of the brightest, most intelligent women I have ever known."

But Clancy didn't want to hear his speech about all her virtues. "You're in love with me," she said. "You have no perspective. I need to be something when I grow up. I'm almost thirty, for Christ's sake."

"I want you to be whatever you want to be." Mathew was sincere, but Clancy shot him a glance that said, *please, I'm not a child you need to humor.*

The next day she spent at the college going through catalogs, but when she was faced with all the different options and choices they became a blur. She didn't have a clue what in the hell she should pursue. Every time she'd ever gone to school, she'd quit. Why would this time be any different? Because she had an impetus to catch up to Mathew? She would never catch up to him. He was already too far ahead.

"You've got a great life," Lisa had said to her not too long ago. "You have a man that adores you, a house that you've made beautiful, a family that thinks you two are God's gift to coupling. Jesus, what more could you ask for?" That was the other part of it: How dare she be dissatisfied? Which in turn only made the struggle more painful.

When they lay in bed that night Clancy curled into Mathew's arms. "It's just that I don't understand what's going on with me. I . . . something is missing. I can't put it into words, but I need to find out what . . . well, what in the hell is wrong with me."

"Nothing's wrong with you," he mumbled groggily.

"Mathew, please, try and hear me. I'm telling you this has been eating at me for months. Something's wrong here and I don't want my problems hurting us." A long silence, and then she realized from the slow rise of his chest that he'd fallen asleep.

The next day she had left before he woke and didn't return for two days. She had driven to Santa Barbara, stayed with a friend. When she returned Mathew wasn't at the house. She stood terrified. Then saw the note tacked to the refrigerator: "Darling, your uncle's had a heart attack. Meet me at the hospital."

She spotted him down the hospital corridor, saw the graceful slant of his body, his thick fine black hair, a little overgrown. He was leaning against the wall, his back facing her, talking to a nurse.

Mathew smelled her perfume. He turned.

"Is he—?" she asked.

"No. He's okay now. They just took him out of ICU." Mathew wanted to touch her, but could feel the barrier she had thrown up.

"Where is he?"

"They've taken him for some tests."

"I've got to get back," the nurse said to Mathew, and left.

They stood still for a moment. Mathew cocked his head to the side, hurt and disappointment written all over his face. By a will not her own, she went to him, put her arms about his waist, and held him close. The minute she made contact, his arms circled about her, familiar, ohhh so familiar, and she was safe. And home.

"Where did you go?" It was later that night; they were wrapped closely together, lying in bed.

"Santa Barbara."

"I was terrified, Clancy."

"So was I." Different fears, same terror.

Finally: "Why?"

It was a long time before she answered. "Because the pressure to be me around the pressure that is you . . . is sometimes too overwhelming. And I lose myself."

When he had fallen asleep she heard him breathing calmly and resented his ease, his ability to take for granted that things would work out fine. He was so naive. And it was easy for him. He was master of his universe. She was simply trying to survive each day.

"Is that the Santa Ana winds I hear? Or are you a wee bit frustrated?" Clancy heard Uncle Sal's voice. She thought he had been sleeping, but he must have been watching her.

"You're awake."

"And you're troubled."

She turned and smiled at him. "Just thinking."

"Come here, Clancy," he said, motioning her to sit by the bed.

She went to him and he took her hand. "My dear, I have a favor to ask you. And it's a big one. But you have to grant it because I'm a dyin' man."

"Uncle Sal—"

But he put up his hand, now frail and wavering. "Just promise me you'll say yes."

"Of course. Anything."

"I want you to play for me, Clancy. Play the violin."

She didn't even consider the option of saying no to him. Had she, she probably wouldn't have returned to the hospital that evening, wouldn't have opened the leather case as if it were the most natural act in the world, would never have taken the violin from its velvet chamber and held it as if it were a part of her being. She stared at the tawny amber hues for a long moment, felt the fine wood in her hands, wondering if she could break the instrument by the mere pressure of not having played in almost twenty years. Wondering if she dared break so long a silence.

"Play for me. Play for me, Clancy."

She took out the bow, adjusted the violin to her shoulder. She preoccupied herself momentarily with tuning, and then with a deep and mournful sigh, let the bow touch the strings and upon contact she miraculously made music.

The first time he heard her play the violin it created an ache so exquisite inside him, that he didn't know if he would survive. It wasn't just her playing the violin—a sad ballad, its sweet melody tensing the lines of her face—it was the tight-jawed, pierce-eyed intensity that glowed from her, that shot into him as he watched her become another person he hadn't yet seen. This Clancy, opened up in a way she wasn't even when he made love to her, exposed a new part of her to him that made him want her so fiercely that he began to cry.

She stopped when she saw his tears. "What's—"

"Please don't stop." Mathew whispered. "I can't bear for you to stop."

So she played, another hour and another and he listened with senses alive, new feelings, thinking, there was no end to feelings. Her playing, hesitant at times, faltering at others, did not distract for a moment from this experience, this gift. He felt both pain and pleasure watching Clancy do the only thing she was truly passionate about. And watching her, he knew Clancy was brilliant. Far more brilliant than he.

"My God, Clancy, why have you never played before?" he asked as they strolled slowly down by the beach, the sun almost setting. "Why did you give it up? I don't understand. You're so talented, why don't you study?"

"Study? For what?"

"For what? Because it's what you do."

"Mathew, I can't exactly earn a living playing the violin."

"Earn a living? Certainly you can. Play with an orchestra, the Los Angeles Symphony."

But her eyes wouldn't meet his.

"Clancy, you are too good, too talented not to do this. I can feel how much you love it. I'm . . . I'm in awe." And as Mathew said it, he realized he was also a little jealous.

"I'm . . . you don't know." She let her hand slip from his, clearly unsettled. "You think I'm good because you have no idea what it really means to be good. The dedication, hours . . ."

"Excuse me, but what do you think my writing is about?"

"I didn't mean that. I mean you are truly gifted at what you do. People respect your work. You have a following. You actually have the ability to earn a living. Be a professional." Her voice got low. "I'm not nearly . . . good enough."

"Or you don't think you deserve it?"

"Please, kind and goodly doctor, don't start with any therapy here, okay?" She tried to make her tone light, but the edge of anger was well defined. "Anyway . . . I'm going back to school to study law and that's it."

When had she decided that? Mathew wondered. During her mysterious trip they never discussed? When he tried to resume the conversation, she wouldn't let it go any further.

But when they made love that night the passionate fight in Clancy was about desperation, an urgency Mathew hadn't felt before, a need he couldn't seem to satisfy. "Talk to me . . . what do you need?" But she couldn't answer. She didn't know.

By the end of the week she was playing Bach.

December 1987

Once she returned to the violin she couldn't put it down. It became a salve to the pain of years, each note healing another moment. Aunt Nora had been right. She spent hours immersed in regaining the basics. Mathew told her about a teacher he knew at Pepperdine and Clancy called and began taking lessons. Within weeks she was playing beautifully, and in the process became a Clancy neither of them had known. She hummed in the mornings as she made coffee, traipsed giddily into the bedroom, serving Mathew breakfast in bed, seducing him with sweet aggression.

Yes, she was happy. Truly, genuinely happy.

Three days before Christmas they packed Uncle Sal, who was feeling much better now, Dirk, Aunt Nora, and Dora all into the station wagon and headed to the Lodge. Lisa joined them a day later. From the moment they arrived it was as if angel dust had been floating through the air, mixed in with the snow and sprinkled magically over every one of them and everything. Mathew cut a tree, they decorated while drinking "Melakalikamaka Tide" as they all sang with Bing Crosby and the Andrews Sisters.

As Mathew unearthed his ornament on Christmas Eve, Aunt Nora walked up to him and Clancy and handed her a present. "Early birthday gift, dear." She unwrapped the box, opened it, and gently pulled the delicate ornament from its packing. It was an interesting mix of images, more impressionistic than real, with a violin at its center, a mysterious montage of what appeared to be places one traveled, like a postcard, with a backdrop of an exaggerated wing that met the small body of Tweety Bird, who seemed in mid-flight. The colors were exquisite, the painting in oils, the glass of which it was made so fragile Clancy was terrified she would break it when she hung it upon the tree.

"What do you think the ornament means?" she asked Mathew later that night in bed. "It's not as well defined as the others; it's made out of material that practically shatters when you look at it. I don't think she thinks I'm made of anything."

"Don't be ridiculous. I know my Aunt Nora and she couldn't be more in love with you."

But it bothered Clancy, especially when she repeated to herself the words she had used to describe the ornament to Mathew. She had studied all the ornaments and it was clear they were as representational of each person's life as a home movie. It frightened her that she might be viewed as insubstantial. She wrapped herself around Mathew, holding him close through the night.

On Christmas Eve they celebrated Clancy's birthday in grand style; Clancy played the violin and everyone shed tears of joy as she wove her special magic. She looked at the faces who had brought this gift back to her: Dora, the grumpy old coot who came to life with these people; Dirk, such a dear man to her uncle; Sal, acting as if he were twenty-five; Aunt Nora, eccentrically wonderful, charming, and unpredictable; Lisa—thank God she had come back into her life; and Mathew. Mathew her one and only. She was filled with the kind of love that heals whole nations, moves mountains, transforms the soul. Because that night she felt perfect happiness. Simple. Divine. All-encompassing.

That night Mathew proposed to her.

Mira spends hours investigating other anticyber sites, ensconced in the world of the early twentieth century. There is a theme that beckons her from the Capraesque morality plays she views: that a single individual can make a difference and they don't have to stand for things the way they are. Mira has no idea how she herself might make a difference but wants desperately to change the lonely life she leads.

She begins to communicate with other anticybers who all share in common the belief that the Cybernet has become an alluring opiate for the masses and that while it might appear to serve society as progressive technology, it has also created a sedentary, semiconscious nation of pawns. The e-mailed rhetoric she exchanges with these unseen rebels is heady and intoxicating, and Mira finds herself drawn into regular communication with one Tarek Simon, a revolutionary thinker who hopes to preach online.

When Tarek first transmits his visage online, Mira is quite intimidated by his physical beauty, but he is gentle and reassuring with her. Although they have not met in person, Mira feels as if she is really beginning to know Tarek and finds herself tumbling from bed to rush to the computer to read his latest posting.

As she pulls up his communication to her this morning, she blushes reading a poem he has written for her. She isn't entirely certain, but considers the remote possibility that Tarek is courting her. She bubbles throughout the day with that prospect.

Carlita realizes she is very close to being caught. Damn, she thinks, closing down the future hologram. If only she could get to where Mira has her baby.

February 1988

She stared at the rings on her finger. They were love and commitment bands.

Clancy had said yes, but that she wanted to wait at least a year before they married. So they window-shopped jewelry stores for the next month, hunting for the perfect ring. Finally Aunt Nora solved their dilemma one evening, when she descended the stairs from the attic with a small teakwood box. Inside were a sensually curved set of bands, one thin, the other almost twice its size in width but with the same exquisite curvature.

"They're love and commitment rings," Aunt Nora explained, but remained evasive when asked where she'd gotten them. "The thin band's love. That's the easy part. And the thicker one denotes commitment. That's the part that takes all the work."

Clancy and Mathew loved the rings, found them perfect. They took them up to the willow tree overlooking the valley and had their own private ceremony, where they made love on the blanket under the tree in celebration, light breeze playing upon their skin, the sun penetrating their bodies. It was as if God were casting a ray of approval, Clancy thought as she stared up into the blue that went on forever, not a cloud in sight, and imagined that if you spotted them from above, say from another planet, you would see them—two shiny objects lit by love.

"No matter what happens, no matter where we are, know that I am with you. Always." Mathew's voice came to her from a million miles away. She had drifted off, huddled beneath the blanket now, as the air had turned crisp. She glanced up at him. He was staring at her oddly, a slight edge of worry to his gaze. She understood. Inside her, it didn't matter how deliriously happy she was at this moment. Good had never lasted in her lifetime and she didn't trust it now. She sat up and Mathew put his arms about her and they watched the sunset, a glorious event that seemed to be created just for the two of them.

But that kind of joy can never last, Clancy thought, and as if proof of that confirmed her belief, when they got home she discovered Uncle Sal's body, crumpled at the foot of his bed, dead.

The funeral was an appropriately flamboyant affair. Drag queens from all over the city attended in full regalia. "I never knew he had such a following," Clancy remarked

"Oh, yes. Your uncle was a legend," Dirk assured her, coughing. He seemed next to death's door himself. Clancy knew Dirk was HIV positive, but they never spoke of it.

Later, after everyone had left, Clancy helped Dirk into bed, sat with him.

"I know what you're thinking," he said.

"What?"

"What are you going to do with me?"

"Dirk, I'll take care of you just like I did Sal—"

"Clancy, you have your own life."

"You're family."

"You don't understand."

"What?"

"Sweetie, your uncle Sal, bless his tarnished heart, was in quite a pickle with the government."

"What do you mean?"

"Sal lived it up in his glory days. When he had plenty of money. But for the last five years he's been broke."

"Broke? But how could he afford this house?"

"He hasn't paid taxes in years, he'd filed bankruptcy right before you came into the picture. The house is in repossession. Bless his soul. Champagne tastes and all that." So even sweet Uncle Sal's other side finally showed itself.

At the time of the funeral, Mathew had been scheduled to leave for South Carolina, where *Aunt Maplethorpe* was being filmed. He put the trip off for several days.

"Please don't leave right now," Clancy asked over and over again.

Uncle Sal's death had hit her very hard, leaving her confused and off balance. She'd loved him dearly, but it was more than the grief. With him went the last remaining member of her family, for whatever they were worth. Suddenly she became aware of mortality. There was a new value to time. A new preciousness to moments she lunged toward rather than experienced. And a desperation for Mathew not to leave hung heavily about both their necks.

"I don't want to go, Clancy. The last thing I want to do is leave you right now," Mathew kept saying, as if that were any reassurance. The fact remained, he *was* leaving her.

Clancy fell into a deep depression, and lay in bed for three days. She slept the first two, the third she spent thinking about her life. The whole thing, from her early days on. She rarely went back to her childhood, but now she felt compelled to make this journey.

And she saw two familiar themes reappear time and again. No one was ever what he or she seemed. And just when her life seemed to be coming around, just when things were finally getting good, it fell apart. She attempted the chicken and the egg equation trying to turn this around, wondering if the responsibility to good things became too much of a burden and she would figure out a way to blow it. She was debating every angle of this when she thought of the violin, how for the past few weeks it had erased the fears, the lack of confidence, took her to a place all her own, a place where she was happiest. But now not even the violin could take away this gnawing certainty that it was time for her to get her life together—whatever that meant. It was time for her to understand what kept her from herself. If she didn't she would never be any good to anyone, much less Mathew. She was so deep inside this conundrum that she didn't hear Lisa knocking at the front door.

Lisa slipped through the side deck door and walked into the bedroom, then directly up to the bed, hands at her hips. "Ah . . . the mental ward look. I hear it's in again."

Clancy didn't respond. Lisa had already seen her at her very worst. "What's goin' on, Clancy?"

"I'm grieving. Is that all right with you?"

"Mathew's worried sick. He's been calling the last two days."

She grunted in response.

"Come on, Clan . . . what's wrong."

"Everything."

"It's more than Uncle Sal."

"It's everything . . . I'm . . . I'm stuck."

"Anything I can do?"

"Yes. Leave."

"Okay. But I'm only giving you a couple more days of this. And then I'm going to haul your ass out of bed."

She saluted. Lisa left.

She woke the next morning in the same position.

But Carlita was unaware there were any problems between Mathew and Clancy, because she was too busy delving into Mira's hologram to get the rest of the story:

Tarek has e-mailed Mira a poem every day for the past three weeks. She has never understood the term romantic until now. It's as if she has gone from the drone of hours at the computer living in a world linked by cyberoptics to a dreamy fantasy land where words are no longer simply bits of information transmitted through cable lines, but language full of wonder and charm describing feelings inside her body she never knew she possessed.

Tarek continues to woo Mira until she can stand it no longer. No matter how shy she is, she is desperate to meet him. As it turns out he is not so very far from her, living in Northwest Inc, what used to be Washington, Oregon, and Idaho. Mira knows it is bold, but she invites Tarek to visit her in San Francisco, where she is attending a conference.

When they meet she can barely contain her nervous apprehension, but Tarek puts her at ease. He is even more handsome in person, and she fears she is more plain. But Tarek makes her feel beautiful as they visit the Museum of Twentieth-Century Art and explore the contrast of a society seemingly filled with chaos, but as they both agree, full of passion for life.

It is in front of the Thomas Hart Benton exhibit that Tarek leans to kiss her. Mira has not been touched sexually in all her twenty years and discovers her body might have more power than her mind. It compels her to fall into Tarek's arms, follow him to his Hotel Unit, and grasp him tightly in her arms as he makes love to her throughout the night.

August 1988

Mathew had come home and she was gone. At first he thought she was simply out. But within seconds, as he picked up the mail, walked around to the kitchen, he realized she was gone. Gone. Everything she owned had been packed up.

He stood in a daze. What was happening? He saw the bedroom door closed and slowly approached it, all manner of insanity entering his head, gruesome haunting flashes of her dead, hanging from the rafters. The fear in him swelled outward and he saw his hand tremble as he put it on the doorknob. But when he opened the door, he saw only the bed, made up, everything in order. He stood in shock. *Stupefaction* would be a more appropriate term, he thought wryly.

An hour later he sat on a chair in the kitchen at the table they'd picked out together at a garage sale, on a day that played in his memory with a sweetness that was beginning to feel unreal. Early they had sat on the deck in their robes, just enough sun in the morning for coffee. That day was a Saturday. They'd called Aunt Nora to join them, but she wasn't in. Then they'd gone garage sale shopping, had a late lunch, caught an old movie, strolled on the beach, and then had dinner with Aunt Nora, good conversation with his favorite people. He remembered the day like yesterday, images burnt crisply into his mind. Everything had seemed so right.

So why?

He called Lisa. "She left."

"I'll be right over."

• • •

"You're right," Lisa said as she walked through the door, like a rerun of a bad nightmare. It felt the same. The absence of Clancy. Almost had a scent to it.

"Lis—" Mathew twisted his hands between his knees. He was bent over as in great pain.

"Sshhhh." She walked to him, put her arms around him. "Hey, let's sit on the couch." Once she got him seated, she put her hands on either side of his cheeks. It was familiar, yet foreign, his male skin. She kissed his forehead. "Okay. What happened?"

He shook his head. "I have no idea."

"No note?"

"Nothing."

"Par for the course." Even though she and Clancy had formed a new bond, the old anger still flared. "When was the last time you saw her?"

"Last week before I left. You?"

"When I came over . . . when she was in bed. Did she call you?"

"Yes. Two days ago. But I was out until late and when I called back she was sleeping so we didn't really talk. I tried to call last night, but the phone had a busy signal. God . . . the last time we talked—really talked—was . . . almost a week ago. We had another discussion about her going back to school. About my always being gone. Always leaving her. She felt desperate to be doing something besides the music. I asked her what she thought about teaching. Teaching music, since she loves it. And she almost got hysterical."

"Jesus, I know . . ." Lisa lit a cigarette. "Then what?"

"She said I didn't understand. I knew what I was doing. I had an identity. That it was easy for me to pay lip service to her concerns, since I was successful. I told her I wasn't." Mathew shook his head. "Paying lip service, I mean."

"Were you?"

He caught Lisa's glance. "Maybe. A bit." He ran a hand through his hair. "Yes, damn it. Well, it's bloody impossible, Lisa. I can't make it all right for her. I've never been able to make it all right. I've tried. I mean, after a while it gets a bit old, you know, her changing her career every other crisis. It doesn't matter how much I love her, how much I tell her I love her. She's still that little girl—"

"Who's no good."

They sat silently for a moment.

"She'll be back," Lisa said.

"I . . . I don't know."

"She's done it before."

"But not like this. This is different."

A few days later with still no word, Lisa was back at the house, holding his hand again.

"Look, we both know from brutal experience that whenever Clancy feels trapped she runs."

"Yes, but what from this time?"

"Who knows. Maybe she doesn't even know. She's done it since she was a kid."

"What happened?"

"What happened?"

"I mean, what bloody happened? She never talks about it."

"That, my friend"—Lisa took his hand—"is an excellent question."

They went for a drive, in silence down familiar streets. Finally Lisa exhaled. "Really there is only one thing you can do."

He turned to her.

"Let her be," she said.

Mathew sat back. Let her. Be.

And so he did.

March 1989

In the rare moments she allowed herself even to think about him, she felt the absolute pull of her feelings toward Mathew. In fact, if she could ever be certain about anything, she knew it was the depth and reality of her feelings for Mathew. It was as simple as sensing the sun when she woke in the morning, hazily filtered through dream-colored drapes, a pastel still life lying in his arms, young lovers basking in the glow of a new day. Basking in potential. In those moments before she allowed her mind to taint the process, she knew what people meant when they said of a particular union, "It was right."

If there was a right for Clancy, it was with Mathew. If there was love at first sight—no, not sight—first moment your ions meshed and didn't simply shake hands but waltzed to a tune that made you giddy and weightless—equal parts lust and compassion, making them partners, not competitors—so it was with Mathew.

But those moments of reflection were rare and brief and would slip through Clancy's fingers, as they did now where she lay in the semi-haze of consciousness, in her little studio apartment in Carmel, alone, just she and Tweety Bird.

"Why Carmel?" Dirk had asked. His voice was thin and frail, especially over the phone from Indiana, where he had gone to live out his final days with his family.

"I don't know. Because it's pretty."

"Good a reason as any."

"Actually, it's where I ran out of gas, and when I stopped I saw a for rent sign."

"Good a reason as any."

"Thanks, Dirk."

"Have you talked to Mathew?"

"Not yet."

"Let him know where you're at, Clancy. It's only fair."

May 1989

Dear Mathew,

I'm sorry. I know this has been difficult for you. As it has been for me. I just need some time. I know I've said this before, it's just I don't feel like you hear me sometimes. Your life is so big and loud, I feel lost in the shuffle. I'm as sick of me changing my mind about things as you are. So until I can make myself certain about anything, I think it's best I subject only me to my insanity. I love you. That's never in doubt.

"Now what?" he asked as he handed the letter to Lisa.

"You wait."

August 1989

Mathew waited. And waited. At first he was so in shock by Clancy's flight he could only walk around, numb and confused. But after several weeks he began to feel a new emotion, one that visited him so seldom he could barely name it. Anger.

"I've bled twenty quarts here," he said to Lisa one day while they nursed a couple of margaritas. "What the hell am I supposed to do?"

"Bleed another twenty?" Lisa responded uncertainly.

"I don't have much more patience for this, Lisa."

"Well, even you can only be Florence Nightingale so long."

"I . . . I don't understand. If I only understood—"

"Would it really make a difference?" Lisa asked not unkindly.

She poured another liberal dose from the margarita pitcher. He drank until he could feel nothing. And then everything.

By the time he returned home it had started. Like an electrical current vibrating through his being, anger pumping through his veins until his whole body reverberated with it, dashing from room to room, grabbing this photo and that, all the little notes she had left him, paintings they bought together, even the antique silverware they'd picked up at an estate sale. He stormed through their house—his house now—gathering every artifact that could possibly remind him of her, threw them in a large box, heaved it upon his shoulder, and walked out to the ocean. One by one he threw things into the tide, the churning waves grabbing them in, swirling a photo here, a love letter there, into the vast expanse of sea. He screamed an epithet for each keepsake, until his voice was hoarse and his intoxication subdued by the cold damp.

He fell to his knees, the box half-empty, and slumped over until his head hit the sand; an unfamiliar choking sound erupted from his form as he began to cry, "Goddamn you to hell, Clancy . . . goddamn you to hell . . ." over and over again, until he voice was raw, his heart empty, and his cool British reserve dissipated by the humanity of loneliness.

December 1989

It came two days after Christmas. A Currier and Ives print. He had told her once the prints reminded him of back home in England.

"But I thought home was here?" she had questioned with a sweet smile.

"Well, it is, but . . ."

"But you need to go back sometime." Sometimes Clancy was so

wise, he thought. The times when he felt like a young boy next to her, how she understood life in the way that Aunt Nora did, on a deeply intuitive level . . . where he floundered.

No signature, but he knew it was she, even before he opened it and read . . . "always with me."

March 1990

Once the anger finally subsided, Mathew experienced a sort of resigned resentment. He supposed he should be over it, this waiting and wanting of Clancy, but the truth was that before he could fully extinguish her from his thoughts, things got worse. So Mathew spent a week at Aunt Nora's beach house alone. Lisa joined him for the weekend, and the following week Aunt Nora made her presence comforting but nonintrusive.

He wrote poetry as he never had. As if the swell of the ocean's tide lifted the pain, wave by wave, and caused the words to gush out in a torrent. He felt an inner voice without judgment and glimpsed a brilliance—a true talent—within himself for the first time. It was as if all the broken hearts through the ages now channeled new ways of saying the same old things. And even as the inner messages slowed, there remained a steady flow, so that a phrase, a word, an image would come to his mind and he would dash to write it down. It never stopped.

Deep dreamless sleep quelled thought. Still she remained inside him.

At first it was relentless, like sharing another self. The way he loved her was so part of him he couldn't separate it from his being. He woke up with her, felt the smoothness of her palm at his cheek when he shaved, smelled her fragrance when he passed the blossoming orange trees, heard her whisper as the wind mingled in his hair. Dreams taunted him, dreams of being together, of making love that felt so real that when he woke, he could no longer distinguish desire from reality.

But as time passed, and Clancy made no contact, he laughed at himself, and thought this is what an alcoholic must feel like, this powerlessness over obsession. And the need to give it up. Completely. Surrender.

"Do you think the great poets ever wrote anything when they were happy?" he asked Lisa as they walked along the coastline, a whirling cloud of gray-blue hovering, poised just beyond them.

"Certainly not. When have you ever heard anyone prattlin' about when they're delirious."

"Well, there are the great love poems, as well."

"Ahhh . . . but don't you know when they're written?"

Mathew simply shook his head. Lisa fell into the role of the intellectual cynic. "Right before the doom. The poet knows this. Not in his head of course. His head's in a cloud of delusional puffery. That's where he comes up with all that saccharine verse. No. His heart knows it will be snatched from him at any moment. It's the despair of the inevitable crash. All creativity is based on pain."

Which Aunt Nora countered the following week. "I disagree. All creativity is based on joy. Of course, it's all in the way you look at it, my dear boy. Pain is about joy of rebirth. It's really semantics, don't you think? Haven't you ever felt the pain of something but then been relieved by its inevitable end?"

Mathew thought about his original move there. The pain of his parents' death was certainly relieved by the new life he'd gained with Aunt Nora. A life, he knew in all certainty, he would never have had the opportunity to experience if not for their death.

"You see? It's not even really sacrifice so much as a balancing of things in the universe." As usual she knew what was in his mind.

"Who is to say if it's pain that is a negative connotation. Perhaps a better word for pain is passage. Journey. And every time one travels they pick up treasures, don't they?"

The nausea and vomiting Mira has been experiencing daily for three weeks now concerns her. But not as much as her distress over Tarek. After their magical evening Mira woke the next morning and Tarek was gone. There was no note, no message with the concierge, and in fact, there was no listing for his reservation.

Mira returns to her small antiseptic abode and searches the web for sign of Tarek, hours devoted to anticyber sites, website investigation through all her contacts. She is terrified that something has happened to him. It never occurs to her until the news posting that Tarek was anything but genuine in his affections for her.

But there has been a new rash of cyberscams recently, and the resurgence of MCPS—multicyber personality syndrome. It started as innocent fantasy: playing roles with perfect strangers as a way of experimentation—a not unnatural response to loneliness. It was too easy for the victims to believe they were the character they had created, because there was so little fear of detection, and MCPS had become a serious illness shortly after the turn of the century. But worse, for others it merely became a form of sport. Perpetrators whose challenge it was to chalk up as many "hits" as they could and score by meeting the person they had set up in their elaborate mind game.

It is difficult for Mira to believe it, but there is Tarek's digitized visage staring at her as one of the last "heart-hackers" who have been caught. But her worry does not seem to end, for she still cannot hold much of anything down. She sends blood and urine samples cyberexpress and waits several hours for Netmedicine to e-mail her the results.

Mira can hardly believe the prognosis as it stares accusingly at her from the screen. She is pregnant.

October 1990

It was Mathew's birthday.

Clancy celebrated it with Tweety Bird.

She lit the candles. Thirty-one this year. She wondered if he were with a new lover . . . or maybe he had been with one for quite some time. She wondered if he were up at Aunt Nora's. Was Lisa there, and Dora? Were they sitting out on the deck, drinking one of Aunt Nora's concoctions, laughing, getting loaded on her weed, smiles, good talks, warmth? She missed her old life intensely, actively; missed it in a way that was very much like devotion.

"It's practically like being there," she told her therapist, an older woman, wheelchair bound, who served her clients from a small room in her home that overlooked moon-shaped Monterey Bay. She was the best in the area and Clancy had waited almost a year to get in.

"Is that good enough?"

"You mean being there in my head?"

"Yes. Don't you want to live it?"

"Well . . . yes, of course, when I'm able."

"And what makes you think you are unable?"

"I can't give anything to anyone until I know what the hell I'm doing."

"What are you doing?"

"I haven't a clue. That's why I'm here." And Clancy got angry.

At first Arlene had watched Clancy walk the parameters of her problems and remained quiet, asking very few questions. Finally, after a long silence she said, "Clancy. Do you want to get any work done here?"

"Of course I do. I don't give you my hard-earned money for the thrill of it."

"Then you'll have to stop."

"Stop. Stop what?"

"Pretending to be a patient." At first Clancy didn't know what she was implying, even when she knew very well she had been caught. "So you've seen some movies and this is the way they act. I'm not a movie doctor and you seem perfectly real to me. Now. Let's dispense with the window dressing and get to work."

It had been the little things at first.

It always was.

But those things were surmountable. So had been the initial conflict of moving in with him. A part of her had danced sugarplums in her head when he had first brought it up, fixing up a house of their own, decorating it, making it a home, fixing dinner. Helping Mathew with his work. Being there for him. There was a certain peaceful resignation at the thought of domesticity. A sense of identity, even though calling herself a housewife was certainly not something she had aspired to. There was also a magnificent terror that came from anticipation, from the certainty that the bliss she had discovered would end. She would figure out a way to destroy it. Or Mathew would turn into a monster, would show a side to him she hadn't seen. She awaited the end and constantly prepared for it. So it had not been a stable proposition, moving in with Mathew. But she had done it, because she could not come up with reasonable arguments not to.

It wasn't long after they settled in that Clancy began having dreams of her and Mathew wonderfully in love, strolling along the beach, sipping coffee on the deck, and suddenly he would be gone. Disappear. She couldn't find him. She would search relentlessly and when she tried to call out to him, the sound that came out of her was a whispered moan, so quiet she knew he would never hear her. What did it mean? And after she began playing the violin again she was haunted by a recurring dream in which she played and played magnificently, brilliantly, but it was Mathew who got all the applause. He would bow, accepting it gracefully, his fans bestowing their greatest accolades, but when he turned to her there would be tears of pain in his eyes. These nightmares plagued her until Arlene helped put it in perspective. "You sensed an incompatibility between your talent and his success."

"But he's always been so supportive."

"That doesn't mean he's not human. That he doesn't envy what comes so easily to you." And she had to admit, it was a strange irony that went unvoiced, but they both knew it was there. They both felt it.

And finally, in the end she realized it wasn't that Mathew had another side she hadn't seen, but that when she was with him she saw a side of herself she wasn't sure she could live up to. She saw potential. And it terrified her. So she left.

But she never took off the more slender of the two bands. She may not have what it took to do commitment. But she knew she had the right to wear the one that signified love.

James Wellington sold art all over the country and Clancy had become his assistant and road contact. She had met him quite by accident, standing in one of the three galleries he owned in Carmel, when he came up behind her as she stared at a beautiful painting in oils of a woman, who was, quite simply, deliciously alive.

"Do you like it?"

"I think she's beautiful," Clancy whispered.

"I don't think she heard you."

Clancy turned and smiled then at the distinguished-looking sixty-plus gentleman at her side. "She's beautiful," Clancy now said with conviction.

"Do you know the artist?"

"No. Am I terribly naive? I just find her so incredibly forceful. Loud. Alive. Independent."

"Works for me," he conceded, then walked a few steps to another painting, an abstract extravaganza. "And what about this here?"

Clancy laughed out loud. "Sort of Picasso meets Salvador Dalí and the result is tragedy. It's one of those obnoxious paintings no one understands but the art critics."

"Then I should just throw this seven-thousand-dollar painting out of the gallery," he said, and began to pick it up. It was then Clancy realized she was speaking to someone who worked there.

"Oh, my God. Just say you're not the painter."

"The owner. James Wellington at your service." A moment passed and he smiled at her. They laughed.

"Did . . . I just make the biggest art faux pas in the world?"

"Not in the least. It was quite refreshing," he responded. He immediately liked Clancy's naive approach, her lack of knowledge about art theory, rhetoric, and mostly bullshit. It would be a unique approach to the art world. He thought she might capture a market he had long ago given up on, so he hired her on the spot.

"But . . . what do you want me to do?"

"I want you to sell paintings like you just talked to me. By being real. If you don't like the painting, don't pretend to. There's a lot of people who look at art and would like to buy, but they're completely intimidated by showy salespeople. Let the viewers respond to what they like in a piece of work; don't try to overwhelm them with obscure references and art double-talk."

And so Clancy had a job with a comfortable base salary and a handsome commission for each painting she sold. Because she only had to sell what she really liked, it was a job that completely made sense to her. And because of that she was good at it, enjoyed it, and thrived. It made the best of her natural ability to sell, gave her something to believe in, and because there was travel involved it allowed her to escape her circumstances virtually at any given moment.

November 1990

"I've got one for you." Lisa would call him every few weeks. "She's great. I mean this is a woman that's got it all. She's been through therapy. She's together. She's hot. I think she's incredibly sexy."

"Good. Then you date her," Mathew would reply, not unkindly.

"You've become the mad Saint of Celibacy," Lisa moaned. "When is enough going to be enough? I'm sick of this woman ruining both our lives."

"Look, I just don't think—"

"Come on, give it a try," Lisa encouraged. "Her name's Sandy. She's a production designer. She loves poetry."

But when he went out with Sandy all he could think of was how much she wasn't like Clancy. How Sandy was like all the others Lisa had set him up with, not because they were the same, but because they were not Clancy, and it only made him feel worse.

"So she wasn't the right one. There's a million people in the naked city—"

"Serial dating is a reasonable approach?"

"It's called defensive dating and it's the only cure. The only way one really gets over a loved one is to fall in love with someone else. Sooner or later, just on a statistical basis, you're going to have to find someone who's going to knock her image right from your mind."

Mira screams and swears if she ever finds him she will kill Tarek for putting her through this pain. Sweat pours off her face as she pushes against a force that feels as if it will split her body in two. But moments later, when she thinks her body no longer belongs to her, that it is merely a limp form that has been taxed beyond physical endurance, she sees two eyes, mere slits, a blood-slickened creature, this reality, this thing she has created. This baby is not part of an elaborate web of shooting electrons through miles of cabling, this is a real squalling screaming entity.

This is Erik, Mira's baby, and in the first moment his wriggling body fights for her breast she knows there will never be anything that ever matters again, except for him.

"What am I to do with you?" Gabriella was elegantly furious.

Carlita was caught peering in fascination at Mira's hologram as she is having her baby.

"That's it. I'm taking you off this case. As your interest has evidently flagged, that shouldn't be a problem—"

"No. No . . . that's not it," Carlita protested. "Please let me explain."

"What's to explain? I've told you time and again, the future lives of these charges have no bearing on our situation."

"But you said"—she searched—"it would have grave implications if they did not get together. I'm just trying to understand how."

"Carlita." Gabriella set her anger aside. "Yes. The pairing of

Mathew and Clancy will have future ramifications. But that is not your concern."

"I guess. It's just hard for me not to know what the stakes are— "

"This isn't a poker game, Carlita. This is life. You will return the hologram to Mathew and Clancy. Do I make myself perfectly clear?"

"Yes, Angel Gabriella." But Carlita knew, even as she did so, that her compulsion to know about Clancy's future life would continue to plague her. She kept telling herself it was about Clancy . . . as the young boy, but there was something more. Something she couldn't even begin to explain to herself. Maybe the horrors of a world gone mad. Maybe just the need to find out, like the end of a good mystery. All she knew was she had to know, and there was no way to access the hologram with Gabriella by her side.

"In case you're interested, all our work has been eradicated. And Mathew is about to meet someone new."

January 1992

They met at an estate sale. She was looking for an armoire, he was hunting old books. He saw her arm in a mirror . . . drawn to it by its long slenderness. She had been a dancer, he would later find out. He was stuck in a mesmerized stare, watching as the arm waded through a wardrobe box.

When he met Janice, Mathew wasn't initially attracted to her. She was as different from Clancy as you could get. Sarah, Tanya, even Sandy had all been brunette, dark, sultry, all reminded him enough of Clancy that he could forget the personality beneath it and betray his own memory. For a few brief moments. But when Janice came into his life, it was as if she were sent to him. She did not come without difficulty, however: she was married with two children.

Janice was fair, very fair, with the shiniest, longest blond hair he'd ever seen, that glittered like gold in the sun. That's what he saw next, her hair, shimmering like a waterfall as she leaned to pick up a pair of vintage shoes. And that's when she saw him in the mirror, looking at her. Caught, she smiled, then returned to her purchase, a bit flustered. He could see she was young and unsure of herself.

Mathew returned to the book he was holding and then walked to the elderly woman with the change box, paid her a dollar, and began to leave at the same time as the young woman.

"Excuse me," she asked shyly. He saw now that she was very young, early twenties, fresh oatmeal-cast skin, freckles on her nose, and high cheekbones, very Californian. "Are you . . . I mean you are—Mathew Maplethorpe . . . I don't mean Maplethorpe but the guy who writes the Maplethorpe series, aren't you?"

"Oh, yes." He smiled, offered his hand. "Mathew Prendergast."

She fumbled with the shoes in her hand and they dropped to the floor. They both leaned down at the same time to pick them up. He gathered the shoes for her and as they stood back up, he saw the flush in her face, the blatant pink that had spread across her neck and chest, shyness that could not be covered.

"Here you go."

"Thank you. I don't know what my problem is today. . . . I've just been dropping things everywhere."

"One of those days." He smiled gently at her, afraid she might break, ready to go, yet not going. They stood awkwardly for a moment. "I was just heading for coffee . . . if you'd like some."

"Gosh. Yeah. That would be great."

Janice was young. She did not have the frame of reference he was used to, lacked the maturity of soul that he missed so much in the ever-ancient Clancy. She had the strangest ability to be a kid one moment, hair tightly pulled back into a ponytail, the next a provocative siren, raking her mane back with long fingers, sensual, alluring. His connection with her was like a stalled car. With Clancy, even when they sped up at every frightening curve, even when they ran off the road altogether, their union was fluid—at least until the very end. It didn't take many years to make a great difference in this culture of quick change; anything over five years might well have been a century. Yes, she was young.

But she was wise in bed.

Coffee had been an embarrassment. She gushed, incoherently, blushed like a teenager. Mathew had no idea what he was doing at this table. He waved the waitress down for their tab. He would pay quickly and leave gracefully. But as he was leaving a tip on the table she reached out and laid a hand on his briefly.

"I'm really sorry I've been such a dork . . . but you're a celebrity and I . . . I feel like I've made a total fool of myself. . . . I just didn't want you going away thinking that I'm a complete goof . . . and I've been nervous."

He looked at her. She seemed so real in that instant, so precious and without pretense that he found his heart making a U-turn and he sat back in his chair.

"I'm . . . I'm really not this . . ." and then she paused, smiling, her lids dropped imperceptibly, eyes alive with sensual longing, "lame," she finished sweetly.

She was as far from that as one could be when he took her to bed that evening. She was tentative at first. After all, she was married. His mind reeled. What was he doing with a married woman who felt like she could have been his kid sister? But she slipped her long dancer's arms around his neck, her smooth fingers, French-dipped manicure tangling with the hair at his neck more aggressively, her lips full and wanting.

"That's never happened," she whispered when they were finished. He thought she was referring to her infidelity.

"I'm sure it hasn't."

"No. I mean I've never . . . I've never come before," she said after, a tear sliding down her face.

"Oh, my dear." Mathew took her into his arms. She touched his heart in a way that was soft and tender, in a way that made him want to protect her. "Oh, my God, what are we doing?"

He studied her, no longer seeing a girl, but someone full of fire and ache and a wisdom that had nothing to do with learning. She was all woman. And a natural with lovemaking. "I believe you are making beautiful love to me."

Yes. All woman.

"Sometimes it's not so much what you're searching for but what you're not that's really the key to what you need." These words came from Aunt Nora as they sat by the fireplace in companionable silence reading, smoking their pipes.

Mathew tried to take that one in. "As in . . ."

"Sometimes lovely and light can fill a hole."

"Aunt Nora—"

"Just a thought, dear boy," and before he could pursue the conversation she wrestled her frame out of her chair. "I'm getting a hankering to go above."

She walked to him, kissed his forehead, and ascended to the attic. She did not reappear until three days later.

"What is she, five?" Lisa asked.

It was three weeks later and they were having dinner with Lisa and her new love, Arianna, who was now with Janice in the ladies' room.

"She's older than she looks."

"Oh, Jesus Lord, Mathew." Lisa's eyes rolled. "Mathew . . . do I even have to have this conversation with you? Tell me you haven't gotten so befuddled in denial that you recognize the fact that, even though she's beyond babe-o-licious, this kid's barely out of braces, that she's got kids for christsakes?"

"Lis—"

"What about her husband? What about that minor detail?"

"He's been gone for over a year. Rarely communicates with her . . . never sees her kids."

"Then why the hell are they still married?"

He was silent.

"Mathew. What. Am. I. Going. To. Do. With. You."

"Just be my mate, like always."

"Tell me," she challenged, "what do you think—"

"Don't."

But they did. They both thought then of how Clancy would take this information. Mathew worried about it. Lisa knew she wouldn't be threatened on the surface, but that it would kill her to know Mathew was clearly sexually inflamed by this child. But she also knew it couldn't last; fires like that always burned themselves out.

They caught each other's eyes. "Maybe she'd be happy for you," Lisa offered weakly.

Janice and Arianna returned. When Janice sat and her eyes met Mathew's, Lisa saw the complete and utter adoration in them, thought about the flame burning out, and crooked her neck in consideration. This one might burn a good long time.

And it did for a while, but as time passed Mathew wasn't certain. When Janice left for a week to visit her grandmother, he started out missing her, then realized he was quite miserable, only to discover it was Clancy who visited his dreams, Clancy whom he thought of throughout the day, Clancy for whom he yearned.

Late one night he got up and walked to the deck. He took out his pipe, lit it, but did not smoke it. He then lit it again, again let it go out. It was as if things were being summoned to him from another plane. He was not quite awake. Not quite here or there.

Janice. He felt a wistful twist in his gut. It was clear, ultimately, she could never be what Clancy was for him. But why? Was it, as Lisa always pointed out, that the relationship one had with another was merely the by-product of the brain? Why couldn't he fall into Janice, with her willingness to empty herself before him, giving him far more access than Clancy ever had?

She gave. That was a distinction. He didn't have to dig. He didn't have to wonder about the mystery. Janice loved without encumbrance. She was embryonic, fresh, new and young. Certainly not as worldly as Clancy, certainly she did not possess the savoir faire, the skilled grace, the languid motion that spelled seduction. Her sensuality was not an art form, honed and skilled by experience. It was raw and pure.

"She'll never challenge your mind in the way Clancy does," Lisa remarked dryly.

"I have you for that," he threw back.

Janice was without guile. She did not manipulate situations. She simply was.

"Her simplicity is her gift," Aunt Nora remarked upon meeting her.

"Lisa's concerned she won't challenge me."

"But she already has." Aunt Nora picked up her iced tea, could see by Mathew's confused expression he needed further explanation. "To be a different person than you have been. To be new, Mathew."

Is that why she was sent? To finally break the spell he'd been under since he'd laid eyes on Clancy seven years ago now—seven years that seemed like an eternity? Could she? Or was it up to him? And if the challenge was up to him, did he want to meet it?

Finally. A moment away from Gabriella. Carlita signed wildly to the hologram. She had learned a few things since last being caught, like how important it was to set up her aura for detection. She coated her wings with a fine golden force field, radar for anyone who entered the realm of the hologram. While Mathew's screen edged forward with their disintegrating union, she fast forwarded Clancy's to find Mira. She couldn't help herself. She just had to know.

Mira loves her baby with feelings so expansive it is difficult to put them aside, shelve them during the hours she needs to devote to her web work. But all she wants to do is be with her son, this shape that comes from her body with flesh, heart, and soul. She studies his toes, fingers, the fine miniature sculpting of his delicate ears and is fascinated with his perfection.

Deep into the night she lies with Erik sleeping peacefully by her side, smelling his baby smell, powder mixed with satin skin, his fragile form curled against her, rapid heartbeat and gentle scufflings through the night. There is nothing more precious. Nothing more sacred than this being. A tear of joy trails Mira's cheek as she caresses Erik closer, for she has now found a reason to be alive.

Carlita was mesmerized by the love that showed in Mira's eyes for this baby. It felt as if she knew this moment, somehow, knew this experience, but that was completely insupportable. Oh, no. Her wings vibrated. Someone was entering her field. She immediately rewound the hologram and there found herself faced with Clancy's tears.

September 1992

She woke and found Tweety Bird dead, a small lump on her pillow. It took her a moment to figure out what Tweety was doing there. Clancy picked up the limp form and sat with it until Tweety's body turned cold and hardened. Tears followed. Forever it seemed. She didn't know how long. All she knew was that it was dark and she had to call him. She had to.

He felt a heaviness in his heart.

"I guess I should be getting home," Janice whispered softly, her lips pressed against Mathew's chest. They had just finished making love. Quickly. Janice needed to get home to make dinner for her kids. He didn't have a response for her.

It had only been a flock of angels passing, but it made Carlita realize she should have been paying more attention to Clancy. Now Tweety Bird was dead. She'd become so absorbed in Mira's life—the baby—she'd completely left Mathew and Janice to their own devices. She found Janice irritating anyway, even if she did give Mathew a measure of solace. But now . . . oh no . . . this mustn't happen.

Clancy gazed at the phone. Could she do it? After all this time? Decision was like heavy tar sticking to her shoe, messy and inescapable. The phone. She felt like it was now staring at her. Waiting. Waiting.

"Anything wrong?" Janice put a slender hand to his chin.

He didn't answer. This relationship was going nowhere and they both knew it. Janice's eyes filled with tears. Mathew leaned to kiss her. But when she moved toward him, he cut her off. "You want to shower first?"

"No . . . go ahead."

Clancy picked up the phone and sat it back down. It had been over three years now. She was just going to pick up the phone and call. It was simple. After all, they were adults. They'd grown. They say time heals all wounds. But she had this new gaping hole now, and only Mathew could help fix it. Her hand reached for the phone.

Janice lay in the bed, wondering what she should do. If Mathew gave her even the slightest encouragement she would divorce her husband.

Clancy dialed.

Carlita didn't think twice. It was stipulated that no prefect ever leave the realm of Angelica unsupervised but Carlita couldn't be bothered with that right now. She had to stop Janice from picking up that phone. She had to stop Janice from answering Clancy's call for help.

Traveling at the speed of light, she transcended her form, morphed into the smallest particles of energy, and dove head first into the phone lines, jamming the transmission after the first ring.

That was strange, Clancy thought. She knew she had heard a ring, then nothing. Like it just went dead. She dialed again, heart still pounding out of control, but the line seemed to be cut off. Was this a sign? A sign from the gods? She smiled, wryly. She sat several minutes justifying another try. She picked up the receiver three times, set it back down. This was ridiculous. One more try. If the phone did the same thing, then surely that was an indication not to call him. But she had to give it one more try.

Mathew walked from the shower, towel draped about his midsection, hair ruffly wet. The phone rang.

Carlita sighed. There . . . she felt so much better. Who knew what would have happened if she hadn't intervened and Janice had picked up the phone?

"What would have happened would have been what was supposed to happen!" Gabriella was furious. Before Carlita even broke the barriers of Earth's stratosphere, Gabriella was waiting for her. She directed her back to Earth where they landed on the first cluster of clouds that floated by. Gabriella was silent for a long time. Then, "Do you realize if I took you to Magdalena right this moment you would not only be taken off this case, but your wings would be clipped to nubs and you would spend the rest of your stay on Angelica as a cherub aid!" The thought of being surrounded by the plump patrons of sainthood chilled Carlita. "How dare you! How dare you transgress the Holy Order of Fate!"

"But . . . the whole point of our mission is to get them back together."

"Yes . . . when the time is right."

"But if Janice had answered—"

"If Janice had answered, Clancy would have dropped the phone and returned to her healing And then—and only when she becomes ready—would we intervene. Do you think vortices are picked out of thin air?"

"I'm—"

"Don't even say it."

Gabriella fumed several seconds, then regained her graceful bearing. "I don't know what to do with you, Carlita. You have really taxed me beyond all divine patience. Now I want you to sit here and see what needless pain your little antic has caused these two."

"Yes, Angel Gabriella." Carlita could barely get the words out. She couldn't remember a time she felt less like an angel.

Later, when she had come to her senses, she wondered if she had gone temporarily insane. She would call him back. Tell him not to come. Tell him she had been overcome with grief. That she had called him on impulse. But the longer she waited, the more "too late" it became, until she knew he would have already gotten in his car. And that he would be there in the next couple of hours.

As Mathew drove his mind alternated between numb and wildly terrified. And yes, excited. He traveled in a heightened sense of reality; everything seemed bright, sharpened, full of clarity. There had been nothing for over three years. And now they would be seeing each other. Every exit he came to he thought of turning off, of calling her, telling her it was best just to leave it . . . leave it as it was. He felt so close to letting it go. And still at every exit he passed he knew he was one exit closer.

When he saw her he was startled by the sameness of her. Her hair and smile—they were the same. The fine misted lines about the eyes—maybe a bit deeper. But her essence was as if they'd never traveled these years. And yet they had to be different people now, different after all they'd been through. Or maybe not. Maybe they would never be different with each other.

Although she had been crying over the death of Tweety Bird

and had a terrible head cold in the bargain, to him she was completely lovely. But more than anything, when they embraced, although quite awkwardly, the smell of her hair, the touch of her smooth skin, and the scent of her being moved him to understand what he could not escape. He was still completely in love with her.

Even after Janice.

Even after his heart had stopped living.

After their embrace, they stood shyly. It almost was as if they were meeting for the first time, yet knew everything there was to know about one another. She led him into the apartment, a studio, put together with her graceful sense of aesthetic. She was wearing black slacks and a cream-colored top, deeply veed at the neck. It made him very much aware of her breasts and he wondered if she had worn it on purpose. He found it difficult to track their stilted conversation, the inimitable fragrance of her perfume pummeling his senses, as she showed him around, showed him things she had acquired over the past few years. He saw the slender band on her finger. His eyes caught hers. Penetrating. He glanced away.

"Will you get a new bird?" he asked.

"Only one Tweety Bird." The subject was closed. Then she told him she had to go back to the gallery, that she had a client who was picking up a delivery, and it wouldn't take more than an hour. She seemed different in that moment. Sure of herself.

"Fine. I'll wait," he responded. It wasn't real. That he was there. When she left he walked around the studio, studying the bed she slept in. Lovers? How many, how often? He lay upon the bed as if to move closer to her, saw a book of poetry on her nightstand. He knew he shouldn't, but picked it up, hunted for a lover's inscription. There was none. He sighed with relief. Then he went into her kitchen, opened the refrigerator. A few staples. So undomesticated, yet so feminine. Then scanned her music and books, saw his novels set aside from the others on her shelf. He lay on the couch for a few minutes, taking in her space. Just being in it. He ached for her, always had—despite the time apart, it had never gone away.

When she returned he was busy editing the pages he'd worked on that morning. She came up behind him, as she used to, laid her hands gently upon his shoulders, so conscious of her every touch, what it meant, what it didn't mean.

"What are you working on?"

"My next book."

"An Aunt Maplethorpe mystery?"

"No. A real book. A novel."

"Your mysteries are real books."

"Not for me."

"Good, Mathew." Genuine. "I know you've wanted to do that for some time." She put a hand to his hair, then abruptly stopped, laughed awkwardly. "I . . . I guess I don't know how to be around us."

"Yes. It is a bit awkward." But Mathew smiled reassuringly. "I guess we should just try and be ourselves."

"Okay." They glanced at one another, both sighing deeply, letting the tension out.

"How about some tea?" she asked.

"Sure."

They drank tea, sitting on the couch, her knee inches from his.

"So . . ." he started.

"So." She grinned, self-effacing, a bit weary. "So, how have you been?"

"I've been . . . well, great on and off. Then there have been other times, I haven't been so great. And you?"

"The same."

"So you're an art dealer?"

"Yes."

"You like it?"

"It really suits me." She smiled. "And, surprisingly enough, I'm good at it." There it was. The self-deprecation. Neither one of them wanted to continue on this particular path.

"Lisa said to say hi."

Clancy shifted uncomfortably. "Does she . . . hate me?"

"Of course not. She's got a new lover, Arianna . . . she seems great."

"So she's happy." Clancy lowered her head.

"I think so. What about you, Clancy?" Mathew put his teacup down. "Are you happy?"

When she raised her face to his, he saw the tears streaming silently down her face. He couldn't stop himself. He moved to her and grabbed her up in his arms. "Oh, Clancy."

"Mathew, make love to me."

They lay naked in one another's arms, after the explosion of their first repressed connection, half on the couch, half on the floor, clashing together, each moment of need more intense than the one before, each one's hunger more demanding. It was ruthless, selfish, and wonderfully explosive. Side by side, sweat-pressed, half-clothed, their legs entwined, panting, trembling.

And then Mathew picked them both up, led her to her bedroom, undressed her, urgent tenderness as his hands found their way home to her skin, then lying over her, already hard again, her arched body meeting him, arms clasped to his back, "Oh, please, Mathew, please," begging him to enter her, and telling him, "yes, oh, God yes, oh, Mathew, stay inside me," somewhere between a whisper and a prayer as they moved together, their rhythm building, slow and rolling, like a wave that never ends, beckoning them to the place they both belonged, a place they could reach only together, their union a gasping stretch to oblivion and a moment called perfection.

They made love all weekend long, finally the second day ordering in moo shoo chicken, pork fried rice, and spring rolls. They fed one another, struggling with the cheap wooden chopsticks, then pigged out on Häagen-Dazs ice cream she had in the freezer.

"I hate Chinese food."

"I know. So why'd we order it?" Mathew asked as he propped himself against the pillows.

"Because it's the only place that delivers in this town." And then she said something he didn't catch.

"What?"

"What, what?"

"What did you just say?"

"Nothing."

"Come on, Clancy." Mathew smiled, gently. "After all this . . . let's have no secrets, okay?"

"Fine. I said Chinese food reminds me of my mother."

"Hmmm. Your mother." Mathew patted his lap, indicating for her to lay her head there, so he could run his hands through her hair. She smiled. She loved it when Mathew touched her. Outside of making love, having him run his hands through her hair was the single best sensation she could think of.

"You've never spoken about her," Mathew said.

Clancy lay still as she felt his strong hands wind the hair from her neck and gently tug so that grand shivers ran down the length of her body. "Oh, Mathew . . . she's such a not good subject."

"I'd really like to know, Clancy. What happened?"

"To my mother? I don't know." Clancy took a deep breath. "All I know for certain is what Uncle Sal told me about his own childhood. Their mother meaner than my own—if that's conceivably possible—bitter, angry, churlish. Must be in the DNA." She stopped for a moment, felt the calming motion of his hands. "She got the drinking from my grandfather. He died before I was born. Liver failure. They were devout Irish Catholics, so there was no birth control. My grandmother had eight children, only five of whom lived beyond their first week. My mother left home when she was fourteen, fended for herself. Lived with Uncle Joe and Sal until after they booted Sal out, and then she found a decent job cocktail waitressing and got her own apartment.

Clancy lay silent for a moment. "My mother lied about being pregnant to nab my father. When he found out she wasn't really pregnant I guess he got back at her by screwing everyone on the Upper East Side of Manhattan, as well as my mother because she did get pregnant and that's when he left her. Because she got fat and messy. Anyway, that's about all there is to tell."

But later in the early morning hours, she woke. He was between her legs, making love to her with his mouth. . . . It was delicious to not be quite there. She floated in a consciousness dedicated to pureness. So that afterward when she cried, raw, emptied out, she spoke in broken sentences.

"The night I met my father . . . I'd taken the violin home. I don't know why . . . I just had. It was . . . you know, I can't even remember. I was eleven . . . early bloomer, my mother said I'd be a slut. He arrived at the apartment before my mother got home. I was practicing, so when the knock came I shoved the violin under the couch. It was him. My father. Tall. Handsome. Everything I daydreamed him to be. He was going to save me.

"I was quite the lady showing him in . . . drinks . . . I could mix them like a pro . . . he wanted scotch and soda . . . I gave it to him . . . he said it was fine. 'My, what a lady you've turned into,' real surprised like. I don't know . . . maybe he expected me to turn out like my mother.

"He had a couple of drinks and we talked about this and that . . . what I was doing in school, things like that. He told me what a big man he was on Wall Street . . . how successful he was. And then he saw the tip of the violin under the couch. 'Well, what's this?' he asked and pulled it out, and then set it on his shoulder. 'Why, don't tell me you play this, young lady?' and I didn't know what the right answer was, terrified he would hate me if I did, but he smiled and said, 'Oh, play Daddy a tune.'"

"I played my favorite Bach . . . a slow second movement. He was smiling . . . and I was in heaven. Finally, someone letting me be who I was . . . I closed my eyes and played my heart out for him . . . wanted to give him back this gift he must have given me . . ." She sighed heavily. "I don't exactly remember how it happened . . . I finished the piece and he had walked around behind me and said, 'Ohhh, that was sweet. Go on, play Daddy another song.' But his voice was thick with something unfamiliar, so I turned. He had come back from around the couch and exposed himself. I froze. I stopped playing, but I sat in the same position. Then I can't . . . everything happened like in a dream. He grabbed himself, 'Oh, keep playin', baby, keep playin' . . . started to jerk himself off . . . grabbed my ponytail . . . shoved my head into him . . . and then my mother was there—screaming—'you fuckin' pervert!' and then they were both scrambling on the floor . . . she was whaling away at him with her purse. 'Pervert!' she kept screaming. Over and over again . . . Finally they both got back on their feet . . . she hit him again . . . shoved him out the door. 'If you ever come near her again I'll kill you.' And it was the first thing she had ever really done for me. For me." Clancy paused a long moment. "But then she turned, her eyes flames . . . zeroed in on me like a torpedo, grabbed my violin, knocked me flat with the back of her hand. But I didn't even feel the lump growing on my head because she'd taken my violin . . . banged it over the armrest of the couch, over and over and over again until there was nothing left but a mass of splintered wood and broken strings. 'Here, play this,' she said bitterly." Clancy sighed. "But I'll tell you, nothing really mattered, because for that one moment, that one horrendous moment, I loved my mother. For her fierce loyalty . . . for her saving me."

Clancy was crying, and her skin had turned cold, as had Mathew's, chilled to the bone with the horrific nightmare Clancy carried daily. He drew her to him, held her, pulled the covers over them. "I love you. I love you so, Clancy."

But she couldn't hear the words. She only heard the echoes of yesteryear.

A week later when he could finally think about their time together, he wondered if he was fated to a terminal connection of ill timing. How could they have shared what they shared, how could she reciprocate yet not be here with him now?

Was it that she had laid herself bare to him, made him witness to her terror, the information now with him always, as it had been with her? Or was that her way of saying good-bye? *Here . . . now perhaps you can understand me and know I can't be with you.* Because later that morning when he had to leave, to get back to Los Angeles, they had wrapped themselves up in each other, entwined, long kisses of good-bye and she in her throaty, husky morning voice, "I love you. Beyond all reason." Soft and sweet before she was awake enough to have any defense and it had burned in his ears, through to his heart. "Beyond all reason."

They were the last words from her mouth that would echo in his mind for the years to come.

And then she disappeared. Again.

"See?" Gabriella said, but her voice was soft with kindness.

"I just don't get it. They love each other so much."

"Love isn't the problem here. It's interfacing two humans whose psyches are at obverse positions of mating. Now we will have to find a new vortex, somewhere, in which to relink the two." Gabriella pressed her lips together and exited.

Carlita thought heavily about Gabriella's observation and then examined the words "beyond all reason" and knew they could be applied to the love Mira felt for her baby, Erik. Erik, who had Mira's fine blond hair, her deepset, gentle eyes. Wise eyes for a baby so young. And Carlita loved this baby too . . . this Clancy of another time, so compellingly, in fact, that it was simply beyond her control; she had to find out how Clancy's future life ended up.

Mira spends every free second away from her computer with Erik as he develops rapidly, walking at eight months, jabbering excitedly with his stuffed animals, creating games with a fierce imagination. There is only one area in which Erik does not excel and that is with his computer learning. Preschool e-mails grade him satisfactorily but indicate a tendency toward wandering when it comes to web theory and history. When he turns five, Net teachers reluctantly recommend education for a physical vocation, as he is good with his hands. Mira is secretly pleased.

When Erik turns six Mira takes him on a trip, where they play on the last remaining stretches of uncontaminated beachland. There are only a few people there, as it is more convenient for people to recreate by Virtual Destination. Erik loves the real treks they take, enjoys hiking in the upper reaches of Topanga, sitting with his mother as the sun sets against an oceanscape.

Mira thinks back on the old movies she now shares with Erik at night before he goes to sleep and knows that in her own way, she is fighting the system and giving Erik the best—maybe not to excel in this world, but to live up to the best in himself. If it is the only thing Mira is able to do for her son, she wants Erik to know about the real world, the flesh-and-blood world, not the electronically synapsed mindscape she was forced through as a child.

"Now what are you doing?!" Was there nothing that escaped Gabriella's senses? And how had she gotten through Carlita's detection shield?

But it didn't matter. When Carlita turned, a golden tear plopped itself gently from her eye and shimmered down the translucent membrane of her cheeks to her satin chin.

"You're . . . you're . . . crying." Gabriella couldn't believe her eyes. Tears were only for humans. And the rare moment of galactic phenomenon. "Oh, Carlita . . . what have you done? What have you done?"

December 1993

It took him almost a year after that weekend to accept that he could not have her; finally, when he did, he felt peace. The wonder still swirled lightly through his heart at times, but he had split off and become two men. One who loved Clancy and couldn't have her. One who loved Clancy and would have her again. In his heart he believed in the latter, but his head kept him focused on the former.

"I fully expected to find a bag of tortured bones up here," Lisa confessed when she brought Arianna up to visit him and Nora for Christmas at the Lodge.

"Why's that?" Mathew puffed thoughtfully at his pipe.

"Hello!?!" Lisa decried. "Because she did it again."

"Did what again?" Arianna asked. Aunt Nora had left a tray of "Nog Tide" and had already retired to her room. Lisa poured liberally from the batch and in the space of several eggnogs, she performed the saga of Clancy and Mathew and Lisa as they slouched around the fireplace.

Arianna's cheeks burned with more than the brandy. "This . . . this is incredible. You don't mind if I use it in my next book, do you?"

Mathew smiled, then turned to the fire.

"She will," Lisa stated. "Look, Mathew, none of it's ever made any sense. If you love someone, you fuck all the rest and go for it. Right, sweetie?"

But Arianna was watching Mathew, seeing the set of his jaw, knowing the faraway glaze in his eyes was reserved for another reality, that was about him and Clancy, what they were, what they could be. She moved from Lisa and went and put an arm about Mathew's neck, embraced him with all the feeling she still reserved for the woman of her dreams. She wished it could be Lisa, but it wasn't.

"Hope ray," Arianna whispered into his ear, then sat across from him. "That's what I call it: hope ray—the single most convoluted line between two points."

Mathew now saw Arianna for the first time. She was a strange electrical current. Originally he hadn't thought of her as attractive, but now he saw her lit up and she was incredibly appealing. No wonder Lisa had fallen so hard. He imagined it happened a lot for this woman.

"I met a woman, fell so crazily in love with her I couldn't begin to unravel what it meant . . . karmically, et cetera. The point was she was ten years younger than me. We were a match in ways I couldn't have dreamed were possible. The usual crap was there. She had no idea who she was or what she wanted to be when she grew up and every other week she was either going to be a brain surgeon, a therapist, or sell flowers for Greenpeace. She thought her meanderings, her tangential reality bothered me. I had no issue with it. What I had issue with was that she resented the fact that I had an identity. I think she'd have felt safer if I was as lost as she was. But I wasn't. And it didn't make me love her any less." Arianna leaned over. "May I?"

She took a puff of his pipe, a peace offering, a heart offering, in the tale of love gone wrong.

"Anyway we lasted a year. It was the most intense year of my life. This woman touched me in ways there are no words for. We did the usual back-and-forth thing, and then a year after we break up, we end up running into each other. She's been with a new lover and broken up since, I'd been with three, trying to drown my heartache through flesh. We decide to go to dinner. We end up in a hotel, make earth-shattering love, ease into a place we both call 'home,' swim in one another's soul space, and tell each other nothing's changed. We love one another with all our hearts. The point being, *nothing* had changed, including all the things we couldn't abide about one another. We still couldn't put it together."

"But why?" Mathew asked.

"Probably for the same reasons you and Clancy can't put it together. It's not lack of love, lust, complete and utter feeling. It's because you jumped the destination chart. The timing isn't right."

"Yeah," Lisa jumped in, "but we all know timing is everything, so maybe the chart wasn't jumped. Maybe it just wasn't meant to be. Sure. You're madly in love, but it's just not gonna happen. For whatever reason. I'm a fuckin' pragmatist. You let go. You let go and let live and if you're one of the very lucky few, you find the right match."

Lisa was hurt now. She'd heard Arianna's tortured story just a few too many times. If she'd just let go of this damn viper, she'd have a chance.

Mathew sighed. "But she *is* the match."

"Oh, Mathew, grow the fuck up." Lisa got up and stomped out of the room.

"I better go after her." Arianna stood, then put a gentle hand to Mathew's shoulder. "Don't give up. I did and I've regretted it ever since."

Arianna left him alone. She and Lisa were flip sides of a coin representing both halves of him. His mind was becoming cynical like Lisa's. His heart was all Arianna. How did he get the two to make peace?

February 1993

She stood at Point Dume. Stormy. Rain threatened to drench her. She was so close to him, only ten minutes by car up the long winding hill to Aunt Nora's. Her heart raged. She wanted nothing more than to go to him. But even though this time had passed she knew she still wasn't ready. And there was no way she would subject him to another weekend.

That weekend. Filled with so much hope. It wasn't until she actually saw him, felt the rightness of him like a brand on her heart, what they were, how it took over her, how it commanded her submission. Never before had the words "bigger than the both of us" made such clear and overwhelming sense. And even though she had wanted nothing more than to follow him back to Los Angeles, back to their lives, to each other, she wasn't ready. She just knew it was too soon. It would destroy them. Her.

She'd finally come to believe self-destruction was not an option. Had actually, for the first time in her life, celebrated her own birthday, as she did Mathew's. She spent the day pampering herself, bought a new dress, and then drove to Carmel for dinner with James. She still worked for him, but less of the time and only out of San Luis Obispo now. Then she'd driven back home, turned on the lights of her small Christmas tree, and played the violin late into the night. She had a student now, a young Asian girl that lived down the road. It gave her great joy to watch her play, and smiled when she thought back to Madame Jones.

She still saw Arlene on occasion, when she felt buckly, perhaps misguided, but mostly as something she did that was good to herself. She dated very little. She spent most of her free time now reading, taking long walks near the ocean, playing and teaching. She was becoming used to herself, a self she was beginning to like, even treasure at moments. She wasn't lonely, although missing Mathew had become a slow dull ache that lived inside her like her other involuntary functions. And like them, she needed it to live.

Gabriella and Carlita stared one another down. She pointed to Clancy's screen. "This was when they should have connected. But now that weekend got in the way. Do you see now how every moment impacts another?"

"Uhum . . ." Carlita knew there was more.

"You shouldn't have done this, Carlita." But now Gabriella was referring to Carlita's obsession with Mira and Erik.

"I've said I was sorry. What do you want me to do?"

"You don't understand," Gabriella said, more weary than angry. "And it's too late to take you off this case."

"But why would you want me off? I mean, so I've seen Clancy's future. It only makes me want to do my job better."

"No. It can only make you do your job worse," Gabriella snapped.

"Angel Gabriella, please . . . what have I done that is so terrible?"

"Carlita, come with me."

May 1995

He lay flat on his back, suffering from a herniated disk. Picking up the mail one afternoon. That's what did it to him. Picking up the mail and then trying to bend to his desk, he felt skewered in the center of his body as if he been thumbtacked flat. He couldn't walk. He tried. Walk, hell—he could hardly even move. Eventually he shuffled to the phone and, screaming in pain, he picked it up, dialed for an ambulance.

He was in prime physical condition, the doctor said. It apparently happened to a lot of people who worked out. His running up and down all the trails might have caused an injury he wasn't aware of, kept exacerbating it, then bam! Had one patient who picked his nose and his back went out.

"Lovely." Mathew grunted in pain.

Laid up. The first three days after the operation he slept, long vague hours, never certain if it was morning or night when he woke, drugged on Percodans, muscle relaxers, and Valium. "Sleep as much as you can," the doctor had ordered when he sent him home.

And Mathew did sleep at first, but then boredom set in. He created an organized little desk on the other half of his bed, his laptop never far from his side. Aunt Nora dashed in and fussed over him, brought him juice, tea, dinner, and videos, mostly of all his favorites. She'd go into town and rent up to five or six at a time. And then, of course, he rewatched all his Fred Astaire movies. And they had a noir festival on AMC and he watched Rita in his favorite, *Gilda,* and back to back Humphrey Bogart and Lauren Bacall in the *The Big Sleep* and *To Have and Have Not.*

Wild dreams came to haunt him. Remixes of the movies he'd seen earlier in the day . . . in and out of dozing. But one morning he dreamt of her. Vivid. Oh, God, so vivid. He was semi-dozing and she walked in the room. He didn't even wonder how she'd gotten there.

"We have to get you cleaned up." She smiled. So beautiful, he could smell the clean sweetness of her skin, and her hair, so thick, fell half over her face, and he saw Lauren Bacall from *To Have and Have Not,* and her seductive turn of head as she beckoned him out of bed.

"I . . . I can't walk."

"Sure you can, Johnny." Now she was Rita Hayworth in *Gilda.* She walked to the curtains, turned, and asked with Rita's savoir faire, but now she was Clancy again, "Let's hate her, shall we, Johnny."

"I don't hate you, Clancy."

"You said you couldn't love anyone who didn't love themself. Same thing, isn't it, Johnny?" And then she sauntered to him, "Walk for me, Mathew." It was Clancy, full-blooded Clancy, so real now. "Just walk with me on the beach. One more time."

And then they were on the beach and he was in jeans and a sweatshirt and she was in the pale peach summer dress Aunt Nora had bought her and they were walking, sand on their feet, he could feel it, prickling his right foot, hand in hand, smile in smile, laughing. They were young, and carefree, and in love.

He woke from the pins and needles in his right foot. His heart was pounding and he'd worked up a sweat. He started crying. "Damn you, Clancy."

Gabriella watched as Carlita viewed Mira's hologram, watching Erik as he grew from a baby to toddler, watched him baking bread with Mira, full of flour and laughter, his eyes full of life, playing with the Erector set, watching Mira as she came into the room and lavished praise on her son for his building her the wonderful castle where they pretended they lived.

Between the pain Carlita had caused Mathew and Clancy and having experienced the unbreakable bond between Mira and her son, Carlita's wings felt paralyzed, her head was bent, and another golden tear flowed from her diaphanous eyes.

"Do you want to know why we are watching this, Carlita?" Gabriella asked.

"Yes," Carlita responded, a bit defensively.

"The point is, Carlita, Erik isn't supposed to happen."

"What? What do you . . . what are you saying?"

"It's what I probably should have told you sooner. But how was I to know you were going to go dabble in future realities?" Gabriella sighed. "Carlita, Tarek is only born if Clancy and Mathew don't get together."

"You're confusing me."

"If Clancy and Mathew don't get together, Mathew will marry in England. His offspring will beget offspring, and so forth, until Tarek is born, whom Mira meets."

"And if Tarek doesn't exist . . ." Carlita slowly starts to put the puzzle together. "Then Erik isn't born."

Gabriella floats close to Carlita, nearly touching her. "Do you understand, my dear? Mira will never have this son. This son that finally gives her reason to get up in the morning. This son who takes away all the pain and isolation of the world she lives in."

It's a bit difficult for Carlita to comprehend Mira without Erik, but yes, she understands.

"You are now in a terrible conflict of interest. You've been assigned to put Mathew and Clancy together, and if you are successful, then . . . well, then Mira's life will be void of the experience of having her son. Erik simply will not exist." Gabriella's voice hardened. "And now, to compound problems, Magdalena is terribly concerned that you simply aren't ready to be an angel."

Carlita stared despondently.

"She has requested that I relieve you of your duties."

Carlita stared at her in horror. "Oh, please, please, Angel Gabriella. Let me do my work. I . . . I just need time to adjust. I . . . I—"

"See how much difference a moment can make?" But Gabriella's voice was not unkind. "A moment can be a whole lifetime, and it takes just as much responsibility and care."

Carlita merely stared at Gabriella.

"What am I to do with you?" Gabriella asked, bowed her head and floated away.

Gabriella entered a beautiful sitting area of billowy colored clouds. Magdalena was waiting for her with a chalice of celestial tea.

"Well?" Magdalena asked.

"She doesn't know."

"Good." Magdalena sipped the heavenly tonic. "And have you pulled her from the case?"

"No. And with your permission I would like to keep her on. If she can make it through this situation we will have accomplished what we set out to do. She will be an angel of the highest standing and integrity."

"Yes, but we're talking about Carlita here."

"I know." Gabriella looked thoughtfully at Magdalena. "And from what I sense of Carlita I believe she is up to the task."

December 1995

The pass was snowed over so they unpacked the car and decided to have Christmas at home. Aunt Nora didn't seem to mind. In fact, she was particularly festive this Christmas Eve. She'd come from the attic, made "Johnny Mathis Tide," fussed about the tree as she warbled, "Giddy up giddy up giddy up let's go, let's follow the snow" over and over and over, like that was the most fascinating part of the song.

"There are other words, dear." Mathew came up behind her. Hugged her.

"Yes, but I can't for the life of me remember them."

They glanced at each other. Both of them were thinking of her. Thinking it was her birthday. Wondering where she was.

"I'm sure she's okay. In fact, certain of it," Aunt Nora said, but Mathew changed the subject.

"You spent a long time up there."

"Had to finish."

"Finish what."

"Well . . . everything, actually." She turned to him. He noticed her cheeks were flushed.

"Feeling okay?"

"Never better."

"Old age," the doctor said the next morning. "Simply old age."

"But she was fine last night. She's been in perfect health."

"I know." The doctor found it as confusing as Mathew did.

He had gotten up Christmas morning to answer the door when Lisa arrived with Marilyn, her newest lover, and her two children. They gave the kids presents to play with until Aunt Nora joined them. The adults drank coffee, quietly chatting in the kitchen, but when an hour had passed, Mathew decided to wake her. The children were getting antsy.

There was no answer when he knocked on her door. He waited. Knocked again. Then he let himself in. When he walked to her bed, he saw a faint smile on her lips, and it was only when he bent to nudge her that he realized she was pale as a ghost. Dead.

Marilyn took the kids home with her and Lisa stayed with Mathew.

And then he cried. For hours. And Lisa held him.

When she woke she felt something was wrong. Mathew. No . . . it must have been a dream. But it felt so strong. She was in Hawaii, with John, one of Wellington's clients. They'd been lovers for three months. John hated Christmas, so they decided to bypass it altogether and go to Hawaii until it was over.

They'd strolled into a brilliant sunset the night before and had a wonderful dinner, then went back to the hotel. Made love. It was sweet, comforting. She hadn't told him it was her birthday. It was something just for her and she celebrated it in her own quiet way. When he drifted off to sleep, she got up and peeked out the window, at the moon. It was a very clear night. She saw a shooting star. And for some reason Aunt Nora came to mind.

He called Clancy but got her answering machine.

"Hi. It's me. I . . . I got the number from the gallery." Long pause. "I wouldn't have called, but I thought you might want to know. Aunt Nora passed away. We're having the funeral tomorrow. Thought maybe you'd like to attend." His voice broke then. "Jesus, Clancy . . . I . . . I can't bear that she's gone." Another long pause as he mustered his British reserve together, for the next was polite, remote. "Anyway . . . hope you are well."

When she heard the message after she returned from her trip, it was several days after the funeral.

Five months later, Mathew packed up Aunt Nora's things. The pain of her loss still lived at the base of his throat, but he had to do something. And he knew she would have wanted her clothes to go to one of the many women's shelters she supported. As he folded her wild garments, he would remember the times she'd worn each outfit, and he'd be filled with memories . . . some of which included Clancy, and he found himself mourning both the women he cherished in his life.

When he'd finished, he walked out of the bedroom and was about to head downstairs to the kitchen to make a cup of tea when he glanced at the attic door. It was funny how it had escaped his mind, but Aunt Nora's room had been off limits for so many years that Mathew simply forgot it was there. He'd never felt the need to pry after Maria had sternly set him straight, and as he grew to adulthood, and had his own need for privacy, he honored that of his aunt.

But now . . . now he wanted to see her workroom, her place . . . the place she spent so many hours "going off." The room where she'd created the ornaments . . . his ornament, that had expressed the future of him and Clancy. How had she known? But then Aunt Nora's eccentricity and psychic abilities walked hand in hand.

His heart started beating wildly as he approached the door. He saw his hand tremble as it clasped the handle. He turned it. Slowly made his way in. He stood in shock for a long time. Walked about the perimeter in slow motion, struck by the revelation. He finally slouched by a wall to a sitting position, a long sigh accompanying him as he sat. In this room, this room his aunt had spent all her time in, where she traveled to "go off," where she did God only knew what, they would never know. For in this room, there wasn't a clue to be found. Not a trace of solution. But it was just like her. Keep them guessing.

It was empty.

March 1996

"You know you could always call him," Arlene said. "Try and start over."

"If I were Mathew and I heard from me after all this time, I'd run a million miles the other way."

"Why don't you let Mathew decide for himself?"

"Well, hasn't he?"

"You mean that he hasn't charged after you? Come in like a knight in shining armor? Proved to you his love?"

"Yes! I mean if he really wanted this, he'd come after me. But he got as sick of my indecision as I did. Besides . . . too much time has passed. For all I know he could be married. And truthfully, I'm only just now getting to the place where I know what I want. At least for each day. Not much beyond that. But there is a modicum of consistency." Clancy smiled. She had come a long way.

Since she'd lived in San Luis Obispo, she had learned to come to terms with who she was. Having told Mathew about her father and her mother, she had for the first time allowed the horrors of her childhood to be spoken out loud. That weekend had served more than "to torture the hell out of them both" as Arlene put it, but turned out to be the pinnacle on the road up, and now she was slowly making it back down, slowly coming to terms.

"Maybe that's what Mathew was for me. A road map."

"Think so?"

"I don't know. I guess the question is, can I get anywhere without him?" But she really didn't know. And so she wasn't able to let go of him. Not yet.

She still got frustrated at herself, but she finally understood that she was simply a woman who wasn't a "something." She could claim no profession, but she could claim a job that suited her, and it was one she performed well. She now had four students, and was excited by each of their unique and individual talents. She'd discovered a quartet of very fine musicians at a street fair, a straggly bunch but very much like herself in that they loved their music but hadn't made it their life. They invited her to join them, marveled at her talent, which made her blush, but gave her no end of pleasure. They even performed occasionally in public.

Her personal life didn't amount to much. After she'd found Arlene she devoted most of the time she wasn't working to therapy, reading a mass of self-help books, finally getting an understanding of her relationship to her mother after a grueling three-hour session, during much of which Clancy lay in a puddled heap on the floor, crying, allowing herself to hate the demon that had anchored her to the dark. Once the phantom of her mother was faced head-on Clancy felt a lightness she'd never known.

So life went on. She became lovers briefly with one of the guys in the quartet, but he became too involved, so she ended it, not wanting it to interfere with her music. She had another brief affair, with a married man, but she didn't like how it made her feel, so she ended that one as well.

"Good," Arlene said.

"Why good?"

"Because it shows you have a sense of value about yourself."

"What? That I sleep with married men?"

"No, that you don't."

And then she had met John, at one of Wellington's galleries in Carmel. He did much the same thing she did, so they had a lot to talk about. He lived in Portland, which was an interesting coincidence, she thought, but suited her fine. They both seemed to want the same thing: a long-distance relationship with no strings. But as the affair continued, their meetings became more frequent. She flew up to Portland more often, they'd meet at remote places where one or the other of them was delivering art. John had a delicious sense of humor so they laughed a lot. They had fun with each other. The more time they spent together, the better it felt until eventually he began to talk of a future.

When she was with him Clancy felt calm—nothing like being with Mathew. The way she felt about Mathew was never calm.

"Is it settling?" she asked Arlene one session.

"What do you mean?"

"I . . . I don't think I'm in love with John."

"Are you supposed to be?"

"Isn't that the point of having a relationship? I mean, isn't that what we're striving for?"

"First of all, there are an infinite number of ways to be in love. And being with someone depends on where you are. On what you need. Sometimes," Arlene sighed, "one simply needs a rest from passion. And sometimes, one needs to work one's way back to it."

"Like training?"

"Precisely." Arlene smiled. She liked Clancy. "And sometimes, one is simply trying to learn how to be passionate with themselves."

"But does it have to be mutually exclusive?"

"You tell me."

She almost called twenty times after she got the message about Nora. She wanted so much to make contact. But each time she got near the phone, she just couldn't pick it up. After torturing herself she decided she would just send a card. But when she looked for one, they all seemed so ridiculous and besides, what would she say? What *could* she say? What could anyone say to another when someone who was a part of themselves was gone? But she couldn't not make contact with him.

Finally she called. He answered the first couple of times and she hung up. When she got his answering machine, she said, "Mathew . . . I got the message about Aunt Nora. I'm so sorry. I really am. She was one of the most wonderful . . . well, you know that. I . . . um . . ." and then she froze. And hung up.

She called Lisa instead.

"Lisa?"

"Clancy???" Disbelief. "Clancy, I don't believe it!"

"Yeah . . ."

"How are you? Where are you? Are you in town?"

"No. I'm home. I just wanted to make sure Mathew was all right."

"Yeah, he's okay. It's been hard on him, though."

"Yeah . . ."

"Clancy!" And then she heard Lisa laugh.

"What's so funny?"

"I don't know. Mathew and I were just talking about you the other day, and, well, we just wondered how your life was going and all."

"Things are good."

"Good. That's good."

"And you?"

They continued with the small talk, catching up on each other's lives, Lisa's relationship with Arianna and how that led to Marilyn. "Ahhh . . . .Marilyn. She's wonderful. I think I've finally found the one."

Silence.

"Do you mind if I cut to the chase?" Lisa asked.

"You will anyway."

"Are you seeing anyone?"

"Yeah," Clancy said, adding quickly, "sort of a long-distance thing." She wanted to ask. It burned in her, but she was afraid to know.

"Why don't you call him? I know he'd really like to hear from you."

"Well, you know . . . so much time has passed and—"

"He's leaving, Clancy." Lisa's voice was clipped. "For England."

"For a trip?"

"No. He's moving back."

"After all these years?"

"I think Nora's death really did a number on him. He said he would be gone for at least a few years, anyway. Wants to find his roots. Change of scenery. Get new material. You know."

"New material. Of course." An edge crept into her voice.

"Clancy—"

"Never mind," Clancy remarked. "Look, I gotta run. I'm late for an appointment. It's been great talking with you. Take care." She hung up before Lisa could respond.

"Yeah, don't be such a stranger."

Christmas Eve

"How? How the hell would I know?" Lisa asked. "It's just something I know, inside me."

"But you said that with Arianna."

"I *wished* it with Arianna. God, how I wished it. You have to have two people there together. Arianna was always drifting into some writer's fuckin' dreamworld." Lisa laughed after she said it. "Okay, apply it to yourself, you miserable hack."

They had just finished dinner. Marilyn was putting the children to bed, and Lisa and Mathew were drinking "To Aunt Nora Tides."

"It just doesn't have it, does it?" Lisa asked.

Mathew stared at her drink. "I don't know what she put in them . . . but no. It's definitely not a 'tide.'"

"Ohhh, Mathew. I miss her."

Later when they'd all gone to bed, he lit his Dunhill pipe. Communion with Nora. He heard her voice in his head: "It will all be okay," she whispered, but he wasn't sure. America had been his home for so long. He would miss Lisa. The irony in their being best friends was like a warmth that shielded him from the cold outside.

It was a quiet night. He stared up at the stars, wondered where she was. But all was quiet inside. He'd let go. All quiet except for the final scream deep inside. He rarely heard it now. Had gotten used to shutting out the sound.

The next morning, he and Lisa woke before everybody else. He made her coffee. She made him tea. They sat. Lisa reached across the table for his hand.

"We should have gotten married. Clancy could have been our child."

He winked at her. "You're my dearest friend."

"I'm going to miss you . . . you gentlest of men . . . you poet." Lisa started crying. Mathew went to her. They held each other. Lisa smashed the tears from her face. "Tears and Christmas morning—not a match."

The world outside was make-believe. Frost painted the frame of her window as she stared at the hillside of chilled baby's breath, smoothed over the surface in faint tinted blue. Taking in its cold beauty, she could truly imagine that she was the only one in the world. She breathed that in for a moment. She had felt like that so much of her life. The hermit of her soul. There was only one person who could ever meet her there.

Now she sat on a Greyhound bus. Destination: Portland. Musing as she stared at the passing scenery, beautifully cold, untouchable. How many birthdays and Christmases had she spent alone? How many had she cared about? The only one that had really mattered was the one at the Lodge. Christmas morning when she and Mathew had gotten up before everyone else, winterblue dawn, snuggling in front of the fireplace, presents under the tree, the lights on. No words. Just union.

Mira and Erik put the last of the Christmas ornaments on a plastic tree they have found in an antique store at the underground. It is illegal to have a real one—they have been on the endangered list for years. But they make the most of it, spraying the house in pine and lighting cranberry-scented votives, singing along with an old Julie Andrews album, another treasure they had found.

The image jolted through Carlita even though she was trying to stay focused on this critical vortex of her charges. It was imperative she stayed focused. Gabriella was giving her one last chance, and she wasn't going to screw it up.

The bus revved its hoary engine, pulled out of the pit stop, and started down the road. It was just brightening over the tip of the hill, southeast.

She was visiting John. He'd finally decided they should try Christmas together and that she should meet his family. It was quite a commitment for him. And for her. In truth, she wasn't sure she was ready to take that step. When it came time to get on a plane, flights into Portland were delayed because of the weather, possibly as much as twenty-four hours.

She decided to fly to San Francisco and take a bus the rest of the way, but when they finally got over the pass and were heading through Medford, they hit another storm and were stopped for the night.

She'd rented the only room she could find, a scabby imitation of a Hotel 6, sat and watched TV, and felt him. Intensely. As she had for the past few days. Memories and images of him were much stronger than usual. Probably because of the holidays. Yes, that and the realization she had when she saw the local map in the lobby, of how close she was to the Lodge. But still, she couldn't shake the sense of his nearness. Of course, she knew she was being silly. He was in England.

She called the front desk, asking where she could get a rental car and how far they were from the Mount Hood area. Four hours, but she'd never make it in this weather, the clerk said flatly. She rented the car anyway. In any event, she could drive it from there to Portland. She had called John, told him she wouldn't make it until late Christmas Day.

• • •

They sat companionably in the living room, drinking tea in the hour before dawn, the hour before the children would get up and shatter the easy silence of the morning.

It was only then that he saw it. Even though they'd been there a full day. A package under the tree. Mathew crossed the room, bent and picked it up. It had been addressed to the Lodge, but there was no return address and the post date had been smeared by weather, or . . .

"Did you send this?" he asked, turning to Lisa.

"No," she said. She joined him, and they both hunched on their knees inspecting the brown paper wrapped gift. They stared at each other.

"No . . . couldn't be."

"Should we?" Mathew asked.

"Do it," Lisa commanded.

Mathew carefully unwrapped the paper. Underneath was another layer of hunter-green Christmas wrapping. When that was shed, he sat with the ornament box in his hands. He stared at it for a moment, then glanced at Lisa. "Why would she send this . . . and when?"

"Maybe it's been here since before she died."

"But that would mean she knew she was dying."

"Sweetheart, with your Aunt Nora . . . anything is possible." Lisa touched his face. "Open it."

He lifted the hinged lid and they both peered inside, then he gently extracted the contents, held it up between them. They stared at one another in disbelief.

Christmas morning Clancy paced the hotel room, turned to the window, but couldn't see beyond twenty feet in the white-out. She'd rented the car last night and then bought chains. She knew.

She was going to do this. Arlene would call it closure. She wasn't certain what she'd call it, aside from crazy, but she knew that if she didn't do it, she could never get on with the rest of her life.

The room filled with the noises of Cece and Todd scrambling about under the tree. Marilyn and Lisa cooed at each other as they exchanged loving gifts. Mathew took pictures, sat beneath the tree as they gave him a handmade scarf to help ward off all that damp English air.

It had taken her two hours to make the first fifty miles, but she never thought of turning back. Her mind became a single focus. Onward.

Later in the morning, after Christmas breakfast, Mathew sent Lisa and her new family off. They had to get back so that Marilyn's kids could spend the last half of Christmas with their father. Lisa put chains on her Ford Explorer, packed the kids in, and ran back to the house and found Mathew staring at the mysterious gift.

"Are you sure it's wise of you to brave the elements?"

"Wise? Probably not. But the sooner we get the kids to their father, the sooner we have some alone time."

Mathew laughed, then frowned. He picked up the ornament and put it out for Lisa's appraisal. "And what is this supposed to mean?"

"Wishful thinking," Lisa said gently, and then embraced him. Held him. Loved him.

She was about an hour away now, her neck stiff from craning forward to see through the snow, trying to distinguish fact from fiction. Her eyes were beginning to play tricks on her . . . the white seemed almost as bright as the sun. Still she never wavered. She was on a mission. She'd had a chance. She'd seen the fork in the road and laughed at the metaphor. One way to John. Another to Mathew and her past. She had to do this. Self-preservation. She had to put an end to it. To kill it once and for all.

Mira tucks Erik into bed, sifts her hands through his silky hair as she tells him a bedtime story. He struggles to keep his eyes open, desperate not to fall asleep, but his mother's soothing voice finally gets the better of him.

Mathew stared through the Lodge windows at the thick snow and checked his watch again. He'd never make his plane. But he had to make his plane. It was too important. Lisa had kept asking, "Why now? What's the urgency."

"I don't know. It's just one of those 'it's now or never' kind of things." He had only waited to celebrate Aunt Nora's favorite day, and now he wanted to get on with his life. If the caretaker didn't get there soon, he'd try using the old four-wheeler the grounds-keeper kept in the garage.

He glanced about him, annoyed at feeling as if he was forgetting something. The caretakers would be there in the morning to take down the tree, fix up the place, modernize it a bit. He had decided to leave the property in their hands, rent it out to other people so they might enjoy its magic. His watch hadn't moved from the last time he glanced at it, but he called the caretaker's number, anyway. His wife said he was on his way. Would probably be a little late, what with all the snow. . . .

But something still bothered him . . . what was it? Mathew shuffled aimlessly through the Lodge, feeling somewhat like a ghoul, and then laughed at his own absurd thoughts. "The ghost of Christmas past. Mathew, get a bloody handle."

Gabriella thought what she must be feeling was something close to what earth people called panic. She'd sent Carlita to oversee Clancy. To stay with her until she made it, while she stayed by Mathew's side. They were coming down to the wire. This was it. This would be their last chance to make this happen. But now she wondered if she should have let Carlita go? Was this a big mistake? Should she have told her the truth? The whole truth? Would Carlita do the right thing? Then she floated to Mathew. How could she keep him here?

The hairs at his neck bristled. He'd turned the heat down an hour ago and it was getting chilly inside the Lodge.

He walked up the stairs to get his suitcase. In his room, he headed to the window to check for the caretaker's Jeep. The snow finally seemed to be letting up, he thought.

Wheels spun. Clancy was stuck. She put the car into first gear, then in reverse, let it rock in neutral. Finally. It pulled out, crawled at snail's pace.

Mira bends and kisses Erik's forehead, turns the light off, and goes to where she has hidden Erik's presents. She hums to herself as she wraps several books and toys. But the important gift, the one she cannot wait to share, is the red clay, wet and unformed. She packs the sculptor's tools into his stocking and envisions Erik, so talented with his hands, creating work as an expression of his expansive soul. She almost wants to wake him and give him the gift now, and then laughs at herself, feeling more the child than her son.

Carlita shook the vision from her head. Images of Mira's hologram simply would not leave her. She had to know. It was as simple as that. She knew she was to stay with Clancy, but the need to get to the bottom of the mystery was overwhelming her.

She dematerialized and floated to Gabriella, reappearing.

"What are you doing here?"

"Please, Gabriella."

"What—"

"I have to know."

"This isn't the time."

"You must tell me. I need to know."

Gabriella stood on one side of Mathew, Carlita on the other, as he continued to peer out the window.

"Yes." Gabriella nodded solemnly. "I suppose you do."

She spun out again, wheels skimming like a skater on ice, one fluid motion right across the road. The motor was stilled by the frozen embankment.

Clancy gripped the steering wheel. "Damn."

She opened the door, almost slipped on the patch of black ice by her feet. She grabbed her purse and started in on the trek. By her calculations the Lodge was roughly another mile farther in. She wrapped the scarf about her ears.

◆ ◆ ◆

Gabriella knew it was against the Interplanetary Guardian Angel Code, adverse to every Angel Maxim she knew, was something she could be called up for and lose her standing as a Superior Angel for, but she was in an impossible situation, and she didn't know what else to do.

Using the glass of a mirror to bounce a reflected light beam, she created a mini-hologram that displayed itself in the window of Mathew's bedroom.

"Carlita, we don't have much time," Gabriella said anxiously, as they could now just see Clancy barely visible in the distance through Mathew's windowpane, trudging forward slowly. On an adjacent pane was the hologram. As a split screen they watched the parallel lives of Clancy in this world and Erik and Mira in the other.

> Mira carefully places the packages under the tree, steps back, and picks up the gift Erik gave her earlier, wrapped in soft tissue paper. She returns to Erik's room, and as with every time she lays eyes on her child, her heart fills with love and warmth. She cannot bear to be without him this night. She picks him up, realizing he will almost be too big to do this much longer, and carries him into the living room. She wants him to see all the presents when he wakes. But just as strongly she wants to sleep next to him, feel his body next to hers.

Clancy trudged through the thick snow. The packed drifts slowed her progress. She began sweating. "This is ridiculous," Clancy thought. "What am I doing?" But still she continued forward.

• • •

Mathew turned from the window just as Clancy became a speck in the distance. He went to pack the last of his books into the suitcase, picked up a volume of poetry, opened it, and read the inscription aloud. "For my dear poet, my muse, my love, C." There was a photo peeking out from the center of the book. He pulled it out. It was the first picture he'd ever taken of Clancy, when they'd first met. He held it before him a moment, then put it back into the center and closed the book, breathing deeply. He began to put the volume into the suitcase, then took it out again. He walked to a bookshelf, slid it in among those already there. He shut the suitcase. He walked back to the window, but all he saw was the caretaker's Jeep. "Finally," he whispered.

Mira carries Erik into the living room and lays him on the couch. She oh so carefully brushes his flaxen hair, now matted in child sweat, to the side. She pulls a blanket over them both as she cuddles close to him and sighs deeply with contentment. She watches the tree lights blink on then off, entranced by their beauty, trying to stay awake to feel this moment for as long as she can. The last thing she remembers before she falls asleep is the scent of Erik's hair, the pureness of him, the perfect smell of his child essence.

"It's me. Isn't it?" Carlita stares at Mira, sleeping with her son, inside the scene. Living it. And now she knows why she has not been able to let this go. Why it is she has felt so connected to Clancy and why she has loved Erik as her own.

Gabriella turns to her. "Yes," she says gently. "It is."

"I'm Mira." Carlita's voice, an angel whisper.

"I'm sorry." Gabriella truly feels for Carlita, this upstart angel

whom she's grown quite fond of. But even in this predicament she must perform first and foremost as a Superior Angel with a mission. "If only you hadn't seen the destifate screens. It's put you into an absolute conflict of interest." Gabriella's voice gains urgency. "But now that you have, you must find a way to put this behind you. We are at an imperative."

It was her. She was Mira. It finally all made sense. Why she loved Clancy so. Why she felt her in a way that was part of her.

"Carlita."

Carlita's wings trembled. How could she decide? How could she give up her son, the only thing that she would ever love in this way? And how could she not? Why was this decision left to her?

"But . . ." Carlita can barely tolerate the choice. "What happens . . . to me?"

"That I cannot tell you."

"But there will be no Erik."

"No. Erik will not exist."

"And that means she . . . I will be lonely."

"I guess that will really be up to you, won't it?" Gabriella's voice was filled with warmth. "I cannot tell you your future. You have to have faith. Faith in what is supposed to be."

Carlita stood for a long moment, caught in the vortex of parallel realities. She peered at the hologram, Clancy's struggle on one side, Mira sleeping with her beloved son on the other. Carlita gathered all her strength, a brilliant glow emanated from her aura as she looked Gabriella straight into her translucent visors and stated unequivocally, "I am an angel, Gabriella, and my charge must never suffer."

And with that Carlita whisked her form through the window.

Gabriella glanced pass the holograms and saw the caretaker's Jeep as it drove up the hill.

• • •

Clancy's movements became slower, her legs leaden weights.

Come on Clancy. Faster. Carlita hovered about her.

It was as if her legs were no longer receiving messages from her brain, overtaxed, the deep snow fighting her every step of the way.

Carlita spun about her, frantic. Faster, Clancy. Faster. And then saw a way to speed her progress, dashed below, and knocked a cluster of snow beneath her feet.

Clancy slid halfway down the hill. When she hit the bottom, it knocked the wind from her for a moment. She got back on her feet, dusted the snow off, and continued the last two hundred yards to the house.

The Jeep pulled into the driveway.

Carlita saw that the Jeep was making far better time than Clancy. What could she do? She completely divorced Mira and Erik's vision from her mind, shot past Clancy, and flew directly inside the cab of the Jeep. She glanced at the panel. It meant nothing to her. She'd never even learned to drive a car in any of her other incarnations. Then she watched as the caretaker put his foot to the gas pedal. It gave her an idea.

Clancy felt a surge of adrenaline and renewed determination.

Gabriella panicked. She saw the Jeep heading to the house, and then just as quickly it swerved to the left and plowed its way into a snowbank. She smiled. If nothing else, Carlita was resourceful.

• • •

Clancy stood before the Lodge's thick oak door. It brought back every memory. Every single thought and feeling she'd ever had. Maybe this wasn't such a great idea. My God. What had she been thinking?

The door was slightly ajar, a suitcase stood close by. She wondered if Mathew had sold the place, or rented it out perhaps. She pushed the door and moved inside, breathing in the smells, all of them; the sweet permeating tobacco and cinnamon of Aunt Nora, the seductive musk of Mathew's cologne. She grinned self-effacingly at the power of suggestion.

She heard sounds from the living room.

"Hello?" she said. But no one answered, and then she thought she heard footsteps.

"Hello?" She felt like an intruder in her own life.

More footsteps. And then he was there, walking in from the kitchen. Just like that. They both stopped. It seemed their being there, standing opposite each other, was as normal as breathing. Except they had both stopped. Except there was nothing at all normal about them facing each other after years of separation.

Inescapable moment. Neither could move or talk.

"Clancy . . . ," Mathew finally said.

"I . . . I thought you were in England."

"I am—I mean I will be. I'm heading out this evening."

"Oh."

They continued to stare at each other but stayed clear of each other's eyes.

"Lisa told me you were leaving in the fall . . . this past fall."

"I changed my mind. Wanted one last Christmas at the Lodge." Mathew wanted to step forward, but his feet wouldn't move. "When did you speak with Lisa?"

"After I heard about Aunt Nora." Their eyes caught each other's briefly, then Clancy glanced away. "I was so sorry to hear about her, Mathew."

Another silence filled the room, until the caretaker stomped through the door. "Mr. Prendergast?" Then he saw them standing there. "Oh, there you are. Damn Jeep got away from me. Don't know what the hell happened, but I'll have her out in a sec."

Mathew glanced from the caretaker to Clancy to his watch. "How long will it take?"

"Maybe five minutes."

"No—to the airport."

"Couple a hours."

"It's cutting it close."

"I'll do my best." The caretaker tipped his hat and left.

"What . . . what are you doing here?" Mathew finally asked.

"Well . . . um, I was on my way to Portland."

"For Christmas."

"Yes."

"Visiting friends?"

"Yes." But they both knew what they were saying. He was leaving the country and she was visiting a lover.

Utter uncertainty.

The caretaker stuck his head back in. "Ready when you are."

They both knew the next moment would change their lives forever. One way or the other.

Carlita and Gabriella floated by in suspension.

"Now what?" Carlita whispered.

"It's now or never."

"We have to do something. Anything," Carlita begged.

Gabriella glanced at Carlita, who had clearly proved her genuine heart and soul—a true angel—her selflessness unquestionable. Yes. Carlita's aura of gold was no accident. Pure goodness. She would make an excellent Superior Angel at some point, not too far off in the future. Faced with information that could have spelled disaster, she had taken her own needs out of the picture and done what was right for Clancy. What was right by the universe. Gabriella could now do something in return.

She sighed. It meant confronting the core of her angelosophy and everything she had ever believed about being an angel. She liked to operate from the interior out with her charges. Playing magic rarely worked. The effects were too superficial. But it appeared they were at the moment of no return. Carlita's frustration echoed in her mind: What was the point in being an angel if they couldn't affect their charges for the good? And if she was to be completely honest with herself, she knew if Carlita was willing to go the distance, then so could she.

"This will be our little secret."

She stretched a wing. Gabriella's glorious lavender wing gracefully whipped forward like a toreador's cape, creating a ripple that floated softly through the space they call air on earth, until the current reached the ornament with the book and violin, touching it with such gentle velocity that it was swayed by the force and fell to the ground.

The shattering glass reeled them back to the moment.

Mathew and Clancy stared at the tree and then at one another. Mathew walked slowly to the broken ornament, as if moving too fast might create another calamity. Clancy followed, almost tiptoeing.

It was his ornament. Their ornament, really. The first thing

Aunt Nora had given him. How fitting, he thought, and his look said as much when he presented it to Clancy. Finally shattered. He felt a lump tighten his throat. His jaws clenched.

"A grand gesture from the gods?" Mathew's voice was laced with unfamiliar bitterness.

He began to pick up more of the pieces and stopped at the miniature violin. Clancy watched him. His handsome strength, his gentle softness, his grace. His goodness. All the things she had ever loved about him in conflict with the brokenness of who they had become. It wasn't him. It had never really been about him, she now knew. All these years, apart from each other, all these years of missing him, were so that she could finally become who she was meant to be, for better or worse. Her flaws and her strengths could now all comfortably reside inside her skin. What was different about them now was herself.

"Mathew—" She put out a hand to his, gently removing the broken fragments from his palm. "Don't hate me. God, don't hate me."

His eyes met hers. She was crying.

"If you hate me, I can't live."

"All I have ever felt for you, Clancy," his voice cracked into a ragged whisper, "is love."

And in that moment they knew.

They had finally come home.

Gabriella sighed.

Carlita couldn't stop herself, another golden tear floated from her and out through her, dissipating much like gold dust. She looked at Gabriella. "Thank you. Thank you."

They drifted above Mathew and Clancy as they walked, hand in hand up the stairwell to his room, watched as they stopped to kiss, slowly, deeply, passionately.

As Gabriella led Carlita above and beyond them, they floated toward the bedroom window, where the image of Mira and her son in the mini-hologram began to dissolve. Erik's existence ceased, evaporating from the scene. Mira was alone on the couch, a blanket thrown over her. And then the image disappeared altogether, and they glided beyond the window, over the snowcapped landscape, up through the clouds to the blue-black of the stratosphere and straight toward the stars.

And on the tree, a new ornament swayed, the one Mathew and Lisa could not quite believe had shown up from the mysterious package. On this ornament was a familiar scene: a warming fire, two overstuffed chairs, but in this one the violin and book rested on the same chair, a small teddy bear plopped its floppy ears in the other. And if one looked thoroughly and studied the inset very carefully, there on the mantel of the hearth stood a pair of candlesticks, their form that of two splendid, golden angels.